THE HACK (A MENAGE ROMANCE)

A MENAGE IN MANHATTAN NOVEL

TARA CRESCENT

My editor Jim takes the comma-filled words that emerge from my keyboard and shapes it into a story worth reading. As always, my undying gratitude.

Additional thanks for Miranda's laser-sharp eyes.

Cover Design by Eris Adderly, http://erisadderly.com/

ABOUT TARA CRESCENT

Get a free story when you subscribe to <u>my mailing list!</u>

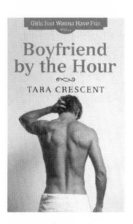

Boyfriend by the Hour

This steamy, romantic story contains a dominant hero who's pretending to be an escort, and a sassy heroine who's given up on real relationships.

Sadie:

I can't believe I have the hots for an escort.

Cole Mitchell is ripped, bearded, sexy and dominant. When he moves next door to me, I find it impossible to resist sampling the wares.

But Cole's not a one-woman kind of guy, and I won't share.

Cole:

She thinks I'm an escort. I'm not.

I thought I'd do anything to sleep with Sadie. Then I realized I want more. I want Sadie. Forever.

I'm not the escort she thinks I am.

Now, I just have to make sure she never finds out.

THE HACK

They're my bosses, and I've been hired to destroy them.

Men are not to be trusted.

My father cheated on my mother. *My ex-husband cheated on me.*

I won't let it happen again.

No more guys. From now on, all I care about is work.

Then I meet my **two new bosses.** My two **wickedly hot,** good-looking new bosses. Finn Sanders and Oliver Prescott.

Brilliant. Charming. Rich. Successful. *And oh-so dangerous.*

I've been hired to **hack** into their systems and **destroy** their company.

Not a problem. I can do this. I have skills. Resources. And

I'm definitely immune to Oliver and Finn. I'm not attracted to their **brooding intensity.** I can resist the **fire** in their eyes. I can ignore this **pull** I feel toward them…

Then they find out who I am and why I'm working for them.

And it turns out that Finn and Oliver have a few secrets of their own…

PROLOGUE

When it is all finished, you will discover it was never random.

— UNKNOWN

Miki:

Thanksgiving should be a time of gratitude and reflection.

Bite me.

The line inches forward. The terminals at Houston's George Bush Intercontinental Airport are always busy, but today, they're practically bursting at the seams. Swarms of tired and cranky passengers are everywhere. Several freak storms in the area have disrupted flight schedules, and the ticket agents are frantically rebooking the travelers, doing their very best to cope with the melee.

Miracle of miracles, my flight is still on schedule. Probably the only thing that's gone right in six weeks.

I queue up in the serpentine line, waiting to check in my

luggage, two big suitcases, bursting at the seams with everything I own in Houston that I want to keep. My clothes, my computer equipment, my collection of silly and impractical shoes. My laptop I clutch to my chest—the the gate agents will pry that from me over my cold, dead body.

Twenty long minutes later, I finally reach the counter and hand the tired-looking agent my ID. She pulls up my details on her computer, and eyes my two suitcases dubiously. "There's a fee for checked luggage," she says, looking like she's bracing herself for an argument.

Poor woman. It must suck to work on Thanksgiving. "I know," I reply. "That's alright."

She punches in more keys, weighs my luggage, charges me for overweight baggage, and then prints out my boarding pass. I look at my seat assignment and wince. 31B. That's the back of the plane, in a middle seat. On a four-hour flight.

Pasting on my friendliest smile, I give her a hopeful look. "You don't have an aisle or a window seat open?"

She shakes her head. "I'm sorry, Mrs. Hickman. It's a full flight."

Ah well. A middle seat is a minor bump in the shit sandwich that has become my life in the last month and a half. "I'll deal with it," I reply. "Oh, and it's not Mrs. Hickman. It's Ms. Cooper. The divorce will be finalized in December."

IN NORMAL TIMES, Thanksgiving is my favorite holiday. It's a day dedicated to eating. There are no crowded malls to wade through, no presents to buy. What's not to love?

These are not normal times.

Six weeks ago, I thought I'd surprise my soon-to-be-ex-husband Aaron at work on a Friday evening. We'd barely seen each other in the last three months, and I'd planned to surprise him with a spontaneous date night.

Except I walked in on his assistant Peggy giving him a blowjob in his office, bobbing her big blonde head on his junk.

Even worse? They'd been doing the dirty-dirty for eighteen months. Yup. When Aaron and I were standing up in front of a judge, promising to love and honor one another, he was having an affair with his assistant.

Let's just say I'm approaching the holiday with an emotion that does not resemble gratitude *in the slightest.*

TWO HOURS LATER, we board the plane. I take my crappy middle seat. The other occupants in my row haven't shown up yet. *Maybe they missed their flight,* I think hopefully, then scold myself for that uncharitable thought. *Just because you're in a craptastic mood, Mackenzie Cooper, it doesn't mean you have to be a bitch.*

Coopers do not complain. Coopers square their shoulders, hold their heads high and carry on.

My family lives in Manhattan, but I haven't told them about the impending divorce. I'm sure my mother will try and talk me out of it, and I'm just not ready to deal with her yet.

I feel like such a fool. My friends tried to warn me that I was jumping into marriage with Aaron, but I wouldn't listen. Aaron was tall and handsome, and I was the nerdy computer chick. I'd been so thrilled that he noticed me that my common sense had fled.

I'd been wearing love-goggles, and I was blind. And stupid. And now I'm paying for it. When I get to Manhattan, Wendy, Piper, Katie, and Gabby will give me pitying looks and ask me questions about what Aaron did and what I'm going to do next.

I'm not ready to talk about it. *I'm not ready to face the future.*

Enough brooding. I pull out my dollar-store notebook with its neon pink cover from my backpack and start making a list.

Top Five Ways in which I'm Going to Reclaim My Life.

1. Move away from Houston. I'm done with this town. I'll always be the woman who walked in on her ex-husband's assistant giving him head under his desk at work, and I'm never going to be able to leave that memory behind.
2. Move back to Manhattan. Find an apartment.
3. Find a job. Manhattan is not a cheap place to live, and my savings won't last long.
4. Get a cat. I don't have to worry about Aaron's stupid *and imaginary* allergies anymore.
5. Sex is allowed, but love is off-limits.

I underline that last resolution several times until I stab a hole through the paper.

That's when someone clears his voice. "Excuse me," an amused male voice says. "If I could get to my seat—"

I look up, and my eyes widen. The two men standing in the aisle are absolutely gorgeous. The one laughing at me is big, blond, and broad-shouldered, like a modern-day Viking. He's wearing a carelessly un-tucked white shirt with dark blue jeans and worn sneakers, and he still looks like a million bucks. And his friend? His friend, with his custom-tailored gray plaid suit, dark hair, piercing blue eyes and lean, taut body, is just as drool-worthy.

I've won the plane lottery, ladies. *Pity I don't care.*

I get up, and the blond man slides into the window seat. It's a tight fit. His shoulders are broader than the seat, and his knees hit the back of the row in front of him. I'm five-feet-three-inches, and I don't have enough room. The Viking is easily six feet tall, and he must be acutely uncomfortable.

"Are you together?" I ask the dark-haired one. "Would you like to change seats?"

"No thank you," he replies. He has light blue eyes, the color of the sky on a cloudless day, and when his gaze locks on mine, my heart beats a little faster. The corner of his mouth quirks up. "I talk to Oliver all the time at work. Right now, you look much more interesting than he does."

Well, okay then.

Is he flirting with me?

What should I do?

I'm a hacker. Ask me about registry settings, and I'm your woman, but put me in front of a good-looking guy, and unless he's talking about brute force attacks or botnets, I'm a tongue-tied, stammering mess.

The noise that emerges from my throat is a mixture of a laugh, a snort, and a neigh. Lovely. *Thank you, universe.* You couldn't make me smooth and sophisticated, could you? No. You had to make me sound like a donkey with a head cold.

My cheeks flushing with embarrassment, I slide into my chair, my shoulder bumping into Viking-guy. "Sorry," I murmur and try to hunch so I'm not making contact with his body.

His smile widens. "Hi," he says. "I'm Oliver. Tell me why you want a cat, who Aaron was and why he pretended to be allergic, and most of all," he bends his head toward me, lowering his voice to a conspiratorial whisper, "why sex is allowed, but love isn't."

"You read my list." Shock makes my voice indignant. *Aren't people supposed to pretend they aren't reading over your shoulder?* "You're rude."

He laughs easily. "I've been accused of that and more," he says. "But you're right. That *was* rude of me. Allow me to make it up to you." He raises his hand, and like magic, a flight attendant is at our side, beaming radiantly at Oliver the Viking.

Good-looking-guy-magic. Aaron had it too.

"I know it's against the rules," Oliver says to the attendant, his smile charming and ever-so-slightly-apologetic. "But you couldn't grab some orange juice from your cart for us, could you? As well as three of your mini-bottles of vodka?"

She simpers at him. "Of course," she says. "It's a four-hour flight, and these seats don't recline. It seems the least I can do."

In about thirty seconds, she returns with a handful of bottles. Oliver takes them from her with a smile, and the dark-haired guy slips her a folded bill. "Thank you," he says. "I really appreciate it."

Whoa. Smooth. I'm pretty sure that was a hundred dollar bill, unless they've started putting Benjamin Franklin's face on smaller denominations.

Oliver hands me my share of the spoils. "Will you accept my peace offering?" he asks, his eyes twinkling.

It seems silly to pout for four straight hours, and this might be exactly what I need. Though I've cried and I've fumed in the last six weeks, I haven't gotten shit-faced. Maybe I do need to get good and drunk.

Closing my notebook, I tuck it into the seat pocket in

front of me. "Okay," I say. Opening my OJ, I take a long drink from it before adding the vodka. "Truce."

Two hours later, I'm chatty, and I'm well and truly on the way to being drunk. Which sadly only takes three of the little mini-bottles, because I'm a lightweight.

I'm sitting between Finn and Oliver, their thighs brushing against mine. Drunk-Miki is much better at flirting than Sober-Miki, or so I think. "Now that we're friends," Oliver says, a smile dancing on his lips, "Who's Aaron?"

"My husband."

Finn's eyes fall to my left hand. I lift it up. "No ring," I announce. "I'm getting divorced." Unbidden, my eyes fill with tears. I was such a fool. I wanted so much to be loved that I ignored all the warning signs.

"Hey, hey." Oliver's voice is soothing. "Don't cry." His big, strong hand covers mine. "It's okay."

Finn hands me a tissue and a bottle of water. I dab at my eyes and take a long sip of the cool liquid. "Sorry."

"It's okay," Finn replies, exchanging a glance with Oliver. "You're not the first person to cry over a failed relationship, and you won't be the last. Let's talk about something else. What do you do?"

I'm a hacker. In today's world of shell corporations and offshore bank accounts, people hire me to track down some-one's assets. I'm not a lone wolf; I used to work for a company that gave me some protection from getting sued or worse. But the work I did was quasi-legal, and I'm too cautious to talk about it. *Even when tipsy.*

"Computer stuff," I reply vaguely. "It's very boring. I stare at spreadsheets all day."

Oliver's hand is still on mine, and I don't know if I

should leave it there, or if I should pull it away. I don't want to be rude.

Finn's face is turned toward me, and he's close enough that if I fall forward, my lips will land on his. It's a tribute to Aaron's asshattery that I resist. His lips look soft. His face is covered with dark stubble, and there's a tiny part of me that wants to rub against it and purr, just like a cat.

I should stay away from vodka.

For the rest of the flight, I sip my water and make conversation. They're easy to talk to. We like the same kinds of what-if TV shows: Person of Interest, Fringe and Sense 8, and the journey passes as we squabble good-naturedly about whether the second and third Matrix movies were any good. There's still an undercurrent of sexual tension in the air, but for the moment, it lingers in the background.

I don't want to leave when the flight lands; I'm having such a good time. I might be fooling myself, but I don't think I'm the only one. Finn and Oliver linger in their seats, ignoring the rapidly emptying plane. It's only when the aisle is almost clear that Finn gets to his feet. "We should go," he says, his voice reluctant. "Miki, it was great meeting you." He smiles warmly. "And my initial assessment was right. You are much better company than Oliver."

I get up as well, grabbing my backpack from underneath the seat in front of me. Call me paranoid, but I don't like leaving my laptop in the overhead bins. I didn't even like leaving it behind when I went to the bathroom, but I also didn't want Oliver and Finn to think I was crazy.

The three of us make our way out. Once we're in the airport terminal, Oliver puts his hand on my arm. "I'd like to keep in touch," he says. His expression is intense, and suddenly, he's not the guy I've been talking to for the last four hours. He's in good-looking-guy mode, and sure enough, I'm back to tongue-tied-and-awkward.

He pulls a business card from his wallet and holds it out. "Call me?"

My heart lurches. What the hell am I doing, flirting with these guys? My marriage has just ended. I don't have a job or a home. My life is one big, tangled, complicated mess, and Oliver and Finn will make it worse.

I swallow hard. "I don't think that's a good idea," I say, unable to meet their eyes. Then, before they can try to talk me into it, I run away.

~

Finn:

I watch her leave, my gaze lingering on her back until she disappears into the crowds at JFK. *So that's Mackenzie Cooper.* "She's not what I thought she'd be," I say out loud.

Three months ago, a prototype security system at Imperium got breached by a hacker. One of our clients, Howard Lippman, had hidden his assets in shell corporations during a contentious divorce. The mystery hacker uncovered the scheme and unmasked Lippman's fraudulent behavior.

I don't give a shit about Lippman's troubles—he violated our terms of service by breaking the law, and we terminated his account as soon as we found out. But I do care, passionately, that my code was cracked.

It was a few minutes' work to close the vulnerability that led to the data breach. It's taken us considerably longer to find the hacker that pulled off the feat.

Then yesterday, we were able to get a hold of a name.

Miki Cooper.

At my side, Oliver's lips curl up into a sly grin. "You mean, she's a girl. You got hacked by a girl."

I roll my eyes. "Grow up, Prescott. I'm not being sexist. My grandmother is the strongest person I know, man or woman." My lips tighten. "Until Miki, we've never been breached. She's a problem."

He nods. "Let's look at the bright side," he says. "She's not a rogue operator. She cracked Imperium as part of her job."

"A job she quit last week." We know as much about Mackenzie Cooper as it is possible to know legally in twenty-four hours, which isn't much. "She's a free agent now. That makes her dangerous."

She's not on social media; she doesn't post her pictures on Facebook, and she doesn't tweet about whatever is on her mind. She's someone who knows that everything she does online is a link back to her, and she's careful.

"Let's keep an eye on her," Oliver says. "She's on DefCon's forums. We'll find her there and make contact."

Imperium, the company Oliver and I founded five years ago, is going public in six months. "We can't risk another data breach."

"I know," he replies, his expression grim. "It won't come to that."

We walk out of the airport and hail a cab. It's Thanksgiving. Nana will have made a feast, as she does every single year. There will be three kinds of pie, maybe four. For the moment, work can wait.

But only for a moment. Tomorrow morning, it's back to the grind.

"We need to stop working with high profile clients," Oliver remarks in the cab. "We're spending far too much time vetting these guys, and assholes like Lippman slip through. I don't want to be in the business of protecting drug lords and mafia dons."

Our private security division is one of our oldest groups, but it's increasingly become a liability for Imperium. This breach is the last straw. "Agreed," I reply. "You want to close it right away?"

He shakes his head. "There'll be too much chatter ahead of the IPO," he says. "Let's take it slow. No more new clients, and we won't renew any packages that expire."

"The board isn't going to like this."

Oliver shrugs. "I'm not going to run our business by Ambrose's ethics, Finn. I'm going to run it by mine."

We both fall into silence. The taxi navigates the snowy roads and the back-to-back traffic, inching its way into the city. I should be reading and replying to the hundreds of emails I've received in the last six hours, but my thoughts are elsewhere.

I was attracted to Miki Cooper. And I haven't been attracted to someone in a really long time.

1

Yield to temptation. It may not pass your way again.

— ROBERT A. HEINLEIN

Miki:

Three months later...

I'm not awake before noon very often, but today's a special day.

'Special' is code for 'craptastic.'

It's my thirtieth birthday. It's also Valentine's Day. For someone still shaken by the end of her marriage, it's quite a double whammy.

"Surprise!" A chorus of voices cries out. My bedroom door is thrown open, and the gang crowds in, Piper in the lead, holding a birthday cake covered with candles.

I cover my head with my blanket and pretend I'm not here.

"Happy birthday, Miki," Bailey says cheerfully. "I'm going to tug the cover free. If you sleep naked, now's the time to let us know."

"You guys, I'm pregnant," Wendy quips. "If I catch a glimpse of Miki's pasty ass, I can't even drown my sorrows in drink."

I stick my head out of my blanket fort. "Pasty ass?" I ask indignantly. "Do you mind? Isn't it traumatic enough that I'm turning thirty?"

"Yes, yes," Gabby says. "And you're divorced, and Aaron's dick was in Peggy's mouth. We've heard it before." She perches at the foot of the bed and gives me a hopeful look. "If you blow the candles out, we can eat cake. It's Katie's carrot cake."

Ooh. Fine. I guess I can get out of bed. I sit up, and the five of them launch into a rousing rendition of 'Happy Birthday.' Once they're done singing, I blow the candles out. Piper gets a knife from the kitchen, along with some plates and forks, and efficiently slices each of us a piece.

Wendy waddles over to the armchair in the corner of the room and sits down. "Okay, Miki," she says. "Eat some cake, because you're going to need it."

I take the plate that Piper hands me. "Why?" I ask warily. When Wendy gets a look of battle in her eyes, anything can happen.

"Because this is an intervention," she replies. "Right, ladies?"

The other five nod. "Let's wait for her to finish eating," Piper says kindly.

I sit up straighter. "Why am I getting an intervention?" I ask, though I already know the answer.

Top Five Reasons I'm Getting an Intervention

1. I haven't left Wendy's apartment in four days.
2. I stay up all night and spend all day in bed. I'm like a vampire, and Wendy's comment about my pasty skin is dead on.
3. No new job. I'm living off my savings and the cash I earn by doing one-off jobs for people.
4. I've worn the same pair of sweatpants for a month. Every single day.
5. In preparation for the horrid awfulness of my thirtieth birthday, I drank a bottle of wine last night. My mouth feels like sandpaper.

Well, hell. If I'm going to get an intervention, I need another slice of cake. My mother's not here to tell me that I need to watch what I eat. I can already hear her voice in my head. *Oh dear, Mackenzie,* she'll sigh. *You're going to get fat, dear. You just turned thirty. How will you meet someone? Failed marriage, wrong side of thirty, and carrying an extra ten pounds?*

I hold out my empty plate and Piper, bless her Southern heart, gives me another slice. Armed with cake, I'm ready. "Okay," I tell my friends. "The intervention. Bring it on."

ONCE THEY LEAVE, I get out of bed and into the shower. Instead of wearing my navy blue sweats, I slide on a pair of jeans and a red sweater. "You're going to conquer the world this year, Miki," I tell the too-pale woman in the mirror. "Forget Aaron. Look at the future, not the past."

I don't know if it's the intervention or the pep talk or even just the shower and clean clothes, but I'm feeling positively hopeful by the time I crack open my laptop and navigate to DefCon, where there are three private messages waiting for me.

I open Lancelot's message first. *Happy birthday, mouse.*

Grinning widely at the fact that he remembered, I click on Merlin's message. *Lancelot and I have a present for you, mouse, but since you won't tell us where you live, you'll have to pick it up yourself.*

Merlin's attached an address to his message. I instantly type it into Google Maps. It's a furniture store. Huh.

Lancelot doesn't appear to be online, but Merlin is. Ignoring my third message, which is from someone called User0989, I click on his icon. *You're buying me furniture? I don't have an apartment yet.*

He replies almost immediately. *Is your friend kicking you out? Do you have another place to live?*

His concern warms my heart. I hastily type out a reply before he worries too much. *Of course not. I can stay here as long as I want. They threw me an intervention today.*

Is that a New York birthday tradition?

I giggle. *No. They're worried about me. They don't think that it's good for me to sit in my sweatpants all night, glued to my computer. They think I should go out, be more social.*

Are they right?

A little, I admit. *I promised them I'd work on it.*

I've never been the most social person in the world, but before Aaron cheated on me, I enjoyed going to movies and listening to jazz bands play in small, intimate venues. I've meant to do all those things again, but I can't seem to find the energy. Maybe my friends are right. Maybe I do need a metaphorical kick in the pants.

Then there's money. My bank account took a serious beating from the divorce—Aaron decided to be a pig and contest it, and I had to hire a lawyer, Wendy's friend Lara, to help me deal with my uncooperative ex-husband. Lara didn't come cheap. I'm living rent-free at Wendy's, and that helps my finances somewhat, but I need to find a steady job.

I don't bore Lancelot and Merlin with all this. I haven't given my online friends my real phone number, and they don't know my real name, just my handle—*Mouse*—but I still tell them almost everything. I've told them about my divorce, my difficult relationship with my parents, my feelings of failure when I compare my life with my sister's, and they're always there to listen, to offer comfort and bracing advice.

It's weird. I don't know anything about them, but they're my best friends.

Merlin doesn't reply right away. I stare at the screen, waiting for his answer, but after three minutes of nothing, I click on my third message, the one from the person I don't recognize.

It's a job offer. *I'm looking for someone with your set of skills,* User0989 writes. *The job pays a hundred grand. Interested?*

Whoa. I'm barely making minimum payments on my credit card bills. A hundred grand sounds amazing. Unfortunately, I doubt it's real. I don't believe in unicorns, I don't believe in fairies, and I don't believe anonymous users who promise mysterious jobs with huge payouts.

I'm about to delete the email when a chat window pops up. It's User0989. Persistent dude.

Are you interested?

I roll my eyes and type out a sarcastic reply. *In a hundred grand? Yes. In your job? How the hell would I know? You haven't told me anything about it.*

What does this guy think? He says a hundred grand, and I'll pant all over him? I might be bummed about Aaron, but it hasn't interfered with my ability to be snarky.

I need you to get me Imperium's client list.

This guy's a lunatic. Imperium is a data security company, one of the best in the business, if not the best. They can't be hacked. Dozens have tried; all have failed. The person in charge of their operations is a genius.

It can't be done, buddy, I type. *Don't waste your money.*

You're wrong, he writes back, oddly confident. *It can't be done from the outside. But if you're inside their firewall, you might have a shot.*

Imperium isn't hiring. About the first thing I did when I moved back to Manhattan was ask around to see if they had any openings, but they were in the middle of a hiring freeze.

If I get you in, are you interested?

Okay, I've had enough of this guy's fantasy. It's my birthday, and I have better things to do with my time. Talk is cheap, and this guy hasn't given me anything tangible. I switch to Merlin's chat window.

Where were you? he asks.

Since I like Merlin, I refrain from pointing out that he's the one that disappeared first. *Some guy's trying to offer me a job.*

Who?

Merlin and Lancelot are entirely too nosy. They don't think I can look after myself. Then again, given that I've been moaning on and on about Aaron for the last three months, I don't blame them.

I'm about to answer, but User0989's icon is flashing at me. I switch to that conversation to tell him to knock it off, but then I read his message.

I've put you on the guest list for the Imperium party tonight. If you want more details about the job, show up and tell them you're M. Mouse.

There's an attachment. I open it to see a flyer for the party, and I immediately realize this event is way out of my league. I'm a hacker, most comfortable with chatting anonymously with people I don't know. The Imperium event is a themed, formal party. I'll have to talk to actual flesh-and-blood people.

Well? User0989 prompts. *What do you think?*

One hundred thousand dollars to hack into a company and steal their client list.

You'll get arrested if you get caught, Miki.

I hesitate, frozen in indecision. I don't want to go to jail, but my financial situation is getting desperate. Call me stubborn, but I don't want to ask my parents or my friends for help. My husband cheated on me. I'm staying rent-free in Wendy's apartment. All my friends have successful careers and happy, healthy relationships. I already feel like a failure; I don't want to make it worse.

A minute later, another message appears on my screen. *What do you have to lose?*

He's right. I have no job. No money. No husband. It's my thirtieth birthday and my plan for the evening is to sit at home and watch TV.

I don't want to be pathetic and miserable any longer. Aaron cheated on me, and I'm the one who's suffering as a result. It doesn't seem fair, and I'm tired of it. I want to take matters into my own hands. I want to control my own destiny.

Before I can second-guess the decision, I type out my reply. *Fine. I'll be there.*

I switch back to Merlin, who's still waiting for me to tell him who wants to hire me. I'm starting to type my answer when a thought strikes me.

Merlin and Lancelot are protective. They're going to talk me out of hacking into Imperium. They're going to point out I'll get into trouble if I get caught. They're going to warn me that I don't know who User0989 is and what his motivations are. They're going to tell me it's not safe.

Just some random guy, I reply, my cheeks heating as I lie. *Dunno who he is.*

I've never lied to them before. *It feels wrong.*

Experience is simply the name we give our mistakes.

— OSCAR WILDE

Oliver:

There's a blonde woman in my bed, and I don't remember what her name is. Even for me, the self-professed king of one-night stands, this is a new low.

I sit up, and the pounding in my head intensifies. Getting drunk was a dumb idea. Bringing the blonde back to my Manhattan penthouse? Even dumber. It's Valentine's Day. Bad, *bad* timing.

Groping for my phone, I tiptoe out of my bedroom and into the kitchen.

Today's Miki's birthday. *Happy birthday, mouse,* I type while I wait for the coffee to brew. She's not online yet, neither do I expect her to be. Miki's a night owl.

Three months ago, Finn and I decided to go on DefCon's

forums and get to know Miki in order to keep an eye on the talented hacker. Our plan worked only too well. The three of us are friends now. Really good friends. *And if she finds out the truth...*

She's not going to find out.

"Hey there," a sultry voice purrs, interrupting my dark thoughts. It's my one-night stand. Her name suddenly comes to me. Bethany.

Bethany's wearing my shirt and her hair's artfully tousled. She's going for the 'I just woke up' effect, but it's spoiled by the fact that she's wearing makeup.

"Good morning." I smile at her cheerfully, even as I wonder how quickly I can get her out of my place. Paul Fryman, my divorce lawyer, is going to be here in thirty minutes. He called yesterday, insisting he needed to speak with me urgently, but he wouldn't tell me why over the phone. "Coffee?"

"Thank you." She pulls up a chair next to me, and sits down, leaning forward, her breasts spilling out. "I hope you don't mind that I wore your shirt," she says, fluttering her eyelashes. "I couldn't find my clothes."

How hard did she look? "They're on the armchair," I reply, getting up to pour her some coffee. "Milk, sugar?"

She shudders at the mention of the dreaded s-word. Sugar. "No thank you. Just black."

I set the mug down in front of Bethany. "I have a meeting in twenty minutes," I tell her, pasting a look of regret on my face. "I'm afraid I'm going to have to rush you a little."

"Oh." She bites her lower lip. "It's Friday. I thought you could take the day off."

"Sadly, no."

She gives me a hopeful look. "Maybe we could hang out later tonight?"

I take a deep breath. Contrary to what my ex-wife Claudia would like the world to believe, I'm not a jerk, and I have no desire to hurt this woman's feelings. At the same time, I made things perfectly clear last night that I wasn't looking for a date or commitment.

All I wanted was one night. No strings attached. Unfortunately, things are never that easy. "I'm sorry," I reply, as gently as I can, given the circumstances. "I don't think that's a good idea."

"Oh." Her mouth contorts into a snarl. "I was warned about you," she snaps. "Oliver Prescott never goes on a second date, right? It's all about the chase and the conquest."

I don't need Bethany to analyze me; my therapist Dr. Hutchins has already pinpointed my flaws. I won't see someone more than once because, after Claudia, I will never again put myself in a position where I'm vulnerable. My broken marriage has left me deeply cynical and deeply mistrustful.

Bethany storms away to my bedroom. When she emerges in five minutes, she's fully dressed. She pauses by my front door, waiting for me to stop her, but when she realizes I'm not going to, she flings the door open and pivots around to face me. "Rot in hell, Oliver," she says angrily, and she walks out, slamming the door shut behind her.

"Pleasant woman," I say out loud to the empty room. Then again, I'm not being fair. Compared to Claudia, Bethany is an angel.

"We have a problem." Paul Fryman looks like someone stole his lunch money. "I received this in the mail from Ms.

Weaver's lawyer." He pushes a manila envelope across the counter.

I open it, and half-a-dozen glossy black-and-white photos spill out. In the first one, Claudia is on the floor, her arms tied behind her back, her legs bound together, a ball-gag in her mouth. In the second, I'm kneeling next to her, a whip in my hands. In the third, she's flinching away from the kiss of the leather.

"Oliver, this is bad. You should have told me about these photos."

"I didn't know about these photos," I reply, tamping down my anger. There's no point yelling at Paul. "Claudia took them without my consent."

He gives me a frank look. "As your lawyer, I need to ask the question, Oliver. Was this activity consensual? Claudia's implying it wasn't. She's implying that she was coerced into this."

"It was her idea," I reply flatly. "Our marriage hit a rough spot, and she suggested BDSM. She thought it might spice up our sex life."

It didn't. Two months later, I came back home from a business trip to find out she was cheating on me.

I take a deep breath. "I assume she's trying to blackmail me with these pictures. How much does she want?"

"She doesn't want money," Paul replies carefully, collecting the photos and sliding them back into the enve-lope. "She wants half your Imperium stock, and she's made it clear that she won't negotiate. If you don't play ball, these photos leak."

Of course. Imperium is on the verge of going public, and there's a lot of money at stake. And Claudia was always greedy.

But this time, she's gone too far. Had she wanted money,

I might have complied, but I'm never going to give her half of my company.

I get to my feet. "I'm not playing ball," I tell my lawyer. "The photos can leak."

Paul shakes his head. "Oliver, Imperium is about to go public. The last thing the IPO needs is compromising photos of its CEO. It casts doubt on your judgment."

He's right. I'm sure that I'll be hearing the same thing from the board of directors, and possibly from my co-founder Finn. But my mind is made up. I'm not going to budge on this.

"I'm not giving her a portion of Imperium. That's a non-starter."

He nods, unsurprised. "I figured I'd give it a shot. You should alert your PR team. They're going to need to manage the fallout."

"I'll see them tonight at the party," I reply. "I'll give them a heads-up. Are you going to be there? Janine should have put you on the guest list."

"Oh no," he replies at once. "I've been married for fourteen years, Oliver. If I work on Valentine's Day, I won't make it to fifteen. Laura and I have dinner reservations at *Masa.*"

I've met Paul's wife, Laura. A more good-natured woman would be hard to find. Paul's a lucky guy. "Fair enough."

I'm just showing him out when my phone rings. It's Sam, my building's doorman. "Mr. Sanders is here, Sir," he says. "Should I send him up?"

Finn? I frown in confusion. I was supposed to meet him at the office this morning, and Finn never deviates from the plan. "Sure." What else is this day going to bring?

~

Finn:

As I ride the elevator up to Oliver's penthouse, I check my phone, but Miki isn't online yet.

When we'd chatted a week ago, she'd mentioned that her neck had been bothering her. We probed a bit and learned that her friend's apartment doesn't have a desk or a chair, and Miki's been spending long hours on the couch, hunched over her laptop.

That won't do.

Miki doesn't talk about it very much, but she's got to be hurting for money. Top flight divorce lawyers don't come cheap, and she's been out of work for three months.

I almost want to hire her at Imperium, but every time I resolve to broach the subject with Oliver, I chicken out. Miki's smart. If we work with her on a daily basis, our identities as Lancelot and Merlin won't remain hidden for long, and when she finds out—

We shouldn't have done it. Miki trusts Lancelot and Merlin, her friends on the DefCon forums. If she finds out the reason we befriended her was to keep an eye on her and make sure she didn't hack into our company, we're going to lose more than her trust. We're going to lose her friendship.

I don't want that to happen.

I type out a message to her. *Lancelot and I have a present for you, mouse, but since you won't tell us where you live, you'll have to pick it up yourself.*

An Aeron chair and a desk might not be exciting presents, but they're useful ones.

That bastard Hickman did a number on Miki. Every once in a while, I see a flash of the laughing woman that sat between Oliver and me on the plane, drinking vodka and having a passionate debate with us on whether Peter

Capaldi made a better Doctor than Matt Smith. But mostly, she's gloomy, withdrawn and isolated.

My phone rings just as I knock on Oliver's front door. It's my grandmother. "Hello, Nana."

"Finn, a lovely young woman just delivered two dozen baby pink roses," she says. I can hear the pleasure in her voice. "Thank you so much, honey."

The corners of my mouth tug up. I send my grandmother the flowers every year for Valentine's Day, and every single year, she has the same note of pleased surprise in her voice when she thanks me. "You're welcome, Nana."

"Are you going on a date tonight?" she asks slyly.

"You aren't even trying to be subtle anymore," I chide. "No, I'm not. Oliver and I have a work party to go to."

"A work party." She sounds disgusted. "Of course. One day, I would like to hear you mention a woman, Finn. Not just work. Even Oliver was married once."

"He was married to Claudia, who you loathed," I point out.

Oliver opens his door and overhears my last sentence. "Is that Nana?" he guesses. "Tell her I wouldn't wish Claudia on my worst enemy."

"You heard that, Nana?"

"Yes, I heard him." She sighs into the phone. "You're busy with work all the time, Finn. Life is for more than that. Life is for living. I want to see you find a woman to care about, to grow old with."

An image of Miki laughing on the plane flashes before my eyes. I blink it away. "I promise, Nana," I reassure her. "As soon as Imperium goes public, I'll make time for other things."

I hang up, and Oliver quirks his eyebrow at me. "Weren't we meeting in the office?"

I take a deep breath. Claudia and Oliver were married for two years, a rocky, contentious marriage that was marked by unhappiness. He's not going to like what I've found.

"Yeah," I say. I walk past him and pour myself a cup of coffee. "It's about Claudia…"

"How did you find out already?" he asks, running his hands through his hair, a frustrated expression on his face. "I thought I'd have a couple of months before the shit hit the fan."

I give him a puzzled look. "What are you talking about, Oliver? I came to tell you that Claudia has been dating Seb Fitzgerald for the last two months."

Sebastian Fitzgerald was a classmate of ours in college. He's always had an unhealthy competitive streak, and he's obsessed with besting Oliver. When Oliver and I announced the formation of a data security firm, Fitzgerald did the same thing. When Oliver started dating Claudia, Sebastian found himself a blonde, blue-eyed girlfriend who looked so much like Claudia I was embarrassed for him.

But now, Fitzgerald's upped the ante.

Kliedara, Fitzgerald's company, is Imperium's biggest competitor. They were never a major threat, but they've upped their game in the last six months. I suspect that Fitzgerald's stealing our technology, but though I've looked long and hard for the source of the leak, I haven't found it. *But I will.*

He inhales sharply. "She's dating Fitzgerald? Of course she is. It all makes sense."

He fills me in on his conversation with Paul, and I suck in a breath. "Claudia's not interested in Imperium, just money. This isn't her idea. It's Fitzgerald's."

Oliver nods in agreement. "Sebastian Fitzgerald would love for me to be publicly discredited," he says grimly. "He's been wanting me to fail since college, and this could be his best chance."

Oliver's right. If the board decides that Oliver is a distraction ahead of the IPO, they have the authority to fire him. He'll still own half of the company, but he won't have any say in the day-to-day decisions.

"Still," he continues, "they might make you CEO."

"Not for all the money in the world, Oliver," I say at once. "I'm terrible at motivational speeches."

That draws a chuckle from him.

I straighten my shoulders. Oliver's my best friend. He's an excellent CEO. He's strategic. He's a great leader, charming and personable. Imperium can't afford to lose him. "The next few weeks are going to be rocky," I say firmly. "But we'll survive it."

We've been dreaming of taking Imperium public from the day we founded the company five years ago. I've worked too hard to let anything or anyone screw it up.

3

Success depends upon previous preparation, and without such preparation there is sure to be failure.

— Confucius

Miki:

What on Earth does one wear to a themed ball?

Bailey wouldn't have a clue, neither would Piper nor Katie. Wendy might, but she's swamped with work, and I don't want to bother her.

Gabby.

I dial her number, and she picks up on the first ring. "I'm sorry about this morning," she blurts out before I have a chance to tell her what I'm calling about. "The Miki I knew was friendly and spontaneous, and Aaron's ruined all of that. I don't want him to win, Miki, but I still shouldn't have been so harsh. I'm really sorry. I feel like a complete jerk."

"No," I rush to reassure her. "The intervention was necessary. I needed to hear it. I've been pouting about Aaron too long. I didn't call about that though. I'm going to a super-fancy party at the Waldorf Astoria tonight, and I have no idea what to wear. Help me?"

"You're going to a party?" Her voice rises to an excited squeak. "Whoa. When you decide to get out of a funk, you don't do it in half-measures, do you? Okay, we're going shopping. I'll be right over."

She hangs up before I tell her I can't afford much. *Think of it as an investment in your career, Miki.* But though I can try and fool myself, I doubt the Visa people are going to be that understanding.

GABBY LOOKS at the electronic invitation. "The theme is 'Pretty in Pink'?" She wrinkles her nose in disgust. "Ugh."

"Tell me about it. I'm going to look like I'm going to prom."

She chuckles. "Don't worry. Friends don't let friends buy ugly dresses." She gives me a curious look. "I didn't know you were going to a party tonight."

"It's for work," I admit. "A prospective job opportunity."

The two of us leave Wendy's apartment and get on the subway, heading to a boutique in SoHo that Gabby swears by. "Is this connected to your forum buddies?" she asks me. "You know, the Knights of the Round Table ones?"

I laugh. "Lancelot and Merlin? Nah, this has nothing to do with them."

"Just as well," she replies. "Don't take this the wrong way, but I don't think they're good for you. You're up all hours of the night chatting with them, and you're substituting online friendship for real life social interaction."

"I know." I bite my lower lip. "I realize I'm avoiding people, but it's been hard. My parents think I'm a failure because I'm thirty and single. They keep telling me how perfect Leah is, and what a mess I am."

"And it doesn't help that your friends are in relationships," Gabby adds. "I can relate. When Bailey got together with Daniel and Sebastian, I'm not ashamed to admit I was a little envious." She squeezes my hand. "I'm here for you," she says. "Whenever you need me, you just have to call." She grins widely. "Now, let's go find you a dress for this party."

"Frothy."

"I'm not a ballerina."

"Prom hell."

"Too much pastel."

Okay, finding a pink dress isn't easy. We've been to three different boutiques, and so far, we've turned up empty-handed. It's four in the afternoon, and time's running out. *So much for my hopes of researching Imperium before the party.* I would have liked to have spent some time learning about the company, but it's looking increasingly unlikely.

"Look, I give up," I sigh after the third boutique. "Let's just pick one of the ugly ones. Nobody's going to be looking at me anyway."

"Nope." Gabby shakes her head firmly. "It's your birthday, and you're going to find an amazing dress, and you're going to look fantastic."

"And at midnight, I'll still turn into a pumpkin, fairy godmother."

She rolls her eyes. "Your ball starts at eight," she says. "The party will be in full swing at midnight. You better not leave early, or I will kick your ass. Okay, let's try Valentina's."

The shop she's standing in front of looks expensive.

"Gabby," I gulp, looking at the designer gowns in the front window, "I don't want to be all Pretty Woman, but this place isn't in my budget."

She's not listening; she's pushed open the door and walked in. Sighing, I follow her into the fancy boutique, feeling awkward and out of place. This is the kind of boutique my mother and sister would shop at. Not me. My tastes are too weird for them.

"This one." Gabby swoops in and picks out a layered magenta chiffon dress. "It's perfect for you, Miki. You have an edge, and so does this dress. Try it on."

I catch a glimpse of the price tag and almost faint. "Gabby, this dress is nearly three thousand bucks."

She holds up a black credit card. "You're not paying for it," she replies with a sly grin. "Happy birthday."

I'm seriously horrified. "Gabby, I can't let you do this," I stammer. "It's too much."

"Stop telling me how to spend my money," she replies, pushing me toward the changing room. "This is *the* dress. Now, try it on so I can see if I'm right."

I SLIP out of my jeans and t-shirt and try on the dress. When I look in the mirror, I'm torn between shock and awe. The gown has a black vee-shaped yoke, and the neckline plunges almost to my belly button. The chiffon in the bodice is ruched, and the skirt has seven layers of delicate fabric.

It's a princess gown, and I don't recognize myself.

"Come out." Gabby knocks on my dressing room door. "I want to see."

I open the door and step out, and she inhales sharply. "God I'm good," she says. "Miki, if you tell me you don't like this dress, I might have to smack you. You look amazing."

She's right. "You're an excellent fairy godmother," I admit. I can't tear my eyes away from the mirrors. The deep pink flatters my coloring in a way that the black t-shirts I live in don't. The dress makes my small boobs appear gently curved, not inadequate. I feel transformed. Gabby might as well have waved a magic wand and said *'Bibbidi Bobbidi Boo.'* It is, in short, the perfect dress. Cinderella has nothing on me.

I can't let Gabby pay for it; I'll have to figure out a way to pay her back. But one thing is clear. Even if I'm going to eat ramen for the next five years, I'm buying this dress.

Oliver:

My day starts out horribly and doesn't get much better. Our new virus scanner needs work, and the team that's built it is overwhelmed and dispirited. We need fresh talent, but that's not an easy task. Imperium hires only the best, and good software engineers are hard to come by.

At lunch, I swing by Mary MacDonald's office. Mary heads up Human Resources. She's eating a salad at her desk, but when she sees me, she puts down her fork and waves me in. "Don't stop eating," I say, sitting down across from her.

I wonder if Miki's figured out what we got her for her birthday. Probably not. The furniture store is in Brooklyn. We'd have picked one closer to her, but since both Finn and I need to keep our identities secret, our choices were limited to places that would let us pay in cash without asking any questions.

With effort, I pull my mind back to work. "We need to

get some talent in here for Block," I tell Mary. "Dmitri's overwhelmed."

She raises an eyebrow. "You told me to freeze all hiring until the IPO," she replies. "You were afraid of a security breach." She picks a slice of cucumber out of her salad with a disgusted look and sets it on the plastic lid. "You have no idea how much grief I've had to take for that decision."

"Trust me, I've heard." I grab the slice of cucumber and take a bite. "Once the executives are done bitching to you, they complain to Finn. When that doesn't get them anywhere, they bug Janine, get on my calendar and whine to me."

She holds out another piece of cucumber, and I nab it. "Who's the whiniest?" she asks wickedly. "I'm willing to bet it's Larry."

I roll my eyes. Until the company goes public, we can't make major executive changes, so we're stuck with Lawrence Kent, our Chief Financial Officer. Hiring him was not my best decision, and I've regretted it since the day I made it two years ago. "What kind of bet is that? Of course, it's Larry."

Mary grins in satisfaction. "You're the boss," she says candidly. "If you want to hire someone for the Block project, I'm not going to stop you."

Hmm. "Let's do it," I reply. "The team looks like they're going to miss their deadline badly, and that's not good."

"Okay," she says agreeably. "Talking about teams that are going to miss their deadlines, Shield looks dicey too. I'm sure Finn's on top of it, but Sachin's sent me three increasingly desperate emails this week asking for additional staff."

"Why?" I frown at Mary. "Sachin's got six people. He doesn't need more than that."

She shakes her head. "He's down to four," she says.

"Larry poached one of his developers to work on some kind of finance tool, and Alessandra, their security expert, was in a bad car crash two days ago."

Larry has no business taking developers from Shield; Finn's going to go ballistic when he finds out. I'm more concerned about Alessandra. "I'm assuming you sent flowers?"

"And a fruit basket," she replies. "Imperium was very generous. Poor girl. She just came back from maternity leave too. I have no idea how they're coping with the baby. Alessandra's got three broken ribs, her lungs were punctured, and her leg's smashed in three places."

I wince. "Let's make sure her husband gets all the help he needs. I don't want to lose Alessandra."

"Kliedara sniffing around our team again?"

I nod. "So far, they haven't succeeded, but let's not give them any openings. Fine, let's get Sachin a security person."

"Got it." She sets her fork down and scribbles something on her legal pad. "Two hires." She looks up with a grin. "By the way, Bob wanted me to thank you for throwing a party on Valentine's Day. He said it made his life a lot easier."

I chuckle. That sounds exactly like something Mary's husband would say. "We're golfing in a couple of weeks," I reply. "Tell him to buy me a drink."

I GET BACK to the office I share with Finn, and Janine, our assistant, who sits in a cubicle just outside, looks up. "Mary just called me," she chuckles. "You left your phone in her office. You want me to go get it?"

"No, I'll go." I head back to Mary's office and she hands me my phone with a grin. She's used to me leaving my phone around everywhere; everyone at Imperium is.

It buzzes as I walk back. It's Miki. Rather, it's her forum moniker. *Mouse.* She's replying to my morning message. *Thank you. What's in the furniture store? Merlin wouldn't tell me.*

I grin. *I'm not going to tell you either. You'll have to go find out.*

It's in Brooklyn, she types. *I don't know where you live, Lancelot, since you duck the question every single time I ask, but for the record, Brooklyn is not close by.*

I live less than five miles from her, a fact that I'm going to keep a secret for as long as I humanly can. *You can get to Brooklyn on the subway, can't you? Go today. Unless you have birthday plans?*

No, she replies. *I'm planning to spend the evening in my PJs, drinking wine and eating ice cream. Maybe I'll even crank-call my ex-husband.*

Don't be a cliché, Mouse.

I can close my eyes and picture Miki sitting in the airplane seat between Finn and me. When I offered her my business card, I hadn't been thinking that it was a way to get closer to the woman who had succeeded in hacking one of our prototype systems. I'd been responding to the obvious chemistry between us.

Thank heavens she said no. That would have made a complicated situation even more so.

I sigh heavily as I reach my office, and Janine looks up. "Paul's news?" she asks sympathetically. "He gave me a heads-up."

Chatting with Miki, I'd almost forgotten about Claudia's latest kick in the teeth. "I'll deal," I tell my assistant.

"I'm sure you will," she replies. She frowns. "No offense, Oliver. If Claudia were here, I'd kick her ass." She looks at her computer. "I've got Susan Dee from the PR team scheduled to meet you on Monday morning. Unless you need to see her earlier?"

I shake my head. "Claudia knows that the moment those photos are leaked, she has no leverage over me. We have time."

"Claudia is a bitch," she mutters under her breath.

Yup. She sure is.

This whole situation with Miki is problematic. When we first came up with the idea to keep an eye on her through the DefCon forums, I hadn't expected to become friends with her. Now, I talk to her at least once a day, and if I don't hear from her, my day feels like it's missing something.

Our entire relationship is based on a lie.

Don't drink too much wine, Mouse, I type. *And definitely don't call your ex.*

I can't explain why that idea bothers me as much as it does.

4

Buy the ticket, take the ride.

— HUNTER S. THOMPSON

Miki:

There's a small part of me that wonders if it's all an elaborate prank. What if *User0989* is pulling some kind of scam, and I'm not on the guest list? When I arrive at the Waldorf Astoria, I'm half-prepared to be turned away.

I'm not. There are a handful of staff members dressed in neon pink milling about in the reception area, carrying iPads. I navigate to a friendly-looking young man in glasses, feeling sorry for the ridiculous costume he has to wear, and tell him I should be on the list. "M. Mouse?"

He's too well-paid to crack a smile. He taps on his tablet and confirms my attendance, and slips a pink wire bracelet over my wrist. "You'll need to check in your coat and all your belongings," he explains. "There's a strict 'No Electronic Devices' rule. The coat check is on your right."

"Thank you." No electronic devices. That's to be expected, I guess, for a data security firm such as Imperium.

I approach the coat check, removing my gloves and stuffing them in the pocket of the black winter coat I borrowed from Gabby. The woman at the counter takes it from me along with my handbag, and she hands me a metal token and shows me that it slips onto my bracelet like a little charm. "Clever idea," I murmur, and she smiles, nods and directs me to the next step, which is to walk through a metal detector.

This place is locked down tighter than JFK.

I clear security and enter the ballroom. The decorators have gone overboard with the theme. The room looks like a cotton candy explosion. Pink heart-shaped balloons are everywhere. A thousand glittering silver stars cover the ceiling. The wait staff wear Pepto-Bismol-pink jumpsuits, same as the crew that was in charge of checking people in. The decor is, quite honestly, ridiculous, but it's nowhere as over-the-top as the outfits some of the guests are wearing. A woman near me appears to be wearing a pink feather boa *and nothing else.* Another guest is wearing skin-tight pastel-pink spandex. She's got the body for it, and I have to give her props. She's a braver woman than I am. I would have never thought of wearing Star-Trek-style gym clothes to this party.

I'm going to need a drink to survive this evening.

I make my way to a corner of the bar. The bartender comes up almost instantly and gives me a friendly smile. "What can I get you?"

I open my mouth to ask for a glass of red wine, and then calculate that the likelihood of spilling my drink on myself is pretty high. "A vodka and soda, please."

He brings me my drink. I stay in my corner and discreetly survey the room, wondering if I can catch someone staring at me. User0989 is here somewhere, but I'm not sure how or when he's going to make contact.

Next to me, two middle-aged men are talking to each other. "Some party, huh?" one of them says. "These guys are pulling out all the stops ahead of their IPO."

I eavesdrop shamelessly. I went dress shopping with Gabby instead of researching Imperium, and I feel desperately under-prepared for this evening.

"Did you hear that the shares aren't going to have voting rights?" The guy sounds quite put out. "Prescott and Sanders own the entire firm, and they're not giving up control."

His friend shrugs. "It hasn't stopped the stock offering from being oversubscribed," he complains. "My broker couldn't get me in on the ground floor. The IPO is going to be a wild success. There's nothing that can derail it at this point."

"They could get hacked," the other guy replies. "Imperium is a hot commodity because they've never been beaten. If someone manages to get inside their network—"

A chill trickles up my spine. That's why User0989 wants me to hack into their network. He wants to derail the IPO.

Facebook raised sixteen *billion* dollars when they went public. Imperium might not be in the same league, but there's no denying that there's a ton of money at stake.

I'm desperate, but I'm not reckless. This is too rich for my blood. *I need to get out of here.*

I'm about to move away when a man comes up to the bar. "I'll have a rum and coke, Tom," he says. His voice sounds familiar, and I look up. He turns toward me at the same time, and I experience a jolt of recognition.

It's Finn. Finn from the plane.

For a brief second, there's an expression of shock on his face, so fleeting that I wonder if I've imagined it. I must have; his face lights up with pleasure. "Miki," he says, "What a surprise it is to see you."

Tell me about it.

"Finn from the plane." I smile widely, thrilled beyond belief to see a familiar face. "What are you doing here?"

"I know a couple of people here. This," he gestures to the room, "is the hottest party in Manhattan this month."

"I wouldn't have thought you cared about stuff like that."

"I could say the same about you," he replies with a wink. He leans in closer to whisper conspiratorially, "The drinks are free."

I laugh out loud. He's being evasive, but I don't care.

This close to him, I can smell his cologne. It's a heady scent, with a hint of citrus and lavender and something earthier. Maybe sandalwood. *Resist the urge to sniff him, Miki. You're not a puppy.* "You flew all the way from Texas for this party?"

"I live in Manhattan," he replies, his eyes twinkling. "A fifteen-minute cab ride away. You?"

"Ten minutes," I reply. "I live in Hell's Kitchen."

We launch into conversation. As we talk, I survey him discreetly. Finn looks better than I remember. He's wearing another suit, a dark charcoal one this time. His only concession to the 'Pretty in Pink' theme is his pink plaid tie.

I've thought of the Thanksgiving flight from Houston to New York often. Of being seated between two impossibly good-looking men, of laughing and flirting with them, pretending for the space of a few hours that my carefully constructed life wasn't shattering around me.

I've wondered what would have happened if I'd taken

the business card Oliver offered me. Would I have slept with him? Would it have been good?

Finn's eyes run over my body, taking in the plunging neckline of my gown, lingering at the swell of my breasts. "You look lovely," he says. "That's a very pretty dress."

I swallow as I meet his gaze and see the desire in his expression. "Thank you," I murmur. Daringly, I brush his arm with my fingers and look up at him through my eyelashes. *Flirting for Dummies, Miki-style.* My nerves loosen my tongue. "My friend Gabby took me shopping. Today's my birthday, and she wouldn't let me pay for it."

"It's your birthday?" He leans in, his body inches from mine, and his breath tickles my ear. "Happy birthday, Miki."

Goosebumps break out on my skin. His thigh is touching mine. He's close to me. I can feel the heat of his body, and if I take one more step toward him—

My girlfriends' intervention has worked; I'm not thinking about Aaron right now. I'm thinking about how gorgeous Finn looks. His ice-blue eyes are running all over me, and my long-dormant libido comes alive with a vengeance.

Before I have time to react to his nearness, Oliver appears out of nowhere. I jump like a scalded cat, and Finn bites back his grin. "You startled me," I accuse the blond man.

"Sorry about that," he replies. Like Finn, Oliver's wearing a dark suit. "I thought I saw a familiar face." His lips turn up in a half-smile. "Did I hear it's your birthday?"

He leans in to kiss me, his lips brushing over my cheek. My skin tingles where he touches me, and my stomach clenches with desire. *Oh hell. Both of them?* Evidently, my body has decided that it's done with mourning my failed marriage. My nipples bead under my dress, and since I'm not wearing a bra, my arousal is painfully visible under the chiffon fabric.

Calm the fuck down, Miki. "It's the big three-oh," I reply, trying to sound light and casual.

"It is?" Oliver's eyes sweep over me. "The drinks are free at this party, otherwise I'd insist you let me buy you a drink to celebrate."

A tall, thin woman with long dark hair, slicked back into a tight ponytail approaches us, her gaze locked on Oliver. Finn waves her away. "How've you been, Miki?" he asks me. "You were in the middle of a divorce, if I remember correctly."

"All done." My lips twist into a grimace. "As my mother likes to remind me, I'm now thirty and single, and the odds of meeting a single guy in Manhattan aren't in my favor."

Oliver's voice lowers to a purr. "Your mother's wrong," he replies. "You're talking to two single guys right now."

The woman approaches us again, and this time, it's Oliver who waves her away. "Sorry about that," he says to me. "This is a work event, and Janine wants me to mingle."

He doesn't show any sign of wanting to leave. His fingers trace small circles on my naked forearm, and my skin tingles where he touches me. Finn's eyes follow the movement, but he too stands exactly where he is, right next to me, so close that I can feel the warmth of his body.

"You should probably do what she wants." *Why do I sound like I've just run a marathon?*

"Work will keep," Oliver replies dismissively. "What's been going on with you? Let me see if I can remember the list you made on the plane." His eyes dance with amusement. "Did you buy a cat?" He takes a step closer to me and bends his head to my ear. "Is your pussy happy, Miki?"

I gasp at his bold words. "You're rude," I say, shocked, as a flush creeps up my face. "I can't believe you just said that."

"I'm not rude," he says calmly, unfazed at my reaction. "Just direct. What's the matter, Miki? I thought sex was okay in your rule book. Just not love."

"Maybe I'm picky about who I have sex with," I reply loftily.

He chuckles, a low sound that has my insides throbbing. "Of course," he agrees. Finn's still watching, a smile playing about on his lips. He hasn't moved away. Maybe they're telling me, ever so subtly, that they're interested in sharing?

Don't be ridiculous, Miki. You're imagining things. All your friends are in ménages, and that's messing with your head. Not everyone wants a threesome. In fact, most people don't.

The tall woman, Janine, hovers near us for a third time, a frustrated expression on her face. Oliver sighs. "I think I'm being summoned," he says ruefully. He reaches for his wallet and pulls a business card out of it. "I'd love to take you out to dinner sometime. Call me?"

Three months ago, I'd passed on Oliver's invitation. But my friends staged an intervention for me this morning, and I promised them I'd do better. And what better day than my birthday to start something new?

I pluck the card from his fingers. "Maybe."

He laughs. He lifts my hand and presses a kiss on my palm. He tosses back his drink in one gulp, then he disappears into the crowd.

I half-expect Finn to follow him, but the other man makes no move to leave. "It's your birthday," he says, his sky-blue eyes piercing into me. "Yet you're here, not with friends."

"What about you?" I counter. "It's Valentine's Day. No date, Finn? No special someone you want to be with?"

"I'm happily single." A wry smile tugs at his lips. "Also, I don't believe in Valentine's Day."

"Why not?"

He lifts his shoulders in a shrug. "If I were in love with a woman," he says quietly, "I'd show her how much I care *every day*. She won't need flowers in the middle of February to know she's the most important person in my life."

Aaron took me to the fanciest steakhouse in Houston for Valentine's Day last year. At the same time, he was fucking his assistant.

Don't go there, Miki. Aaron's in the past.

"My friends woke me up with cake this morning," I reply, skipping past his comment about Valentine's Day and focusing on his earlier remark.

Finn smiles. "That's a great way to start the day," he replies. "What kind?"

"Carrot with a ginger cream cheese frosting," I say smugly. "I'm not ashamed to admit I ate two pieces."

"Why would you be?" he asks, his eyes raking down my body again, his gaze appreciative. "You look fantastic."

His fingers trace the black yoke of my dress, skimming over my cleavage. My breathing catches at his touch. "You're flirting with me," I whisper, not pulling away. I'm like a moth dancing around the open flame, chasing danger, and tempting fate. Butterflies dance in my stomach as Finn's fingers lace in mine, and he tugs me closer.

I should be running away, but I'm not. My pulse is racing, my throat is dry, and I'm rooted to the spot.

Finn bends his head toward me, almost in slow motion. He's going to kiss me. My insides clench with anticipation. *Yes, please.* It's been so long since I wanted someone with this kind of raw, aching need.

His lips meet mine, warm and firm. His hand rests on

my waist, drawing me closer. I make a noise of pleasure in my throat and tilt my head up, pressing against him and deepening the kiss.

Finn's tongue slides against the seam of my lips. I open my mouth and kiss him back. The noise of the party recedes to the background, and blood pounds in my ears. Finn's hand moves from my hip to the back of my neck, and he deepens the intensity of the kiss.

Carrot cake for breakfast, and a kiss for dinner. I'm having quite the birthday.

I bring my hand up to his face. His stubble scratches my skin faintly, and the slight rasp of it sends shivers of heat through me. My breasts are smashed into Finn's broad chest. His hips are pressed against me, and I can feel his erection against my stomach. Shamelessly, I press closer to him, and his hand moves lower, cupping my ass before he seems to realize where he is.

He breaks off the kiss and stares at me, his eyes foggy with desire. "Miki," he exhales. "If I told you I have a hotel room upstairs, would you be interested?"

For a second, for one brief second, I'm tempted to throw caution to the wind and say yes.

Then common sense reasserts itself. "Yes," I reply truthfully. "But I wouldn't do it anyway."

His eyes bore into me. "No," he agrees. "You wouldn't." He pulls a business card out of his wallet and hands it to me. "Like Oliver, I need to mingle or risk the wrath of Janine. Will you have dinner with me?"

"So you can try changing my mind?"

His lips curl up. "My intentions aren't completely pure, it's true," he says. "But I'd like to get to know you better as well."

"Oliver asked me to dinner too."

His eyes meet mine. "You can do whatever you want, Miki," he replies. "You can have dinner with him. Or me. *Or both of us.*"

You know what I should be doing? Freaking out. *You know what I'm doing instead?* Being intrigued. Taking Finn's business card. *What the hell has gotten into me?*

"I should go," I mutter. I don't know where User0989 is, and I don't care. I'm not thinking about work right now. I'm thinking about the two men whose business cards I hold in my hand.

"Of course." Finn's ice-blue eyes survey me intently. "Happy birthday again."

IN THE LOBBY, I stand in line to get my coat. There's a stack of brochures on a side table, half-hidden by a tall vase of flowers. Imperium brochures. I grab one and idly start reading it as I wait for the couple ahead of me to retrieve their belongings.

Then my heart stops.

There are photos of Imperium's executive team on the back.

I recognize two of them. Oliver Prescott is the CEO of Imperium, and Finn Sanders is the Chief Operating Officer.

My entire body goes cold. I kissed Finn. I flirted with Oliver. They both invited me to dinner. *And they're the owners of Imperium.*

My mind is churning, and I don't know how to process my reaction.

I reach the front of the line and hand the woman there my token. She takes it from me and fetches my coat and purse. "I hope you enjoyed the party," she says.

"Sure." I put my coat on, and pull my gloves out from the

pockets. It's February, and it's freezing outside, and a year in Houston has decreased my tolerance for the cold.

"Ma'am?" The coat check woman points to a folded piece of paper on the floor. "Something fell out from your pocket."

I pick up the scrap, my heart pounding. I've borrowed Gabby's coat, and there was nothing in the pockets when I arrived at the party. This must be a message from User0989.

I wait until I'm in a cab before I read the note. Sure enough, it's from him.

Your next step is to apply for a job at Imperium. I'll send you more details on Monday. And Ms. Cooper, don't worry. You'll be hired.

5

It has been my experience that folks who have no vices
have very few virtues.

— ABRAHAM LINCOLN

Finn:

"She lied to us." Oliver's expression is dark. It's well
past midnight. The ballroom has almost cleared
out and only a few stragglers remain.

Miki's appearance has thrown both of us for a loop.
We've been chatting with her daily on the DefCon forums. I
spent half an hour talking to her today, damn it, but she
never mentioned coming to our party.

All kinds of alarms are going off in my head.

"I asked Miki earlier today what her plans were," Oliver
continues, taking his fourth glass of rum and coke from the
bartender with a nod of thanks, "and she said she was going
to drink wine and eat ice cream."

"I know." I don't like this. Today's been a shit show. First the Claudia photo bombshell, then finding out that she's dating Fitzgerald, and now this.

I've been spending long hours trying to find out who's leaking proprietary information to Fitzgerald. Now, I have a new mystery to investigate. *What is Miki up to?*

"This isn't a coincidence," I tell my friend grimly. "She's up to something."

Oliver nods bleakly. "I thought we could trust Miki," he mutters. "I guess I was wrong."

I draw in a deep breath. After Claudia, Oliver's trust in women has frayed badly. Miki was one of the few people he still had faith in. But now—

I sigh. Fucking Claudia. She really did a number on my friend. Before he met her, Oliver was mellow and laid-back. Now, there's a darkness in him I don't like. "Don't drink too much," I advise him.

He ignores me. I get the feeling he's going to be at the bar all night long.

Miki:

On Saturday, I head to the Plaza to have afternoon tea with my mother and sister, a weekly Cooper tradition that I've always hated. I don't fit in with the 'ladies that lunch' crowd; I never have.

Then again, the tiny finger sandwiches are amazing, and my mother is paying.

The two of them are seated next to a potted palm tree. A white-clad waiter shows me to their table. "Mackenzie, there you are," my mother greets me, running a disapproving eye over my outfit. Audrey Cooper does not believe in pants, and

I'm sure my red sweater, simple white shirt, and navy blue pants violate some kind of dress code. Pity. I thought I looked quite good in it. Nautical. Very Sea-Captain-ish.

"Hello, Mother." I graze my lips over her cheek, careful not to disrupt her makeup, and sink into my seat. "Hey Leah."

My sister's lips twitch. "Happy birthday, Miki. Sorry I couldn't take you out on Friday."

"Don't worry about it," I reply. "Valentine's Day. I get it. Did you and Benjamin go out?"

Her smile dims. "No, he had to work late." There's a dispirited tone in her voice, and my spidey senses go on full alert. I'll have to ask Leah what's going on when my mother isn't around.

We make our tea selections. "I got you a present, dear," my mother says once the waiter is out of earshot. She hands me a small robin-egg-blue box. "Leah helped me pick it out," she replies. "I hope you like it."

I open the jewelry box and find a ring inside. A chunky jade stone is set into a thick gold band. It's absolutely beautiful. "Thank you, mom. I love it."

"Leah tells me it's quite the rage for single women to wear right-hand rings," she says. "And since you don't have a man to buy you jewelry—" Her voice trails off.

Moment ruined. Classic Audrey Cooper. I should be used to my family by now. Leah looks indignant and mouths 'I did not' to me. I pat her on the shoulder.

"You look pale, Miki," my mother adds. "You keep such odd hours."

"She looks fine." Leah rolls her eyes. "Have some tea, mother. Eat a sandwich. Try not to be snide."

"Well, really," my mother begins, but I cleverly put a fruit tart on her plate, the one with lemon custard, topped with slices of glazed strawberries. That stuff is like catnip, and it works perfectly to divert her attention.

"What did you do on Valentine's Day, mom?"

She gives me a brittle smile. "I just had a quiet evening."

Translation: My father was out banging whoever he's sleeping with at the moment, and my mother is doing her best ostrich imitation.

I shouldn't have asked.

Leah changes the topic hastily. "What did you do for your birthday?" she asks me. "Did your friends take you out?"

I shake my head. "I went to a ball at the Waldorf Astoria." I think back on the day. Shopping for dresses. Gabby carefully doing my make-up and my hair. The pink balloons and the shining silver stars. And of course, Finn and Oliver. "It was very Cinderella-like."

My mother's hand freezes midway to her mouth. "You went to a ball?" she asks. "Of your own free will? Has someone kidnapped my first-born child and replaced her with a clone?"

She's staring at me with a shocked expression on her face. As is Leah. "I go to parties," I reply defensively. "There's no need to look at me like I've grown a second head."

"Wrong, you *never* go to parties," Leah replies. *Traitor.* "I think I could count the number of parties you've been to in your life on one hand."

"Every single Monday night, I hang out with my friends," I retort.

"That's not a party," she says. "For something to be considered a party, you'll have to speak to one person you don't already know, Ms. I-Hate-Talking-To-New- People."

"I don't think that counts as the official definition." Oh My God, this cucumber sandwich. In a perfect world, I'd wear my right-hand ring and marry this cucumber sand-wich. *So good.*

My mother looks at my sandwich-laden plate and sighs. I quickly offer her a petite-four, forestalling her timeworn lecture of eating like a lady. "Tell me about this ball," she says instead. "It was at the Waldorf Astoria?"

"In the ballroom." I know that'll impress her. "A company called Imperium threw a customer appreciation party for their clients. I thought I might find a job there."

Job, *schwab*. Audrey Cooper doesn't care about my employment prospects, just my marital status, and she's a bloodhound in her quest to get me coupled again. "And did you meet any eligible young men, Mackenzie?"

Oliver and Finn's business cards are still tucked in my purse. I tossed and turned all Friday night, wondering what to do about the complicated situation. I still don't know.

Leah chuckles. "You're blushing," she accuses me. "Tell us everything."

I think of the expression in Finn's eyes as he lingered over the swell of my breasts. The way Oliver's fingers caressed my bare arms. The sparks that ran through my body when Finn kissed me. The promise of so much more.

You can have dinner with him. Or me. Or both of us.

"You'd have loved the dress I wore," I tell Leah, knowing that any mention of clothes will distract my fashionista sister from snooping.

It works.

IT'S BEGINNING to get dark outside when we leave. It's snow-ing, and I'm debating hailing a cab when Leah grabs my elbow. "You're walking home, aren't you, Miki? I'm heading your way. I'll come with you."

It takes me a second to catch the tightness in her voice. "Sure," I say readily, hugging my mother goodbye. The doorman outside the Plaza has already hailed her a cab and is holding the door open for her. "See you next week, mom."

"What's going on?" I ask Leah when she's gone. "I doubt you have a sudden desire to walk in the slush and snow."

"I want to talk to you about Benjamin," she replies. She takes a deep breath before blurting out, "I think he's cheating on me."

I stop dead in my tracks. "Oh, Leah," I murmur, lost for words. The Cooper women always seem to draw the short straw when it comes to the men in our lives. "Are you sure?"

"No. That's what I wanted to talk to you about. Can you do your hacking magic and find out?"

"You want me to read his email?"

She shakes her head. "Not email. Our finances. We have a joint bank account, but this year, his Christmas bonus was only half the size of last year's. I want you to figure out if he's hiding money from me."

"Of course." The legalities of what I'm going to do are murky, but this is my baby sister. I would walk through fire for her.

BACK HOME, I go straight to my laptop. I check DefCon's forums from habit, but Lancelot and Merlin aren't online. Neither of them has logged on since Friday night, which is strange behavior for them.

Not everyone is glued to their computers all the time, Miki, I mutter as I log into my sister's bank account, using the account information and password she gave me. I scan the transactions, looking for anything that seems out of place. It's as good a place to start as any.

Three hours later, I hit a wall. A high, impenetrable one. Ben's online accounts are protected by Imperium. Why does my brother-in-law feel the need for top-of-the-line data security? Not a clue.

I guess I'll be applying for that job after all.

6

Know thy self, know thy enemy. A thousand battles, a thousand victories.

— Sun Tzu

Finn:

I spend most of my weekend at work, deliberately staying away from the DefCon chat rooms. I miss chatting with Miki, but I'm not ready to talk to her. Not until I understand what's going on.

Monday morning, I get to work by seven. Fortifying myself with three cups of coffee, I make my way to Lawrence Kent's office. Technically, the CFO reports to Oliver, not me, but I've never let it stop me in the past, and I'm not going to let it stop me now.

Sometime between his fourth and fifth drink on Friday, Oliver mentioned that Kent had borrowed a developer from the Shield team. That's complete bullshit. Kent doesn't need any additional team members—he's the reason every single finance initiative is late. He's unpleasant to work with, condescending, arrogant and petty. He never gives his team any credit and throws them under the bus with regularity. Turnover in his division is insanely high. Nobody wants to work for Lawrence, and I don't blame them.

I'm in a very bad mood as I make my way to the fourteenth floor. Kent's typically in early, and sure enough, he's already in his office, eating a bagel and reading the Wall Street Journal. "Sanders," he says, nodding coolly when he sees me. "How was your weekend?"

"Busy." There's no love lost between the two of us, and I'm too irritated right now to observe the niceties. "I found out on Friday that you poached one of Sachin's team members. What the fuck, Larry? Shield's a critical project for us."

"I mentioned it to you," he argues. "I told you I needed someone with a technical background to consolidate our financial statements ahead of the IPO."

"No," I correct him. "You said that the work would go faster if you had a developer, and I told you that I couldn't pull anyone off one of my projects."

"Well, Sachin didn't think there was a problem," he says huffily. "You're not in kindergarten anymore, Sanders. Learn to share."

Deep breath. "You went behind my back," I tell him clearly. "Sachin is dreadful at saying 'No', and you intimidated him and implied that his job was on the line if he didn't cooperate." My jaw clenches in anger. I'm done with this clown. "This time, you're getting away with it. I'm going to hire someone else. But consider this a warning, Larry." I step into his office and glare at the man. "You pull this kind of shit one more time, and no matter what the consequences, I'll see to it that you're sidelined or fired."

He doesn't reply, nor do I expect him to.

Miki:

At six in the morning on Monday, User0989 sends me a link to a job posting at Imperium. They're looking for someone to act as a security expert on one of their products. It's a perfect match for my skills.

Under different circumstances, I'd be applying to the role in a heartbeat.

Yet, for the next three hours, I'm wracked with indecision.

If I'm inside the Imperium network, I have a fighting chance of finding out what my brother-in-law is up to. I love Leah, and I will move heaven and earth to help her.

But I have no illusions. Once I'm inside the company, I'm committed to doing what User0989 wants. I won't have any other choice. He knows too much. He knows my real name as well as my DefCon username. If he threatens to expose me, I'll have to cooperate with him.

And if Oliver and Finn were to find out the truth, I have no doubt that the easy charm and sexy smiles will disappear. *They will have me arrested.*

I wish I could talk to Merlin and Lancelot about this. I pull my phone out, but they're not online. *Again.*

I went to the furniture store yesterday. When I realized what the two of them had given me, I'd been ready to bawl my eyes out at their kindness and their consideration. In our year of marriage, Aaron never once got me a gift I wanted. Instead, I got jewelry and fancy clothes, so that he could show his colleagues what a wonderful husband he was.

Forget Aaron.

I'd sent Lancelot and Merlin a couple of messages yesterday thanking them for their gift, but I've heard nothing back from either of them. After talking to them every single day in the last few months, the radio silence feels strange and weird and, if I'm being perfectly honest, a little hurtful.

Forget Merlin and Lancelot.

Finally, I give up and apply for the job. *They might not even call you back,* I tell myself. *You're probably stressing over nothing.*

LESS THAN AN HOUR LATER, I stare at my email with total disbelief. There's a message in my inbox from someone called Mary MacDonald, who heads up Human Resources at Imperium.

They want to interview me today at four in the afternoon.

Crap on a cracker.

I'm torn. This job interview is the best thing that's happened to me since my divorce. For the first time in a long while, I'm excited. There's a part of me that wants to do a happy dance around Wendy's living room.

I type out a reply confirming my availability. My heart is pounding in my chest when I'm done. I have to tell someone my big news. I could call Leah or one of my girlfriends, but they wouldn't appreciate what a big deal this is. If you're a hacker, Imperium is the Holy Grail of employers.

Except it isn't real.

But even that sobering thought can't quite quell my excitement.

Lancelot and Merlin would understand. Even though

they haven't been online or seen any of my messages, I still want to tell them.

I pull out my phone and type them a quick line. *Guess what? I have an actual job interview. AT LAST! And it's at IMPERIUM!!!!!!!!*

My euphoria fades in the shower. Oliver and Finn are way, way out of my league, and nothing is ever likely to happen between us. But it had been nice to daydream about the possibilities.

If I'm hired at Imperium, however, I can't let anything happen.

Because I'm secretly plotting to destroy them.

7

Do I not destroy my enemies when I make them my friends?

— ABRAHAM LINCOLN

Oliver:

Monday morning, I have a meeting with Susan Dee, the head of Public Relations at Imperium. "You were quite cryptic at the party, Oliver. What are we dealing with here?"

I slide the envelope containing the six photos across my desk, and she opens it and flips through them. "I'm a little disappointed," she quips when she's done. "I was hoping you'd be wearing leather pants."

I chuckle. Susan's impossible to shock. "Claudia claims that I coerced her into bondage, spanked her without her consent, and took photos of the act."

She rolls her eyes. "How much did she ask for? I'm assuming you're not paying."

"If it were money, I might pay just to get it over with. She wants Imperium shares. That's not going to happen."

Susan nods, unsurprised. "No, of course not." She flips through the images again. "Well, these photos aren't good. How long do we have before this hits?"

"Ten weeks, probably." We go public in three months, and there's a blackout period for six months after that to prevent people from selling their shares. Claudia is going to want to get her portion before the IPO.

"Ouch." She frowns. "This isn't my area of expertise, Oliver. I'm going to recommend we hire a PR firm that specializes in crisis management."

"We need someone discreet."

"Absolutely," Susan replies. "I can have a shortlist of firms on your desk by Wednesday morning."

"Thanks, Sue. I appreciate it."

She clears her throat. "Oliver," she says, "This blackmail attempt is just vile. We're going to fix this."

Her faith in me is reassuring. I only hope the board sees it the same way.

A COUPLE OF HOURS LATER, Finn and I are lost in work when both our phones buzz at the same time. Out of habit, I glance at my screen.

And freeze.

Miki's interviewing at Imperium.

Finn looks like someone's hit him with a baseball bat. "What the hell?" I swear out loud. I pick up my phone and page my assistant. "Janine, I need to see Mary in my office as soon as possible."

Hanging up, I look at Finn. "This is bullshit." I'm infuriated. I don't know where my rage is coming from, but there's no doubt that I'm angrier than I've ever been in my life. "Tell me that it's coincidence that the only person who success-fully hacked into one of our systems is interviewing at our firm."

He doesn't reply.

"Tell me," I continue, my voice louder, "that she's not hiding something. Tell me she's on the up-and-up. Tell me that I can trust her."

Finn meets my gaze squarely, but he doesn't say a word.

"I'm done." I get to my feet and stare out of the window. From my office, I can see the East River. Typically, the view soothes me. Not today. "I'm done being Lancelot. No more DefCon. No more late night chats. If I can't trust Miki, then I'm going to cut her out of my life, Finn. Mary can cancel the damn interview."

My gut churns at the idea of never talking to her again, but my mind's made up. If I wanted to spend time with a lying, conniving woman, I'd call my fucking ex-wife.

"She's not Claudia," Finn replies quietly. "And I don't think either of us can take the moral high ground. We've been lying to Miki for three months."

"So you trust her unquestioningly?" I sneer, ignoring the stab of conscience I feel at his words. "You want to roll out the red carpet for Miki? You want to let her inside Imperium and give her access to our network? The IPO is in three months, Finn. Do you trust her that much?"

"No," he admits reluctantly. "Something doesn't add up." He glances at his phone again, and his lips twist into a small smile. "She sounds really happy about this job," he mutters.

Yeah. She really does.

I remember the first three months after my divorce. I'd been shattered. My emotions had see-sawed from relief that I was free of Claudia, to self-reproach that I could have been stupid enough to marry her. Finn had never liked her. Janine couldn't stand her. Finn's grandmother had taken me aside and asked me if I knew what I was getting into. I'd ignored them. I'd been a fool.

I've poured all of this out to Miki over several late night conversations. No names, of course, and no identifying details, but she knows more about me than anyone except Finn.

Fool me once, shame on you. Fool me twice?

Finn's lost in thought. "I think we should hire her," he says at last.

"Are you out of your mind?"

"Hear me out, Oliver," he snaps. "I'm not suggesting we have her running around without supervision. I think we should hire her, and have her work on something where we can keep an eye on her. There's someone behind this. Don't you want to find out who?"

I give him a questioning look. "Don't you think it's Fitzgerald?"

"He isn't acting alone. Someone inside Imperium is helping him. Possibly the same someone who put Miki on the guest list for Friday's party."

There's a knock on our door, and Mary MacDonald sticks her head in. "You wanted to see me?"

I wave her inside. "You're interviewing Mackenzie Cooper today?"

She looks surprised. "Yes. She sent her resume in this morning. She's exceptionally well qualified."

Yeah, I know.

"Is there a problem?" Mary asks. "I did a quick background check, and there wasn't anything that stood out."

I make up my mind. "No, no problem," I tell her. "Who's meeting with her, Sachin and you?"

She nods.

"Change of plan. Finn and I will be interviewing Miki ourselves."

Finn's right. We need to keep an eye on Miki. My head tells me we're doing the smart thing by hiring her.

But in my heart, I know this is a very bad idea. I like Miki, and I'm attracted to her.

If I felt nothing other than pure sexual attraction for her, I could ignore it. I'm a fucking adult, after all. But I genuinely like her, and that makes her dangerous.

You liked her, I correct myself. *Your friendship is in the past.*

8

True friends stab you in the front.

— Oscar Wilde

Miki:

I get to Imperium's front desk and ask for Mary MacDonald. The receptionist waves toward the couch. "Please take a seat, Ms. Cooper," she says. "I'll let Mary know you're here."

The Head of Human Resources appears in the lobby three minutes later. "Mackenzie," she greets me with a friendly smile. "Thank you for coming at such short notice."

She places her hand over the scanner, and it flashes green. I'm impressed with Imperium's security. Key cards can be stolen. Fingerprints are much harder to fake.

Mary pushes the door open, and I follow her through. "Can I get you something to drink? Coffee? Water?"

"I'm good, thank you." As I walk, my head swivels back and forth, and I check out the office space. It's light and airy, but it's smaller than I would have thought. "How large are you?"

Since Friday night, I've googled Imperium six ways to Sunday, but I've run into some real limitations in my search. Information on the data security company is practically non-existent. Their website has a lot of detail about their suite of products, but almost nothing about the company itself, apart from the one page with a list of their executives. It's maddening.

"We're just over sixty employees now," she replies. "When we talked earlier, I think I said that Sachin Sharma, the team lead of Shield would be interviewing you, didn't I?"

I nod.

"Change of plans. Sachin's slammed. You're going to be meeting with our CEO and COO instead."

My heart almost stops. "I beg your pardon?" I say faintly. Surely I've misheard her. Why would Finn and Oliver be interviewing me personally?

She stops in front of a dark walnut door and knocks. "Come on in," a familiar voice says.

"Good luck, Mackenzie," Mary says. She turns the handle and pushes the door open.

I step into the office, my palms damp. *Run, Miki, run,* a voice inside me is screaming. Get out before it's too late.

But it's already too late; it was too late the moment I wore my pink dress and went to their party. It was too late the moment I replied to User0989's message.

Now, I need to see this through.

"MIKI." Oliver rises to his feet when I enter, as does Finn. He smiles at me, his eyes amused. "I pride myself on being able to remember conversations. When we first met on the plane to JFK, Finn asked you what you did."

The office is huge. It's got floor-to-ceiling views of the river, two huge desks, a large gray sectional in the corner, and a round table with eight chairs around it. It's very fancy. "What did I say?" I ask. Even though his smile seems friendly, I'm still wary.

Finn answers. "You said you stared at spreadsheets all day. Then again, you probably couldn't talk about your work at Blackthorne."

I seize on the lifeline he's thrown me. "Exactly."

Oliver waves me to a chair across from him, and I sit down. Finn's sitting next to me, and I'm acutely conscious of his presence. After the way I'd flirted with them Friday night, how could I not be?

This is a job interview, Miki. Stay professional.

It's hard. Finn's eyes are not running over my body now, but I can't stop thinking of the way he'd looked at me Friday night. Oliver's sitting across the desk from me, acting completely professional, and all I can think of is the way he bent his head toward me and asked me if my pussy was happy.

My pussy would be a lot happier if it got up close and personal with these two men.

Oliver is scanning my resume. "Tell me about yourself," he says. "Why do you want to work at Imperium?"

My brother-in-law might be cheating on my sister, and the proof, if any, is here. Oh, also, someone's paying me a hundred thousand dollars to steal your client list. I'm still looking for a way out of that one, though.

"I believe in data security," I reply. Yeah, I know that's a lame answer. "I enjoy finding vulnerabilities in systems before someone can exploit them."

"Tell me about the work you did at Blackthorne," Finn prompts.

I answer his question, wishing I could read them. It might be my imagination, but I'm willing to swear there's an air of tension in the room. Suddenly, the reason behind their strained expressions strikes me.

"I'd like to say something." God, this is awkward. "I had no idea who you were on Friday. Obviously, if I'm hired, I'll keep things strictly professional."

A smile tugs at Oliver's lips. "Thank you, Miki." He raises his eyebrow at Finn. "Finn, anything you want to add?"

My stomach sinks. They haven't even asked me three questions. So far, my interview has lasted less than ten minutes. When Mary emailed me, I thought I had a real shot at this job. So much for optimism.

I've blown it.

I don't know what passes between Finn and Oliver; I'm too lost in my misery to pay attention.

"Miki," Oliver's voice pulls me out of my gloomy reverie. "We'd like to offer you a job."

"What?" I gape at him. "But you didn't ask me any questions."

Finn chuckles. "I spent twenty minutes on the phone with your boss at Blackthorne," he says. "Wade Beaumont could not say enough good things about you." He holds his hand out. "Welcome to the team," he says. "If you're interested in joining us?"

"Of course." I'm absolutely numb.

Oliver shakes my hand as well. "About your salary," he says, and rattles off some terms that have my head spinning.

It's money. It's pretty good money. It's enough money that I'm going to be able to hit 'Restart' on my life.

Miki, this is insane. What are you doing?

They're looking at me expectantly, and I realize they're waiting for me to respond. "I'm in," I reply quickly. "Thank you."

"Excellent," Finn says. "How soon can you start?"

"Tomorrow?" Everything's moving so quickly that I don't have time to think. I'm acting purely on instinct.

"Good." Oliver rises to his feet. "Oh, by the way. You won't be working on the Shield team."

"I won't?"

There's a dark expression in his deep blue eyes. "No," he says. "Your skills are much more suitable for a project that Finn and I are working on. You'll be working directly with us. In fact," he adds, "until we find you a cubicle, you'll be working in our office." He waves at the conference table. "As you can see, there's plenty of room." His eyes gleam with amusement and something more heated. *Or is that just my imagination?* "Welcome to Imperium."

I won't be able to poke around their network with Oliver and Finn watching my every move. How am I going to find out what my brother-in-law, Benjamin, is up to? What's User0989 going to say?

I'm screwed.

9

The secret of getting ahead is getting started.

— MARK TWAIN

Miki:

I do my best to calm down on my way home. The instant I walk into the front door, my phone buzzes. It's User0989. *Well? What happened?*

I play dumb. *What do you mean?*

Don't play games with me, Ms. Cooper. I know you interviewed with Prescott and Sanders at Imperium an hour ago.

A chill runs up my spine as something clicks into place. User0989 could have learned that I was interviewing at Imperium today by watching me in the lobby. But how could he have figured out I met Finn and Oliver? Even I didn't know that until I got inside their offices.

There's only one way. *User0989 works at Imperium. Someone in their 60-people organization wants to ruin the IPO.*

I take a deep breath and tap out a reply. *I got the job, but*

I'm going to be working with them directly. I can't start snooping right away. I need some time to settle in.

Damn it, he types. *Fine. You're right. Sanders is a suspicious son of a bitch. I don't want him to start asking questions. I'll be in touch in two weeks.*

I've bought myself a little bit of time. I can only hope that's enough.

ONCE I'M DONE with the conversation, I reach for my notebook with shaking hands. I'm in over my head, and everything feels out of control. I need to make a list.

Top Three Things I need to do at Imperium

1. Find out what Ben's hiding.
2. Find out who User0989 really is. Right now, I have no leverage. He knows my identity, and I don't know his. I don't even know if User0989 is a guy. I need answers.
3. Get Finn and Oliver to trust me.

The last item is the most complicated. I refuse to hack into Imperium and steal the client list that User0989 is looking for. The only reason I'm at Imperium is because of Leah.

I'm using User0989's connections as a way in, but sooner or later, he's going to demand results, results I have no intention of delivering. The only way out of this situation is to tell Oliver Prescott and Finn Sanders the whole truth and hope that they decide not to press charges.

But for that, they need to believe I'm acting in good faith. Will they?

I stare at the list for a long time, and then I tear it out of my notebook and burn it. As much as I'd like to start solving the puzzle of User0989's identity right away, I can't. My girl-friends are taking me out for drinks tonight. It's the first time in over a year that the six of us are going to be together in person, and there's not a force on Earth that will make me miss it.

Finn:

It's past midnight when I get to my condo. I grab a bottle of beer from the refrigerator and sink onto the couch. There's not a scrap of food in my house, and it's too late for most restaurants to deliver. Pizza it will be.

I flip open my laptop, navigate to the nearest all-night place that delivers and place my order. I'll pay my penance on the treadmill tomorrow.

I'd had lunch with my grandmother yesterday, about the only human connection I have outside of Imperium. She'd been a little unsteady on her feet. "It's nothing," she'd dismissed when I'd asked. "Just old age."

Time is a funny thing. It feels like just yesterday when I'd moved in with my grandmother. My parents were raging alcoholics who were more neglectful than not. When I was eleven, frustrated with the fact that they hadn't given me my promised allowance for three months, even though they kept telling me they would, I'd hacked into their bank account and transferred the money into my own.

I'd been too young to conceal my tracks. The bank had discovered the breach, and they'd hired someone to figure out who was responsible.

CPS knocked on my door soon after, and after a stern rebuke from a judge and a two-week stint in juvy, my grandmother had taken custody of me.

Life got better after that. I didn't have to take care of my parents when they were in a drunken stupor. I could go back to being a kid.

On Sunday, after we'd eaten lunch, my grandmother had pressed me again about finding a partner. "Life's short, Finn," she'd said. "Don't put off falling in love until it's convenient."

A tab on my browser is open to the DefCon forums. I click on it out of habit, and I see that Miki's online. Her message from this morning is in a chat window. *Guess what? I have an actual job interview. AT LAST! And it's at IMPERIUM!!!!!!!!*

Maybe it's because my grandmother seems frailer than I remember, or maybe because life really is too short, I type out a response. *How did the interview go, Mouse?*

I shouldn't be talking to her.

She doesn't reply for five minutes. I feel every second of them go by. Finally, the words flash on my screen. *You went missing, Merlin. I thought I'd done something wrong.*

Sorry, Mouse. Work's been crazy.

Thank you for the desk and chair. I'm sitting on it right now.

On the desk? I tease. *You know you're supposed to sit on the chair, right?*

Ha, ha, everyone's a comedian, she replies. *I got the job, btw. <Happy dance>*

I smile as I picture Miki dancing around the room. *Congratulations, Mouse. I'm thrilled for you.*

Did you just get back from work? Let me guess. You've ordered a Hawaiian pizza.

Miki does not understand the appeal of my favorite

toppings. *Ham and pineapple for the win, Mouse. What'd you do tonight?*

My friends took me out for a drink.

Are they pleased that their intervention worked?

To a point. Now they're worried that I want to sleep with my bosses.

I sit up in my chair. She wants to sleep with us? My fingers hover over my keyboard as I figure out how to reply to that, but before I do, she chimes in. *Stop freaking out; I'm not going to sleep with them. They're out of my league, in any case.*

The doorbell rings, and I get up to grab my pizza. When I get back, Oliver's joined the conversation. *I've just looked them up,* he writes. *The blond guy looks like a bear, and the other one needs to shave.*

I stifle a laugh. That sounds like the pre-Claudia Oliver. I pull my phone and text him on his real number. *I don't need to shave, asshole.*

That's because you're guys, Miki writes. *Guys never think other guys are hot. Even if they do, they don't admit it. Trust me; they're hot.*

My conscience prods me. She doesn't know who she's talking to, Sanders. She'll be mortified if she discovers the truth. Isn't it bad enough that your entire friendship is built on a lie? Do you have to double down on it?

It's time to change the topic. Oliver must think so too, because his next message is about Imperium. *When do you start?*

Tomorrow, she writes. *And if I don't go to bed soon, I'll be mainlining coffee to stay awake in the morning. And what kind of shitty first impression would that be?*

I don't want to end this moment of connection, but I should sleep too. *You're probably right. Goodnight, Mouse.*

Goodnight, you two.

I stare at the screen once she types those words. She's still online, still typing. I eat a slice of pizza while waiting for her to finish her next sentence. *You don't know someone called User0989, do you?*

Oliver replies before I can. *No,* he writes. *Who is he?*

Just a random guy, she replies evasively. *Listen, I should go to bed, but if you could dig around, find anything about this guy, I'd be your best friend for life.*

We log off the forums, and Oliver calls me. "User0989," he says. "Setting off any red flags?"

"All of them." The timing is too convenient to be a coincidence. User0989 has to be related to Miki's appearance at Imperium. I'm convinced of it. Now, we just need to figure out who this guy is.

10

You can't cross the sea merely by standing and staring at the water.

— RABINDRANATH TAGORE

Miki:

I show up to work on Tuesday morning, wearing a navy blue suit I borrowed from Wendy. "Take it," she'd said to me when I called her asking if I could raid her wardrobe. "The best part about running a construction company is that I can dress pretty casually. Besides, the little monkey has made sure that I don't fit into any of my clothes anymore."

The receptionist smiles at me when I identify myself. "Welcome to the team, Mackenzie," she says warmly.

Intense relief floods through me. "Thank you." There was a tiny part of me that couldn't quite believe that I'd been hired by Oliver and Finn yesterday after a ten-minute interview. Not going to lie, I'd been half-prepared for the receptionist to laugh at me and send me away.

"Mr. Sanders will be down to set you up with your security access," she continues.

That surprises me. "He's doing what? Is that normal?"

She laughs. "Oh, Finn's a workaholic," she says cheerfully. She looks around and lowers her voice. "Also, a little paranoid."

"Thank you, Pam." Finn's voice is dry.

Pam goes beet red, and I jump. "I didn't hear you," I blurt out.

So far, every time I've seen Finn, he's been in a suit of some kind. Today, he's dressed more casually. He's wearing a pair of dark jeans and a chocolate brown shirt, his sleeves rolled up to his elbows, and best of all, he's carrying two cups of coffee in his hands.

He hands me one. "Hello, Miki," he says. His eyes sweep over my suit. "We're pretty casual here. I guess Mary didn't get a chance to tell you yesterday?"

I shake my head. "Thanks for the coffee."

"No worries," he says easily. "I don't start functioning until my third cup, and Oliver's the same way. Okay, let's get you set up."

For the next hour, I fill out forms for insurance, get my photo taken for my employee badge and have my fingerprints scanned so I can enter the office. Finally, Finn leads me to their office.

Oliver's nowhere to be seen. The couch is gone, and so is the round conference table. In its place is a long, rectangular desk, and four Aeron chairs.

The chairs remind me of Lancelot and Merlin, and a smile tugs at my lips. I'd stayed up much past my bedtime last night talking to them, intensely relieved that they were back online after their weekend away. How pathetic is that? The best relationships I have are with people I've never met in person.

"Sorry about the setup," Finn says apologetically, bringing my attention back to the present. "We're pretty tight on space, and it didn't make sense to put you with the Shield team when you're going to be working with Oliver and me directly."

"Umm, about that," I say, shifting my weight from one foot to another. "Exactly what will I be doing?"

"Two things," he replies. "The first project isn't very interesting, but it'll be a good fit for your financial background. Lawrence Kent, our CFO, needs some help with his numbers."

Lawrence Kent. I try to remember what the man looks like. I think he's the one who's got the Draco Malfoy hair and sneer. "What's the second project?" I ask.

"I've decided to do a full security audit ahead of the IPO," he says with a grin. "You're going to be hacking into Imperium."

Well, hell. This is not going to be good.

I have a meeting at ten in the morning with Lawrence Kent. Finn walks me over to the CFO's office. "Where's Oliver?" I ask as we ride the elevator down. "I haven't seen him all morning." As soon as the words leave my mouth, I want to take them back. Oliver and Finn are my bosses. I need to treat them that way. It's none of my business where Oliver is and what he's doing.

"Board meeting," Finn replies succinctly. "And he won't be in the most pleasant of moods when he gets out, so tread warily."

Again, my mouth blurts out words before my brain can

react and shut it up. "Oliver in a bad mood? I can't picture that."

"He's generally a pretty cheerful guy," Finn agrees. "Having a board of directors breathing over us is new for both Oliver and me, but we can't go public without an independent board. It's an adjustment for all of us."

He stops outside a door. "And this is Lawrence's office," he says.

Before he can knock, the door opens. A barrel-chested man with a high forehead and slicked-back blond hair beckons us in. "Sanders," he says, his tone hostile. "I just got off the phone with Chris. He said he'd been assigned back to Shield."

"Yes." Finn gestures to me. "Mackenzie Cooper just joined my team. She's got a financial background and will be helping you out instead. Miki, this is Lawrence Kent."

We shake hands. "Welcome aboard," the CFO says. He turns his attention back to Finn. "Can you get Facilities to set her up in my office?" he asks as if I'm not in the room.

"Nope." Finn seems quite happy to thwart the man's request. "Miki will be working out of my office, and her focus will be on one of my projects. She'll be able to dedicate a day a week to your division, no more."

Yikes. I can cut the tension in the room with a knife. Lawrence Kent is glaring daggers at Finn. "Miki," Finn says to me, unfazed by the other man's irritation, "Lawrence will give you an overview of what needs to be done, and we'll touch base this afternoon. Okay?"

Once Finn's left, Kent waves me to a seat. "So you're the new hire," he says, surveying me with a dubious air. "Prescott and Sanders have a bad habit of hiring pretty faces. Hopefully, you're qualified to do your job."

My mouth almost falls open with disbelief. What an

asshole. With difficulty, I resist the urge to say something sarcastic. "Can you tell me what you're looking to do?"

He launches into a long-winded explanation that's peppered with useless business jargon and remarkably light on specifics. I listen to him drone on about synergies, core competencies, and paradigm shifts, and after fifteen minutes, I don't have the faintest idea what he wants me to do.

My attention wanders, and I glance around the office. A yellow Post-it note on Kent's monitor catches my eye. It's got writing on it. I blink to clear my vision and look closer at it, and what I find shocks me. Lawrence Kent, the CFO of Imperium, has his passwords written down on a piece of paper where anyone entering his office can see it.

You have got to be kidding me.

So much for fingerprint scans, impenetrable firewalls, and top-of-the-line security.

All of this thwarted by a man who can't remember his passwords.

Kent has finished talking, and he gives me an expectant look. I realize that he's waiting for me to reply. "Do you have any documentation?" I ask him, stalling for time.

That's a mistake. He gives me a three-inch ring binder, stuffed with report after report. "Why don't I give you two days to read this?"

I can't get through this in two days—there's just too much information. But Kent already thinks that I am just a pretty face. I'm not going to give him the satisfaction. "That sounds good," I tell him. "I'll schedule a meeting for us on Thursday."

His sneer grows. "Are you sure you can manage?" he asks condescendingly. "Sanders did say that you're going to be pretty busy. What does he have you working on anyway?"

If Finn didn't see fit to tell his CFO about the in-depth security review, then I'm certainly not going to. Maybe playing the ditz will be an advantage after all. "I'm not sure," I say vaguely. "I didn't get a chance to ask him."

First impressions can be deceiving of course, but I really don't like Lawrence Kent.

∽

Finn:

As soon as I leave Miki in Kent's office, I head back to my computer. It was too late last night to follow up on the User0989 lead, but I'm determined to make headway this morning.

Let's face it, Finn. You don't want to admit that Miki might be messed up in this. You like her too much.

User0989 has only been active on the DefCon forums for a month. His profile is private, and he's made no public posts. The only way I can find out anything about him is to hack into his DefCon account, but the forum's securely encrypted and is almost impossible to penetrate.

I stare at my monitor, wondering what to do next. but fifteen minutes later, I still have no idea how to proceed.

It's time to ask for help.

One of the moderators on the DefCon forums is an old friend of mine. Boris Guzman was in juvie with me, locked up for the same reason I was. He is a fellow hacker. I haven't talked to him in over five years. The last I heard, he was helping Tibetan dissidents hide their online activity from the Chinese government.

Finding his number is relatively easy. I call him, and he picks up on the first ring. "Finn Sanders, as I live and breathe," he greets me. "What a surprise. How long has it been?"

"Five years," I say ruefully. "Sorry about not keeping in touch."

He laughs. "Let me guess," he says, "you've been swamped with work. How's the new company doing? I hear you're about to go public."

"In three months," I reply. Oliver and I have founded four companies together since college. The first business failed. The next two were relatively successful; we were able to sell them for a few million dollars each. None of them had the potential of Imperium though. I've been dreaming of this moment my entire life.

"That's awesome, Finn," he replies sincerely. "I'm really happy for you." His tone becomes business-like. "I assume you didn't call me in the middle of a work day to shoot the breeze. What can I do for you?"

I don't beat around the bush. I'm asking Boris to stick his neck out for me. "I need information on a DefCon user. User0989."

"What the fuck, Finn?" he asks bluntly.

"I know it's a big ask," I reply. "Let me tell you why, and you can decide how best to proceed. Yesterday, a woman applied for a job at Imperium. Coincidentally, she's a hacker. One of the best I've ever met, in fact. User0989 hired her. I want to know who he is, and what he wants."

"So put the screws on your hacker chick," he replies. "Threaten her with jail time if she doesn't talk."

I take a deep breath. "She doesn't know who he is."

"Are you sure?" he asks skeptically. "Can you trust her?"

Miki Cooper is at Imperium for reasons I don't understand. I'm wary and cautious around her. But I trust Mouse. "Yes."

He sighs. "What do you need?"

"Everything. Transcripts of every conversation User0989 had with anyone on the forum. The dates and times he logged in. The IP address he logged in from."

"Of course you do," he says sarcastically. "Do you want fries with that?"

"I wouldn't ask if it wasn't critical, Boris."

He doesn't reply right away. "I'll have to think about this, Finn," he says finally.

It's not the answer I hoped for, but at least he hasn't said no right away.

Doubt is a pain too lonely to know that faith is his twin brother.

— Khalil Gibran

Oliver:

Finn thinks we need to keep an eye on Miki, and I agree. But it's hell sharing an office with her.

It's absolutely ridiculous to be attracted to a woman who is in all likelihood plotting to destroy my company. A woman who I've met only once on a memorable plane ride. A woman who is practically a stranger.

Except Miki isn't a stranger. I've spent the last three months chatting with her. We've talked about our hopes and our dreams, our treasured memories and the things that make us happy. We've talked about our failed relationships. Her husband cheated on her; my wife cheated on me. We've both recovered from painful divorces, and we've both lost faith in love.

I have to keep reminding myself that she's plotting against Imperium. I try and hold on to my anger, but especially after she asked us to find out about User0989, I can't hate her.

It's just after lunch on Friday. On Wednesday, Susan gave me a short list of PR firms that specialize in crisis management. "I recommend Aventi," she said. "They represent about two dozen soccer players, and they've had lots of practice dealing with drunken scandals and sex tapes."

"Lovely," I'd said dryly. "Sure, let's go with them."

I'd prefer the problem goes away entirely. Claudia likes money. If I throw enough of it in her direction, I'm hoping she's tempted into abandoning her quest for Imperium stock. Paul Fryman has been authorized to offer her up to ten million dollars, but so far, she's held firm and refused to negotiate.

Between Claudia and the board, I've been in an uncharacteristically bad mood all week.

On my way back from my lunch meeting, I detour to the coffee shop on the ground floor and pick up a couple of cups of coffee and a box of donuts. After a week of working with her, I've learned that Miki gets hungry and cranky in the afternoon.

Janine's eyebrows rise as I make my way back to my office. "Donuts?"

"Yeah. Want one?"

There's a small smile playing about her lips. Damn it. Janine is entirely too perceptive for her own good. She's probably thinking that I've never brought donuts back for Finn or any of my employees. "No thanks," she replies. "I'm on a diet. I put on ten pounds over Christmas, and it's only three months until bikini season."

"You know where they are if you change your mind."

Through the frosted glass window, I can see Miki's outline. "Where's Finn?"

She checks her computer. "He's meeting with the Shield team," she says. "He'll be done in thirty minutes."

Nodding my thanks, I push my office door open. Miki looks up. "Coffee?" I ask her, setting the cup down on the table.

An expression of gratitude flashes over her face. "Thank you," she says. "I was just starting to slump."

"I know." I open the box of donuts. "I come bearing gifts."

She grins widely. "My prince," she says extravagantly. "Coffee and donuts. What have I done to deserve such riches?" She picks a honey-glazed donut and smiles at me warmly. "Thank you, Oliver. I lost track of time. I was starving."

"Donuts aren't a meal," I scold her. "You need to start eating lunch."

"Not according to my mother," she says ruefully. "How will I ever meet someone if I stuff everything in sight into my mouth?"

A vivid image of Miki on her knees, her pretty pink lips wrapped around my cock, flashes before my eyes. "Everything in sight?" I tease her. "Everything?"

She flushes scarlet. "Oliver," she chides. "Have you read the employee manual about sexual harassment?"

Shit. *She's your employee, dickwad. And she doesn't know you're Lancelot. Stop being an asshole.*

"I'm sorry," I say stiffly, moving to my desk. "You're right. I was out of line. It won't happen again."

"Oh no," she exclaims, looking chagrined. "Oliver, I was joking." She laces her fingers in her lap and looks at me with an earnest expression. "I was a little nervous working with

Finn and you, but I'm having an amazing time. I didn't mean to make things weird."

"No, you're right. Tell me about your first week. Are you getting what you need? Is everyone being cooperative?"

"Mostly." She scrunches her face into a pout. "I'm really enjoying the security review portion," she says. "Even though I've had no luck hacking in so far."

I chuckle. "If you break our system in the first week, you'll drive Finn to drink. What about the work you're doing for Lawrence?"

"He's driving me nuts," she replies frankly. Her cheeks color. "Sorry. I have a bad habit of blurting out whatever's on my mind. Let me say that again, this time in corporate-speak. I'm enjoying the challenge of working with Mr. Kent."

She's adorable. I feel my smile widen. "That's okay; I think Lawrence is a pain in the ass too. If he's too demanding, push back. Your priority isn't Lawrence's financials; it's the security review. As we get closer to the IPO, the attacks against Imperium are going to increase. Our competitors would love to see us embarrassed."

"I will." She takes another bite of her donut, her tongue catching a stray piece of sugar. My cock jumps to attention. Fuck.

Just then, Finn pushes the door open and comes in, his laptop in his hands. "Ah, donuts," he says, setting the computer down and shooting me a knowing look. "Is this a new tradition, Oliver? I like the chocolate-glazed ones the best."

Bite me, Sanders.

We each get to work on our projects. Lawrence has prepared a projection of the revenue we'll lose because of my decision to close the private security division. I review it, frowning as I do so. It's wildly inaccurate. Lawrence has assumed we'll lay off the entire team, when in fact, he knows as well as I do that we'll just reallocate the developers to a different project.

Even worse, he's sent his projection directly to the board.

I swear out loud. Fucking Kent. The board has given me endless amounts of grief about my decision to shutter the division. Now, they'll have new ammunition. Not for the first time, I wish I could just fire my CFO.

Both Miki and Finn look up. "What's the matter?" Finn asks.

"Kent told the board it's going to cost us ten million to close the private security division."

Finn's eyes narrow, and I know he's thinking what I'm thinking. We've both assumed that if Claudia succeeds in shredding my reputation and the board votes to get rid of me, they'll appoint Finn the CEO. But this email from Lawrence makes me reevaluate my theory. It appears that Lawrence is jockeying for the role as well.

Claudia's photos. The person who's leaking our technology to Fitzgerald. Miki's true purpose. And now Lawrence. The threats fly at us from every direction, and it's only going to get worse.

Janine sticks her head through the door. "It's four," she announces cheerfully. "You know what time it is. And Finn, don't even think about bailing on us."

"I'm not," he says. He shuts his laptop and gets to his feet. "Come on, Miki. It's time for happy hour."

∾

Miki:

In the space of a week, I've learned that while Oliver works hard, he's not a workaholic. He's left the office at six every evening. Finn, on the other hand, is always at work when I get in, and still there when I leave.

Which is why I'm shocked when Finn gets to his feet. "It's an Imperium tradition," he explains. "There's a bar around the corner, and Oliver and I buy the first three rounds. Come on, Miki. Work will keep until Monday."

I snort. "You're going to be back here tomorrow morning," I accuse him.

He chuckles. "Guilty as charged." He puts on his jacket and raises his eyebrow at me. "Are you coming?"

Should I go drinking with Finn and Oliver? I'm attracted to them. I was attracted to them at the party last Friday, and my desire has only intensified after a week of working with them. All week, I've been dreaming of Oliver and Finn, touching me, kissing me. It's gotten so bad that I've been avoiding falling asleep every night until well past midnight, choosing instead to chat with Lancelot and Merlin.

Then there's User0989. I haven't heard from him, but sooner or later, he's going to demand to know what I'm doing. I'm no closer to finding out who he is, and Lancelot and Merlin haven't been able to uncover anything either.

"All work and no play will make Miki dull," Oliver says, his lips tugging up into an amused smile. "You don't want to end up like Finn, do you?"

Finn flips him the bird, and I smother my laugh. Janine watches us with an avid expression on her face. I'm sure I'm not exactly impressing her with my professionalism. "Okay," I agree. "I could use a beer."

THE BAR we head to is around the corner from Trinity Church. About a dozen of my co-workers are in the back. I recognize Mary MacDonald, Sachin Sharma, and Chris Wilcox. Mary waves me over with a friendly smile. "I hope you've enjoyed your first week, Mackenzie," she says.

"Very much, thank you," I tell her sincerely. It's the truth.

"Good." She pats my arm. "I'm afraid we've thrown you into the deep end of the pool. Normally, things are a little more laid-back around here, but with the IPO around the corner, everyone's quite tense."

"I understand." Oliver occasionally reverts to the laughing, joking man I met on the plane from Houston to New York, but he seems to be under a lot of stress. And Finn practically lives at work. I wouldn't be surprised if he has a cot hidden away somewhere in the building.

"I'm assuming neither Oliver nor Finn has taken you out for a welcome lunch?" she continues. "Why don't we grab a bite together sometime next week?"

An idea occurs to me. Mary MacDonald is the head of Human Resources. User0989 had seemed certain that I would get the job. Mary's not going to know his identity, but if I can figure out why I was hired, I might uncover a clue. "I'd like that."

A waitress comes up to take my beer order. Mary gets roped into a game of pool with Sachin. Chris is studying the beer list as if there's a test at the end of the night. Finn and Oliver are at the bar, deep in conversation.

I'm about to introduce myself to a cluster of people when Janine slides up next to me. "How's it going?" she asks.

I like Oliver and Finn's assistant. She's smart, she's loyal, and she takes no shit from anyone. "Great," I reply. "I'm pretty glad it's Friday though."

"Tell me about it," she says, her tone heartfelt. "Thank heavens for beer. Any fun weekend plans?"

"Nothing too exciting," I admit. "I moved back to Manhattan three months ago, and I've been staying temporarily at a friend's place. I thought I might go apartment hunting."

"Ugh." She grimaces, taking a long sip from the beer the waitress hands her. "Good luck. You're going to need it."

"I know." Wendy has repeatedly assured me that there's no hurry for me to move out, but I can't stay in her place forever, and I can't afford to rent it from her. I need something a lot cheaper, and I'm dreading the thought of the upcoming search.

"Can I ask you a question?" Janine says. "Do you know Oliver and Finn well?"

I frown in puzzlement. "No. Why?"

"Well, I've known both of them for a long time," she replies. "I've worked with them for the last eight years. They seem very comfortable with you, that's all."

"What does that mean?" I ask cautiously. Does Janine think I'm flirting with them? Oh God, I hope this doesn't become some kind of crazy high-school, mean-girl situation. I was horrible at dealing with drama as a teenager, and I haven't improved as an adult.

"Nothing really," she hurries to assure me. "It's just that Oliver's been really guarded since his divorce, and Finn's always been slow to get to know people."

"Oh." I ponder Janine's words. "I've met them once before. We were stuck in the last row on a four-hour flight at Thanksgiving, and we got chatting about Doctor Who and other TV shows. Maybe that's why?"

Her eyebrow rises even higher. "Oliver and Finn flew coach? Really? That's odd."

Huh. Janine's right. The two men are wealthy. They sold the last company they founded for thirty million dollars. Why wouldn't they be in first class? "Well, it was Thanksgiving," I think out loud. "A lot of flights got canceled because of bad weather."

Janine's not listening to me. Her eyes are glued to a well-dressed couple who've just walked into the bar. "That fucking bitch," she murmurs under her breath, her tone outraged. "What the fuck is she doing here?"

"Who are they?"

She turns to me with a grim look on her face. "That woman," she spits out, "is Oliver's ex-wife, Claudia. And the man she's with is Sebastian Fitzgerald. He's the CEO of Kliedara. Imperium's biggest competitor."

Oliver's ex-wife is dating his rival? That's cold.

12

Buy the ticket, take the ride.

— Hunter S. Thompson

Oliver:

I'm having a beer with Finn at the bar, trying to keep my mind off Miki, when my ex-wife Claudia and her new boyfriend Sebastian Fitzgerald walk in.

Finn, alerted by my sudden stiffness, turns around and inhales sharply. "What the fuck is she doing here?" he says angrily.

I've made mistakes in my life, but none I regret as much as Claudia. I didn't even have a good reason for marrying her. Claudia and I had been dating for six months. She'd been hinting that she wanted us to take our commitment to the next level. I'd just turned thirty, and I'd thought that it was time.

Miki's told me she ignored the advice of her friends when she married her husband. I'd done the same thing.

Still, I'd made my vows, and I was prepared to honor them. Claudia, on the other hand, wasn't interested in staying faithful, and that was the one thing I wasn't ready to forgive. We were divorced in June.

"You have got to be kidding me." Finn sounds disgusted, and I shake free of my gloomy thoughts and look up, only to regret it. Claudia has her hands around Fitzgerald's neck, and she's kissing the man passionately, in full sight of the entire room. Several sets of eyes swing toward me, to see how I'm handling this display.

Not well. I signal the bartender. "Rum and Coke," I say, my voice tight with tension. "Make it a double."

"She's trying to get a rise out of you, Oliver," Finn says quietly. "Don't give her the satisfaction."

"Don't you dare condescend me," I snap. "I'm not a robot who only cares about work, Finn. If I want to deal with Claudia's bullshit in a bottle of rum, *then let me.*"

The bartender shows up with my drink, and I drain it and gesture for another. "Don't worry," I say bitterly. "I'll be back to peak efficiency on Monday morning. If I'm not, well, the board's just dying to replace me anyway."

Finn's jaw tightens, but he doesn't respond to my insult. "They're coming this way."

Of course they are. Subtlety is lost on both Fitzgerald and Claudia. I brace myself for the shitshow. Out of the corner of my eye, I can see Miki watching me, her eyes wide. Fuck. That's all I need. An audience.

"Prescott." Fitzgerald's voice is smug and self-satisfied. "I'd forgotten this is the bar you hang out at on Fridays." He puts his arm around my ex-wife's waist and tugs her against his body. "You remember Claudia, of course."

The bartender sets my drink down on the bar. I lift the

glass in the direction of my two least favorite people in the world. "What a coincidence," I say flatly.

"Hello, Oliver." Claudia gives me her most winsome look. "I haven't seen you in a few months. You look good."

She wants to make small talk? She wants to pretend she didn't take those BDSM photos of me without my consent, act as if she isn't blackmailing me?

Fuck this shit. I'm out of here.

I drain the drink in my hand. "I'll see you later," I tell Finn. I don't look at Fitzgerald and my ex-wife. My self-control is hanging on by a thread, and I don't trust it not to snap.

Then I walk out of there.

~

Miki:

I'm watching Oliver as his ex-wife kisses the guy she's with. I see his face go white. He tosses back the drink that's in his hand. Finn says something to him, but whatever he said, it doesn't seem to matter, because Oliver just looks angrier.

My heart hurts for him. I can relate to his pain. Even though it's been almost four months, the image of Peggy sucking Aaron's dick is still vivid in my mind. I still remember the raw betrayal I felt that day. Even now. The scar's healing, but the skin's still tender.

The two of them walk over and say something to Oliver, and it's the last straw. Oliver slams his glass down on the table and stalks out of the bar.

I'm not thinking clearly. I set my half-full glass of beer on the table closest to me. Grabbing my jacket, I leave the bar, almost running in my effort to catch up with Oliver.

It's dark outside. The streets are brightly lit, but it's started snowing. I stop outside the door and look to the right and the left, trying to pick out Oliver's black jacket in a sea of black, but the tall blond man is nowhere in sight. *Damn New Yorkers,* I fume inwardly. *Would it kill them to wear something other than black?*

In the distance, I catch a glimpse of a familiar head. Oliver. He's walking into the building that houses Imperium's offices. I race after him, wondering why he's going back to work.

"Oliver," I call out as soon as I enter the lobby. He's stepping into an elevator, and if I lose him now, I won't be able to follow. I still don't have after-hours access to the Imperium offices.

He looks up and sees me pelting toward him. He extends his arm and stops the elevator doors from shutting, and I slip in. "What are you doing, Miki?" he asks me. "This isn't a good time."

"I know." I swallow. It's too late to wonder if following Oliver is a good idea. "My husband cheated on me. For weeks after I left him, I swore up and down that I wanted to be left alone." His expression isn't encouraging. "My friends listened to me," I continue. "But they always stayed within reach. They let me know they were there for me."

He surveys me with expressionless eyes, then he reaches for the elevator panel and punches a button. "Where are we going?" I ask as the doors begin to shut.

"To the roof."

"I probably should zip up my jacket."

"Probably." He doesn't add anything else, and I fall into silence.

I'm feeling quite foolish. I barely know Oliver. I don't know why I followed him like a crazy stalker. A sudden thought strikes me. "You're not going to jump, right?" I ask nervously. "Because Oliver, I know the benefits are good at Imperium, but there's not enough therapy in the world to help me cope with that."

"Jump?" He looks at me blankly. "From the roof?" His eyes dance with amusement. "I just want to be alone, Miki. That doesn't make me suicidal."

"Should I go back?" I have no idea what Janine's going to think of my mad dash.

He shakes his head. "You can stay if you like."

The elevator jerks to a halt and the doors open to a drab landing. "Stairwell," Oliver says, pointing to the door opposite us.

I follow him up a flight of stairs. I don't know what I'm expecting, but when we get to the roof, it's just a roof. There's graffiti on the water tower, the floors are concrete, and it's utterly freezing. I zip up my jacket and pull the hood up, and shove my hands into my pockets. I had gloves, but I don't know where they went.

It would be nice if Oliver wanted to be alone somewhere warm. Ah well. That's what happens when I invite myself along.

"You're shivering." Oliver shakes his head and puts his arm around me.

His body acts as a source of heat, and as a bonus, he's blocking the wind. My teeth slowly stop chattering. "I'd forgotten how cold the city gets in February," I murmur. "What happened with your marriage?"

"It was a mistake right from the start," he replies. He sounds weary, tired. Drained. "But I didn't want to admit it to myself."

"I can relate."

"Mmm." He lapses into silence. I stay right where I am,

savoring the feel of his body against mine. Held by Oliver like this, I feel comforted and safe, even though I'm the one that's supposed to be doing the comforting. "One night, a business trip ended early, and I flew back home two days ahead of schedule. I called Claudia from the airport. I didn't want to tell her I was back; I wanted to surprise her, but I did want to make sure she was at home."

"She wasn't?"

"No. She told me she was, but when I got to our apartment, the place was empty. She finally returned at nine the next morning, and she reeked of sex."

I wrap my arm around his waist. "It sucks, doesn't it? You start questioning your judgment. You wonder what you did wrong, why they cheated, if you could have done anything differently."

"My therapist assures me that Claudia's cheating isn't about me. It's about Claudia."

"And do you believe him?"

"Her," he corrects. "You know what I believe, Miki?" His voice is flat. "I believe people can't be trusted."

"Is that true?" I don't want it to be. "Or are you still angry with your ex-wife?"

He's got one arm around my shoulder. He turns me so I'm facing him, and he puts a finger on my chin. My heart starts to beat faster at the look of intensity in his sapphire blue eyes. "What do you think, Miki?" he asks me, his voice quiet. "Can I trust you?"

No. I've been hired to hack into your company. If I succeed, I'll ruin the IPO.

But I'm not thinking of User0989 as Oliver's head bends toward me. I'm not thinking of anything. My brain has turned into mush, and even though it's freezing on the rooftop, my skin feels feverish with anticipation as Oliver's fingertips brush over my lips.

I could move away. *I don't.* My pulse races. "I don't think HR will approve of this," he murmurs.

"I don't care," I whisper. For three months, I've wondered what would have happened if I'd taken his card at Thanksgiving. For three months, I've fantasized about Oliver, about Finn, about both their bodies pressed against mine.

My lips part, unprompted, and Oliver doesn't hesitate. His hand wraps around the back of my neck, urging me closer, and then he kisses me.

At first, his touch is light, feather-soft and exploratory. I stand on tiptoe and kiss him back, my eyes fluttering shut. He smells faintly of the rum and coke he gulped down at the bar. "More," I breathe, greedy for him.

He deepens the kiss, and his other hand, the one that isn't curled around my neck, slides down my back and cups my ass. Pressed against his body, I can feel the hard weight of Oliver's erection, and his arousal sends my own need skyrocketing. My fingers grip his down jacket, and I whimper in my throat.

Without breaking our kiss, Oliver moves his hand over my breasts, cupping them through my clothing. Too many layers. I nudge him toward my zipper, and he gets the message, unzipping my winter jacket. His thumb brushes against my pebbled nipple, then he reaches under my sweater to caress my bare skin, gently squeezing my breasts.

Oh. My. God.

I shudder at the shock of desire that shoots up my spine, and Oliver breaks off the kiss. "You're cold," he says, brushing his nose against mine. "Your skin is icy," he whispers in my ear, his warm breath tickling my skin. "Come home with me?"

I'm about to say yes, consequences be damned, when the door to the roof slams open and Finn walks out. I'm still pressed up against Oliver, his hand under my sweater, obviously cupping my breasts.

I kissed Finn at the party. Just a week ago. And I'm now kissing Oliver.

I pull free and fumble with my jacket, unable to meet either of their eyes. I can't even imagine what they think about me. *Slut,* a voice inside me says accusingly.

"Miki. Stop." Finn's words jerk me from my spiral of self-loathing. There's a dark edge to his tone. "Look at us."

Oliver's hands curve around my waist. He pivots me so I'm facing Finn, and he draws me into his body. My back rests against his chest, and my head falls back against his shoulder. My ass grinds into his crotch, and it's definitely having an effect. I can feel his cock react to me.

"Do you want this?" Finn asks, his voice soft and silky. His fingers are on my chin, tipping my head up so I'm forced to meet his eyes. "Do you want both of us?"

I swallow the lump in my throat and stare at him, transfixed. I don't know what to say. I don't know how to answer his question. And underneath the heat and the passion, underneath the vast, roiling sea of my need, is a truth that can't be denied. They're my bosses. I'm plotting to destroy them.

This is a mistake.

Yet I stay where I am.

"Answer him," Oliver says. "Tell us what you need, Miki. Ever since that day on the plane when you sat between us, I've been thinking of you. Fantasizing about you. Picturing you naked and tangled in my sheets, your legs parted, your eyes foggy with lust."

Finn's thumb brushes across my engorged nipple, and then he squeezes it. His ice-blue eyes bore into me, and he leans in.

I'm trapped against Oliver's body, *and Finn's going to kiss me.*

Finn's face inches closer. I have plenty of time to protest and push him away, but I don't move. I can't. I'm a gazelle trapped, hypnotized by the knowledge of what's going to happen. My insides dance gleefully in anticipation and my pussy clenches in desperate need.

His lips touch mine. I'm sandwiched between the two men's hard bodies. I can feel their erections grind into me, and heat engulfs my body.

Finn doesn't hurry. He takes his time, his kiss savage, passionate and through. When he draws away, I almost whimper in protest. "Miki," he says, his voice sounding drugged with need, "Tell me what you want."

"One night," I whisper. "Just one night. Nothing serious. Nothing real."

Finn draws in a breath and nods slightly.

"Both of you."

I close my eyes and wait for the condemnation, but there isn't any. Oliver's chuckle is warm against my ear. "Thank heavens," he says. "Otherwise, one of us was going home with a serious case of blue balls."

Finn zips up my jacket. "Let's go."

My mouth is dry with desire. I ache so much that it's almost painful. Yet I can't help thinking that this is a huge, massive mistake.

13

Keep love in your heart. A life without it is like a sunless garden when the flowers are dead.

— Oscar Wilde

Finn:

Last night, I'd been up late chatting with Miki on the DefCon forums. Oliver had been online too. The three of us had been talking about the latest hour of Doctor Who, and then we'd started discussing our favorite episodes.

The original series or the reboot? Miki had asked in response to my question. *Be specific, Merlin.*

Reboot, I'd typed, smiling as I waited for her reply. Claudia couldn't understand why Oliver loved the show. "It's stupid," she used to whine. "Time machines aren't real."

As if the reality shows she used to watch were so fucking authentic.

The Day of the Doctor, Miki had said at once.

Oh come on, Oliver had written. *Really, Mouse? You just think David Tennant is hot.*

Guilty, she'd retorted. *What about you, Lancelot? Since you mock my taste, what's your favorite?*

Hmm. That's a complicated question, Oliver had typed. *I don't think I have one. Who's your favorite companion?*

Donna Noble, she'd replied. *I don't like young companions gazing worshipfully at the Doctor. Boring. Donna was smart and bright, and she treated the Doctor as an equal. They were friends, you know? I liked that.*

WE GET INTO A CAB, telling the driver to go to Oliver's place, which has the sole virtue of being closer. In the back seat, Miki sits between the two of us, and I'm very aware of her presence.

One night, she said. *Nothing serious. Nothing real.*

She's right. Tonight is a one-time thing. I can't trust her, and if she discovers that Oliver and I are Lancelot and Merlin, she'll never trust us. We've weaved a tangled web, and now, we're knotted in it, and there's no escape.

Miki's the perfect woman. She's smart and funny and kind. Though she's been hurt, she still allows herself to be vulnerable. She's not brittle and shallow, the way Claudia was. She's real.

If the circumstances were different, I'd want to spend a lifetime with her.

～

Miki:

I'm in the back seat of a cab, Oliver and Finn on either side of me, on my way to have sex with both of them.

What the hell am I doing?

"You look nervous," Oliver says, breaking the silence that's fallen between us. "Are you?"

"Yes." There's no point pretending otherwise. "It's my first time doing this."

A ghost of a smile creases Finn's face. "First time doing what, exactly?"

I flush. "It's my first threesome," I reply. "My first time sleeping with my bosses. My first time sleeping with someone I barely know. Take your pick."

Oliver's hand covers mine. "Would it help to know I'm nervous too?" he asks.

"Are you?" I give him an astonished look. Oliver and Finn seem so much worldlier than I am. So much more self-assured. I can't picture either of them being nervous about anything.

"I like you, Miki," he replies. "I'm very aware that I'm your boss, and I don't want to make things awkward at work either."

The one thing I've learned this week at Imperium is how well-respected Oliver and Finn are. In fact, the only person who's said anything negative about either of them is Lawrence Kent, and Kent is a grouch, who rarely has anything good to say about anyone. "We're adults," I say softly. "We'll figure it out."

Finn rests his hand on my thigh. I'm excruciatingly aware of the weight of his touch. My entire body tightens in anticipation of this evening, of what comes next. What I'm doing is foolish on so many levels, but my need makes me reckless. I haven't had sex for six months. Yes, this isn't the most sensible thing I'm doing, but it could be months before I meet someone else.

I just want one night.

For some strange reason, I feel intensely comfortable with Finn and Oliver. Janine was right; there is an easy connection between us. Maybe it was forged on the night we sat at the back of a plane and drank vodka and orange juice. I trust them. When Oliver tells me he doesn't want things to be awkward at work, I believe him, and I know he'll do everything in his power to keep things professional on Monday.

Yes, you trust them. But can they trust you? And what do you think is going to happen if they find out about User0989?

I shy away from that thought.

"You look troubled," Oliver says. His eyes are uncharacteristically serious. "If you've changed your mind, we'll drop you off at your place. There's no pressure, Miki."

No. I don't want to go home. I twist toward the blond man. "Oliver," I say firmly. "Stop talking and kiss me."

His lips curl up, and he puts an arm around my shoulder, tugging me closer. "I can do that," he whispers. Then he kisses me, hard and insistent. His tongue brushes against the seam of my lips, and his hand tightens in my hair, and I push the doubts out of my mind and kiss him back.

Finn's palm still rests on my thigh. I'm very aware that he's touching me, even as Oliver's tongue slides against mine.

I can't believe what I'm doing. I'm going to have sex with both of them tonight.

OLIVER'S APARTMENT occupies the top floor of a turn-ofcentury townhouse in the East Village. It's a great space, with exposed brick walls and wood-beamed ceilings. "You have a fireplace," I blurt out the moment I walk in. "And a skylight. Did you have to sell your soul to the devil for it?"

Oliver laughs. "It's a fantastic apartment," he agrees. "The windows overlook the communal courtyard. I'll give you a tour in the morning. Can I get you a drink?" There's a twinkle in his eyes. "Vodka and orange juice, perhaps?"

That was our drink on the plane. I don't want to be tipsy, but I'm not going to lie. I could use something to quell the butterflies in my stomach. "I'd love one."

Oliver fixes me a drink. "I've been fantasizing about this moment since Thanksgiving," he says. "So many times, I've wondered what would have happened had you taken my business card and called me afterward."

I swallow. "Me too." I gulp down my drink. "I've never had anal sex before."

Smooth, Miki. Very sophisticated.

Neither of them laughs at me. Finn gives me a reassuring smile. "You don't have to do anything you don't want to, Miki," he says. "You set the pace, okay?"

Okay. That's good. Except I'm here, standing in the middle of Oliver's living room, two of the hottest guys I've ever met on either side of me. We're here to have sex, but I have no idea what to do next. Should I get naked? Should I suggest that we move this to the bedroom?

Oliver rescues me. "Do you play cards, Miki?" he asks, with a wicked gleam in his eyes. "Can I interest you in a game of strip poker?"

Yes. Especially if it involves Oliver and Finn taking their clothes off.

Oliver kicks off his shoes and sits down on the plush carpet, his back leaning against the couch. "Settle down," he invites easily. "Make yourself comfortable, Miki, and prepare to lose."

That makes me laugh. "You're really cocky," I tell him, sitting on the carpet as well. "For all you know, I might be a card shark."

Finn folds himself down. "Are you?" he asks, his eyes gleaming with amusement. "Let's find out."

I WIN THE FIRST HAND. "HA," I say triumphantly, as I set my cards down. "Full house." I give Oliver a pointed look. "Take off your shirt, Oliver."

He chuckles and complies. My throat goes dry as his body comes into view. He's lean and tightly muscled, his chest sprinkled with hair. My eyes follow that trail lower until it disappears into his pants. "How," I demand, "does someone who eats as many donuts as you have a six-pack? Life isn't fair."

He grins. "I assure you, it's not effortless. This building has an indoor pool, and I put in my hours at the gym as well. Now, another hand?"

I might have won the first round, but it's going to be near-impossible to win the next. I can't be expected to concentrate when manchest is on display. Somewhat improbably though, I do end up winning again. I glare at Finn. "Did you throw your hand?" I demand.

"I don't know what you're talking about," he replies blandly. "What's your pleasure, Miki? Oliver's pants or my shirt?"

"Your shirt."

Finn strips down to his waist. More male hotness. The room's suddenly too warm, the welcome heat of the fireplace almost suffocating. I take a sip of my drink, my fingers shaking slightly, as Finn deals the next round.

My luck doesn't hold. Finn wins, and a grin curls over his lips. "I've been waiting for this moment," he says. He leans forward. "It's time for the shirt to come off, Miki."

His fingers brush over the hollow of my throat, and then he unbuttons my shirt. "What are you doing?" I whisper. "I can undress myself."

"Where's the fun in that?" He pushes my white shirt off my shoulders and throws it on the couch. Underneath, I'm wearing a flesh-colored lace bra. The dark outline of my nipples are clearly visible, and both Finn and Oliver suck in audible breaths.

"Very nice," Finn purrs. His thumb brushes over the nubs, and the buds pebble at his touch.

"I didn't think touching was allowed," I breathe. My skin prickles with desire, and my insides tighten. My pussy clenches with arousal.

"I've never been concerned with other people's rules," Finn replies. He sits back against the couch, and I'm not sure if I'm relieved or disappointed that he's stopped touching me. "Shall we play again?"

This time, Oliver wins. He surveys me with a wicked gleam in his eyes. "I'm torn," he says. Jeans or bra?"

"You could make Finn take something off," I suggest. It's two against one, and I just have three more items of clothing.

He raises an eyebrow. "Why would I do that?"

His eyes sweep over me, slowly and thoroughly, and I feel myself blush in response to his scrutiny. "You're staring at me," I mutter.

He makes no move to deny it. "The bra, I think."

There's undisguised desire in his eyes as he watches me.

I slowly remove the scrap of lace, feeling the heat of his gaze like a physical touch. "Come here, Miki," he says, his voice gruff.

A sense of daring recklessness fills me. There's no turning back now, not that I want to. I crawl over to Oliver on my hands and knees, my breasts swaying as I close the distance between us. When I reach him, he tugs me onto his lap, and I wrap my arms around his neck and kiss him. Finn's watching, and that's a turn-on too.

"Mmm." Oliver rolls my nipples between his thumb and forefinger, and I whimper in pleasure. His eyes fill with dark heat in response. "We're going to make you moan all night, Miki," he promises me.

He leans forward and takes one erect bud in his mouth. I bite my lip and bury my fingers in his hair, tugging him closer. Turning my head, I make contact with Finn's light blue eyes. "Join us," I urge.

"Not yet," he replies enigmatically. He's not quite as detached as he pretends. A vein throbs in his temple, and his fingers tremble slightly as he sips at his club soda. "We still have a few more rounds to play."

My nervousness has evaporated. I'm ready to speed past foreplay and get to the main act. "We do?" I ask, unable to conceal the note of disappointment in my voice.

Finn smiles at me. "What's the hurry, Miki?" he asks. "We have all night."

All night. But just one night. Finn's right; I'm in no rush. I'm going to savor every second of this strange and exciting evening.

Oliver lets me go, and I move back to my seat, taking another sip of my vodka and orange juice. Finn deals the cards, and I stare at my hand, unable to concentrate on them, lust running rampant in my veins.

Lady Luck smiles on me, and I win. I lean back and survey the two men. "Finn," I decide. Let's see how detached he really is. "Take off your pants."

He shakes his head. "Do it for me," he says.

Gladly.

Finn gets to his feet. I close the distance between us, pressing my breasts against his hard chest. I glide my fingers over his abs, feeling each tightly defined muscle, making my way slowly to the buckle of his belt. He sucks in his breath as I explore his body, and he groans. "If you keep that up, I'm not going to be responsible for the consequences."

I grin. "Is that supposed to be a threat? I guess I shouldn't tell you I'm looking forward to the consequences."

Oliver chuckles behind me. He stands up as well. He trails a finger down my spine, and goosebumps break out on my skin.

My fingers shake as I undress Finn, unzipping his pants and tugging them down. He's wearing briefs, and the thick outline of his cock makes my mouth water. "Touch it," Finn urges hoarsely.

He doesn't have to ask twice. I brush my lips across his bulge, feeling his cock harden even further in response. As I tease Finn, Oliver presses soft kisses against my shoulder blades, against the curve of my spine.

Finn steps out of his pants. Giving me a wicked glance, he pulls his briefs down as well, and his fat, beautiful cock jumps out. "I thought I'd speed the game up."

I thought I couldn't concentrate earlier, when two hot manchests were on display. Now, when one of them is fisting his length, wrapping his fingers around the base of his cock and gliding his thumb over his head? Impossible.

The air seems to have left the room.

I lose the next hand, and Oliver tugs me to my feet again.

He unbuttons my jeans, his palms warm against my skin. I wriggle out of them, almost frantic in my need to feel their bodies against mine. The strip poker was a great way to calm my nerves and get me in the mood, but I'm done with games.

So are the men. Oliver tosses my jeans aside, lifts me off my feet and sets me down on the couch. His casual strength sends a sharp, hot spike of need through my body. "Fuck poker," he says gruffly. "Spread your legs."

My entire body shivers as I obey. Oliver kneels between my legs. Pushing my panties aside, he slides a finger into my pussy. "You're soaked," he says, his tone satisfied. He holds my gaze in his, and lifts his finger up to his mouth, sucking them between his lips.

A shiver runs through me at the carnal gesture. "Please," I beg. My pussy aches to be filled by his finger, his cock, anything.

Finn takes a seat next to me, his naked body pressed against mine. Oliver tugs my panties down my hips and flings them across the room. "So pretty," he rasps. He spreads my thighs wide, and his tongue traces a path down my slit. "So tasty."

Oh. My. God.

I hold my breath. His stubble rubs against the tender skin of my inner thighs, sending darts of molten heat through me. His finger teases at my opening, and the tip of his tongue circles my clitoris, and I whimper and squirm, almost overwhelmed at the surge of pure, unadulterated lust that engulfs me.

"Don't wriggle away," Oliver chides.

Finn's fingers have been toying with my nipples. At Oliver's words, he raises his head. "Do you want me to hold her open?" he asks. His eyes take in my flushed skin and my parted lips, and his lips curl into a naughty grin. "I think she'll enjoy that."

"Hey," I say indignantly. "I'm right here."

Oliver laughs and lifts my legs over his shoulders so I can't clench them shut. Ooh. Clever Oliver.

As Oliver spreads my pussy lips and licks my core, Finn kisses me, long and hard. As Oliver rubs his face along my thighs and kisses my skin, Finn's teeth tease my nipples, the sensation sharp and hot. As Oliver breathes over my clitoris, Finn's fingers tighten in my hair.

I throw my head back and clench my eyes shut. Oliver sucks and licks me with focused attention. He pushes two fingers into my slit, twisting them around until he finds my g-spot.

The feeling is too much. My arousal rises alarmingly fast. I close my fingers over Finn's cock, savoring the weight of his steel length, the velvet softness of his head. "Yes," Finn hisses as I rub my thumb over his slit, spreading the precum all over, "don't stop doing that."

Finn's hand squeezes my breast. Oliver's fingers slide in and out of my pussy, while his tongue pays relentless attention to my clitoris. My body tightens, and my vision goes blurry. Red hot pleasure thrums through my veins, and my orgasm hurtles toward me. "I'm coming," I gasp, my last coherent thought before the tsunami hits.

Wave after wave of bone-melting release washes over me. The muscles in my pussy quiver and throb and my entire body buckles under the overwhelming onslaught. Pinpricks of light pulse behind my eyelids. Oliver doesn't let up. His tongue keeps flicking at my too-sensitive clitoris, and I float from one orgasm into the next, until I'm weak and ragged, my body limp, my skin damp with sweat, completely and utterly sated.

Oliver gets to his feet and settles next to me. He licks his fingers clean with a satisfied smile on his face. "Who says you have to eat dessert last?" he quips.

My hand is still closed around Finn's erection, and though I've just come—twice—I'm greedy for more. I need their cocks in me.

The men read me perfectly. "The condoms are in the bedroom," Oliver says. "Shall we move there?"

Yes. *So much yes.*

WE MAKE our way to Oliver's bedroom. I barely have time to notice gray walls and crisp white bedding, and then Finn throws me down on the bed. Lowering himself on top of me, he cradles my face in his hands. "It's my turn," he says, his eyes hot.

"Yes," I say again. Oliver opens the drawer of his night-stand and tosses Finn a condom. While Finn rolls it on, Oliver, who is the only one of us who is still wearing any clothes, gets completely naked. I ogle shamelessly as his cock comes into view. Thick, long and hard, with a drop of precum glistening at his tip. I can't wait to taste him.

Finn's eyes are hot with desire. "Get on your hands and knees, Miki," he orders. He pulls my hips back until I'm on all fours, then his hand caresses the curve of my ass, and he presses a kiss on the small of my back, the gesture strangely intimate and tender.

Oliver gets on the bed and positions himself so his cock is inches from my mouth. His fingers brush a lock of my hair back from my cheek, and there's a strange expression in his eyes. "You're so beautiful," he murmurs. "I can't believe you're here."

I shy away from the intimacy. His cock is stiff and erect,

and maddeningly out of reach. "If you come closer," I say lightly, "I'll show you how real I am." I lick my lips and reach for his thickness.

He obligingly moves closer. "I'd be a fool to pass up such an enticing offer," he says. His hard cock nudges at my lips, and I open my mouth and take him in.

At the same time, Finn's hands grip my hips, and he thrusts into my pussy.

He's huge. My pussy, unaccustomed to his girth, already puffy and swollen from my earlier orgasm, stretches as he pushes into me, and I whimper as he fills me completely. I stop sucking Oliver's cock, trembling from the surge of desire that roils through my body when Finn's shaft pierces my core.

Oliver waits for Finn to establish a rhythm, and then his grip tightens in my hair. I wrap my fingers around the base of his cock and suck in my cheeks. Oliver groans in response. "Fuck. The sight of your pretty lips wrapped around my cock—" His voice trails off.

Finn's fingers move from my hips to my nipples. He tugs at the hard nubs, twisting them slightly. "So responsive," he says huskily as I gasp. His cock pumps in and out of me, deeper and deeper with every stroke. Each thrust sends a shock of pain through me, and I dig my fingers into Oliver's sheets and slam back against Finn's hips, wordlessly begging for more.

Each thrust makes me rock forward on Oliver's cock until his head hits the back of my throat.

Everything's turning me on. Every moan Oliver makes as my tongue laps at his length. Every grunt from Finn as he drives into my body and fingers my clitoris at the same time.

Oliver's cock swells in my mouth. "If you don't want to

swallow," he says, his voice tight and urgent, "now might be a good time to stop."

There's no power on earth that will make me stop now. I'm lost in a haze of lust, my body lurching out of control in a stormy sea of desire. My climax rushes toward me. Finn slams into me, his strokes wild and jagged, his fingers moving faster and faster over my clitoris. Oliver thrusts into my mouth, and then it's all too much.

He erupts with a loud groan, and I swallow every drop. Finn's fingers increase their pressure on my clitoris, and I can't hold back anymore. My thighs clench and my body flails as I shatter. Through the roar of lust in my brain, I hear Finn's cut-off shout as he too finds his release.

It takes minutes, hours, days, before I can think again. When my senses return, I find myself sandwiched between Finn and Oliver's warm bodies. "That was amazing," Finn murmurs, his arm wrapped around my waist. He kisses the curve of my shoulder, his stubble rasping against my skin.

"I should go." Common sense, ruthlessly suppressed all night, now reasserts itself. What the hell was I thinking, sleeping with them?

Oliver pulls me into his body. "We have all night," he says. "I haven't had my fill of you, Miki. Not nearly enough. Stay here tonight. Please?"

I swallow hard. If I can only have one night, I want to make it count. "Okay."

14

The most pitiful among men is he who turns his dreams into silver and gold.

— Khalil Gibran

Oliver:

In the morning, we make Miki breakfast, but she refuses to stay, and I don't insist. In the cold, clear light of day, I'm filled with regret.

I crossed a line last night.

I shouldn't have slept with Miki, at least until I determine why she's at Imperium. I've just complicated things a million-fold.

Once she's gone, Finn pulls up a chair at the kitchen island and sips his coffee. By unspoken consensus, we don't discuss last night. "Any word from Guzman?" I ask him, popping a bagel into my toaster.

He glances at his phone. "Not yet. I'm going to call him today."

I take a tub of cream cheese out of my refrigerator and set it on the counter. "Want a bagel?"

"Please."

"Let's recap where we are," I suggest as we eat our breakfast. "There's just too much crap going on, and I don't want anything to slip through the cracks."

"Where do you want to start?" Finn asks wryly. "Okay. First, the good news. I've figured out how Miki's name got on our guest list last Friday."

I stop spreading cream cheese on my bagel. "Really? How?"

He looks disgusted. "The hack wasn't on our end. It was the event planners. Their security is a joke. Anyone could have infiltrated their systems."

"How exactly is that progress?"

"Because it isn't on our end," Finn says patiently. "Have another cup of coffee, Oliver. Your brain isn't working yet."

I flip him the bird but pour myself another cup anyway. "Okay, you're right. I guess that's a win."

"A minor one," he replies, a disgruntled expression on his face. "I'm still no closer to solving who's leaking our proprietary technology to Fitzgerald. We don't know who User0989 is and what he wants, and we don't know why Miki is at Imperium either."

A smile spreads across my face as I think of Miki. I wipe it off. "On my end," I tell Finn, "Claudia is still insistent that she wants Imperium stock. Susan Dee has arranged for me to meet with a PR firm on Monday, so we can come up with a strategy on how to manage the fallout. Lawrence Kent is trying to undermine me with the board, and Ambrose Sutton is still bitching that we're shutting down the private security division."

Finn takes a bite of his bagel. "I can't help thinking that

everything is connected," he says. "And User0989's identity is at the heart of it." He gives me a questioning look. "You still think the board will oust you if those photos come to light?"

"There are seven board members," I reply. "I think I can count on three votes. You, me, and Miguel Vazquez. Ambrose Sutton can't stand my guts; he'll be thrilled to see me out. David Blake always votes in lockstep with him. Barbara Rhodes and Virginia Mullins are wild cards. If they believe that I either beat Claudia or that I took naked photos of her without her consent, they're not going to vote in my favor."

"Come on," Finn argues. "It's Claudia. They're not going to believe her over you."

"Claudia can be pretty convincing when she wants to be." I drain my cup of coffee. "Is Miki having any luck hacking into your systems?"

Finn and I have complementary strengths. I'm good at getting people to agree with me. He's the technical genius, the brains behind our data security technology. Miki got past his systems once, though she doesn't know it. I'm sure he's taken every precaution to ensure it doesn't happen again.

Of course, I'm not going to underestimate Miki. I've always known she was smart, but working with her this week, I've seen how hard she pushes herself. She rarely remembers to stop for lunch. She's creative and persistent, and that's a dangerous combination.

"Not yet," he replies with a grin. "She's still getting up to speed on our systems." His face darkens. "And Lawrence is keeping her pretty busy."

Before I can reply, Finn's phone rings. He glances at the screen. "It's Guzman," he says, picking up. "Boris, we were just talking about you."

I can't hear what Guzman says in reply, just Finn's end of the conversation. He listens to what his hacktivist friend has to say. "Yes," he says. "Yes. I understand. Thank you. I appreciate the help."

Hanging up, he looks at me. "Boris has reviewed User0989's conversations," he says. "He wouldn't tell me what he discovered, but he agrees that the guy isn't operating on the up-and-up. He won't send me the chat transcripts, but he is going to send me all of User0989's metadata sometime today and let me comb through it."

Finally, a break.

Once we discover who User0989 is, what happens next? Will his identity clear Miki or incriminate her further?

It doesn't matter, Prescott. Miki Cooper just wanted one night. You have to respect that.

I ignore the sinking feeling in my gut and drink another cup of coffee.

∼

Miki:

Leah calls me Saturday at noon. "Miki," she says, sounding stressed. "I need help. We're having a dinner party tonight, and my friend Maya has come down with a cold."

That doesn't sound like a crisis. "Why are you telling me this?"

"There are four men and three women. We're mismatched."

I roll my eyes. Even by Leah's Upper East Side Ladies-Who-Lunch standards, this seems like a ridiculously trivial problem. "Such tragedy," I say dryly. "I'm sure you'll survive."

"Don't be uncooperative, Miki," she wails. "Tell me you'll come to my party. Please."

"Not a hope in hell," I reply promptly. Have dinner with Leah's boring, stuffed-shirt friends? I love my sister. I'm hacking into Imperium because I want her to be happy, but I'm not going to put myself through an evening of torture because Leah wants evenly matched couples around her dinner table.

"I thought you'd say that, but I have a counter-argument. You can talk to Ben. Maybe you'll be able to figure out what he's up to."

"So you still think he's cheating on you?" I'm not going to lie; I was hoping that Leah's suspicions would have faded by now. Especially after last night, I don't feel comfortable hacking into Imperium.

"He's hiding something from me," she replies. I hear the brittle note in her voice, the tension and pain that she's trying to conceal. "I don't know what."

"You could ask him, kiddo."

"Right. And I'm sure he'll tell me the truth right away. Because men who cheat on their wives are big on honesty."

I sigh. Damn it. All I wanted to do this evening was relive my incredible night with Finn and Oliver, and maybe chat with Lancelot and Merlin. But Leah needs me. "I'm assuming I'll have to get dressed up for this dinner?" I ask gloomily.

"Yes," she says at once. "Wear the black cocktail dress I gave you last year. You still have it, don't you?"

"I do," I reply sulkily. "Fine. I'll be there."

"Thank you, Miki," she says, chuckling a little at my tone. "I'm really grateful. Really."

THE DINNER IS as boring as I fear. As I talk to the single male investment banker sitting across from me, I begin to fear that this is a 'Get Miki to Meet Some Eligible Bachelors' ambush. Jonathan Sherman, a coworker of Ben's, is easy enough on the eye, but he's painfully boring. All he seems to be able to talk about are his car, his boat, and his career. "What do you do?" he asks me during a brief pause in the monolog.

"I've just started work at a data security firm called Imperium." I look at Ben out of the corner of my eye, but if he has a guilty conscience, he doesn't show any sign.

Jonathan's eyebrows rise. "They're going public soon, aren't they? Their IPO is creating a lot of buzz. It's going to make them a fortune."

Stefan Campos, another investment banker, is sitting at my right. He nods at Jonathan's comment. "They're already spending it," he says. "I ran into one of the management team at my realtor's office. He was looking at a forty-million dollar penthouse on the Upper East Side."

"Who?" I can't see either Oliver or Finn shop around for such expensive real estate. The men are pretty wealthy and are going to be even richer, but so far, I haven't seen any sign that they like to throw their money around. No fancy cars, no expensive yachts.

"Lawrence Kent," Stefan replies.

That's weird. I've had three meetings with the CFO this week. The last one was during lunch on Thursday, the only free slot on his schedule, and he spent ten minutes bitching about the cost of his fifteen-dollar sandwich. He certainly doesn't act like he can afford a forty-million dollar condo.

"Your realtor's office?" Ben asks. "Are you moving?"

Stefan shakes his head. "No, Molly and I are buying a summer home in the Hamptons."

"I'd like to live in the Hamptons," Leah says wistfully. "I've always wanted to open a bakery there."

"You have?" I sound surprised. Leah's always glued to the Food Network, and I know she has a girl crush on the Barefoot Contessa, but I didn't think she was serious about her cooking aspirations. "You do know bakers wake up alarmingly early, don't you?"

Ben looks at my sister fondly. "Leah's usually up at the crack of dawn." He puts his hand over hers. "And she's an excellent cook."

Hmm. If Ben's cheating on my sister, he's a really good actor. Right now, he looks like a man who's deeply in love with his wife. Is Leah just being paranoid?

Then again, I thought I was paranoid when Aaron started spending more and more time at work. I thought that I was imagining the looks of pity the women in his office gave me when I visited.

AFTER DINNER, I corner Ben. "Nice party," I tell him, looking around the library with wide eyes. Their apartment has two floors and is at least three thousand square feet. *In Manhattan, on the Upper East Side.* I can't even imagine how much money they paid for it. "You've redecorated since the last time I was here."

"Leah redecorated," he corrects me, an edge in his voice. "I wrote checks." He pours himself a drink from the mahogany bar and drains it. "This bar was custom-built in Italy. It cost fifty thousand dollars. The flower bill for tonight?" He gestures to the tall vases overflowing with bright orange and red orchids. "Four thousand dollars. They were flown in from Ecuador." He looks at my sister, who's chatting with Sharon Hodges on the other side of the room. "Still, Leah's happy."

I'm reminded of Friday night, of the way Oliver downed his rum and coke when Claudia walked in. I don't know my brother-in-law very well, but something's going on with him. "That seems like a lot of money," I say cautiously.

"No shit." He pours himself another drink and tilts the bottle of Scotch my way. I decline the offer, and he shrugs. "We're on a fucking treadmill, and we can't get off."

"It's none of my business, but have you tried talking to Leah?" I ask gently. My sister has always been something of a spendthrift, but even for her, this is excessive.

"It's my job to provide for my wife," he says flatly. "If she wants orchids from South America, she'll get them."

Warned by his tone, I shut up. I'm willing to bet that what Leah really wants is more of Ben's time and attention. They seem to be trapped in a vicious cycle; my sister spends money because she's unhappy that Ben's never home, and Ben works harder to pay for all the things Leah buys.

Is he cheating on her? I can't tell. But there's no doubt: *Something's wrong with their marriage.*

15

A real friend is one who walks in when the rest of the
world walks out.

— WALTER WINCHELL

Finn:

True to his word, Guzman sends me the data I'm
looking for, a list of every single IP address that
User0989 used to access his DefCon account.

Oliver and I divide up the list, and we get to work. I
comb through the information, meticulously tracing each
address, but every single one I try results in a dead-end.
User0989 has been careful. He's logged into his account
from coffee shops, from libraries, and other public areas. All
I learn is that he's located in Manhattan, which does
nothing to narrow down his identity.

"No luck?" Oliver asks, after about two hours of work.
"Me neither."

I don't reply. I move to the next address on the list.

"Hang on," I say slowly. Something's nagging at me. This IP address looks familiar. "You remember that monitor we installed in the small conference room a couple of weeks ago?"

"The one where the technician couldn't get the display to connect to the Internet?"

"Yeah." I wrack my brain, trying to remember what Janine told me. The display wouldn't work with our firewall, so the technician had to use a workaround. "The guy couldn't connect to our network, so he connected it to the building's wi-fi."

"That's not very secure," Oliver comments with a frown.

"Not at all. Janine was going to follow up with the company that made the unit." I log into Imperium and confirm that I'm right. "User0989 piggybacked on that connection on Tuesday."

Oliver's head snaps up. "You're saying User0989 works at Imperium."

"Exactly."

I pull up the conference room's calendar. User0989 accessed the Internet at five in the afternoon on Tuesday. Who was in the room at that time?

Two minutes later, I have my answer. There were three people in that room.

Chris Wilcox, the developer that Larry poached from the Shield team.

Sachin Sharma, the head of the Shield team.

And finally, a name that sends a jolt through me. Lawrence Kent.

I turn my laptop screen toward Oliver. He reads the list and reaches the same conclusion I do. There's only one person on this list who has the means to hire a hacker.

Why does Lawrence Kent want Miki to hack into Imperium? *What is he after?*

Oliver rises to his feet. "I don't understand," he says, pacing by the window. "What does Larry have to gain if we get breached? He's got stock options. He has just as much to lose as we do if our IPO fails."

"I don't know," I confess. "It doesn't make sense. Larry wants to be the CEO, and I'm sure he'd love to see the two of us discredited. But if the IPO fails, he stands to lose a fortune. He's not going to do that."

We're missing something. If we had User0989's chat transcripts, we might be able to piece together Larry's plan, but Boris Guzman was clear that he wasn't prepared to give those up.

"Could we fire Kent?" I ask Oliver.

He shakes his head. "The board won't go for it," he says regretfully. "Ambrose likes Kent. The two of them golf together twice a month. Sutton will do the right thing, but only if we have conclusive proof."

Damn it. This was the trade-off we made for the opportunity to go public. The board of directors had to have a certain amount of control over our decision making in order to satisfy the SEC. "User0989 hired Miki," I say out loud. "If she discloses that to the board..."

Oliver voices the flaw in my plan. "Miki mentioned User0989 to Lancelot and Merlin," he says. "Not to Oliver Prescott and Finn Sanders."

I lapse into silence. In order to fire Kent, we're going to have to reveal our true identities to Miki.

And if we do that, we will lose her.

Oliver opens his mouth to say something but changes his mind. His expression is conflicted.

Neither of us is prepared to give her up. Not after last night.

Miki:

I get back home after Leah's party, change out of my black cocktail dress and into my comfortable Hello Kitty pajamas and curl up on the couch.

My thoughts are confused and tangled, and my mind refuses to settle down, jumping from topic to topic. I turn on the TV, but nothing holds my attention. Finally, I confront the thing I've been avoiding thinking about.

Last night.

I force myself to admit something I've been denying for the last week. I should have never responded to User0989. Though the money was tempting, I should have never agreed to hack into Imperium. Even for Leah. Even to figure out what Ben was up to.

That's the real reason why I didn't tell Lancelot and Merlin about User0989. I was ashamed. I crossed an important ethical line when I agreed to go to that party, and I was afraid to admit what I did to Lancelot and Merlin. Even though I've never met the two men, their opinions have become incredibly important to me.

Last night, I slept with Oliver and Finn, bringing matters to a head.

Who are you, Miki Cooper? I ask myself. *Finn Sanders and Oliver Prescott are good men. Are you the kind of person that will destroy their dreams?*

I can't do that to them.

I've already gone over the line. If I hack into Imperium

for User0989, I won't be able to face myself. My pride will be wounded if I borrow money from my parents or my friends, but my sense of right and wrong will remain intact. And that's far more important.

What now?

I could quit my job. Ignoring the sinking feeling in my stomach at the thought of never seeing Finn and Oliver again, I force myself to examine the option objectively. If I quit, User0989 might still expose me, but he won't be able to cause the IPO to fail.

Unless he hires someone else. Someone who isn't bothered by inconvenient scruples.

I need to talk this out with someone. I flip my laptop open. Merlin isn't online, but Lancelot is. *Tell them, Miki,* my conscience urges. *They're your friends. They'll help you.*

Or they'll be disgusted by what I did.

I take a deep breath. Either way, it's time to face the music.

Do you have a minute? I type.

There's a long pause, and then Lancelot's reply appears on the screen. *Of course, mouse.*

You remember the other day when I asked you to track down a user called User0989?

Yeah... he replies.

I didn't tell you why I wanted to know. My fingers pause over my keyboard, then I force myself to keep typing. *User0989 hired me to hack into Imperium.*

Lancelot's reply comes almost immediately. *He did?*

God, I feel about two feet high. *He offered me a hundred thousand dollars if I was able to crack their network and retrieve their client list,* I admit. *I should have told you earlier.*

You want our help cracking Imperium? Lancelot asks.

No! I can't go through with it.

Too risky?

That's not it. My cheeks heat as images from last night flash in front of me. The outline of Finn's cock against his briefs. Oliver's blond head bent between my legs as he ate me out. Finn flipping me on my hands and knees and thrusting his hard shaft into my pussy. Oliver's erection nudging my lips.

Imperium has never harmed me, I type out at last. *Oliver Prescott and Finn Sanders have been great to work with. If I hack them ahead of their IPO, they stand to lose a ton of money.*

So you're scared?

No. I don't feel good about what I agreed to do, Lancelot, but I had my reasons, and it wasn't just the money.

Why'd you do it?

My sister thinks her husband is cheating on her, I write. *His information is protected by Imperium. I shouldn't have got involved but after my own divorce—*

I don't continue. Lancelot will understand. His wife cheated on him. Before Aaron, I naively believed that people didn't cheat very often on their partners, that my father was an exception. After all, my friends were perfectly happy with their partners, and Leah and Ben always seemed content.

Not anymore. Aaron cheated. Lancelot's wife cheated on him, though he's never mentioned the specifics. Yesterday, Oliver told me about Claudia. Ben might have a mistress on the side. It's enough to make me lose my faith in love.

I can understand that, Lancelot says at last. *Thank you for telling me the truth, Mouse. So what are you going to do?*

Probably quit my job.

Really? He seems surprised. *That's rather drastic. Don't you need the cash?*

It doesn't matter, Lancelot. I can't be involved in this.

If you quit, the guy's just going to hire someone else off the forum, Lancelot writes.

I exhale in frustration. *What should I do then? Tell me. I'm out of options here. I just know I can't hurt Oliver and Finn. They don't deserve it.*

He doesn't reply for almost a full minute. *What if you told them everything?*

I wish I could come clean with Finn and Oliver, but even the thought of telling them the truth makes me cold all over. There's no good scenario here. Either they're going to think I slept with them hoping to sway them not to press charges when they found out, or they're going to think I slept with them to try and worm information out of them.

Let me see, I write back. *They're on the brink of an IPO, and I've been hired to hack into their company and ruin it. If I tell them, they'll call the cops faster than I can blink.*

You're just a tool in this, Mouse. If they're smart, they'll try and figure out what User0989's end game is.

I stare at the monitor, wondering if Lancelot is right. What he's saying makes sense. User0989 is up to something, and if I were Finn and Oliver, I'd want to know what he's after.

But the truth is, despite sleeping with Oliver and Finn, I don't know the two men. I don't know what their reaction will be when they find out that I was hired to hack into their company.

I'd like to tell them everything, but I can't take the chance.

16

There is no fool like a careless gambler who starts taking victory for granted.

— HUNTER S. THOMPSON

Finn:

What a fucking tangled web we weave.

After Miki's chat session with Oliver last night, he called me, and I'd gone over, and the two of us had stared at the screen for the longest time, unsure how to proceed.

Almost a day later, I still don't know what to do.

I'm intensely relieved that Miki isn't plotting to destroy us. I'm delighted that she's told us everything. I want to tell her not to worry. We will figure out what Lawrence is up to, and we will stop him.

But I can't do any of those things because she doesn't know the real identity of the two men she's been chatting with on the DefCon forums since Thanksgiving.

And if she finds out what we did and why, we will lose her.

"You're preoccupied today," my grandmother says, as she ladles another helping of her delicious beef stew into my bowl. "What's the matter? Something wrong at work?"

I shake my head. "You're going to love this," I tell her. "I'm thinking about a woman."

She sets her spoon down with a clatter. "Will wonders never cease," she exclaims. "Who is this magical woman who has managed to distract you from your company?"

"Her name's Miki. You'll like her."

"So, what's the problem?" she asks. "You don't look happy."

"It's complicated," I sigh. "Oliver and I met her under false pretenses. If we come clean…" My voice trails off helplessly. "She'll never talk to me again."

"You care about this woman." My grandmother's sentence is a statement, not a question.

"Yeah, I really like her. She's special."

My grandmother frowns at me. "Then you have to tell her the truth, Finn. Love can't be built on lies. If this relationship is important to you, you have to be honest."

"I could lose her." My throat tightens at the thought of never seeing Miki again, at never talking to her online. I can't imagine my life without her in it.

"You could," she agrees. "That's a chance you'll have to take. You know it's the right thing to do."

We're both done with our meals. I carry the saucepan back into the kitchen, waving off her attempts to stop me. "I can do dishes," I tell her. "You made dinner. That's more than enough."

She snorts. "I know what you're doing," she says. "You're worrying about me. Stop it. I'm old, not decrepit."

"And I'm capable of washing a plate," I retort. She's putting a brave face on it, but my grandmother isn't walking too well. Her knee has been bothering her, but she's too stubborn to use a cane to get around. "Go sit down."

"There's ice-cream in the freezer if you want dessert."

"None for me." I smile at my grandmother, who never met a flavor of ice-cream she didn't like. "Let me load the dishwasher, and I'll bring you a bowl."

We settle in the living room once I'm done, and the conversation turns to her new neighbors. "Nice young couple," she says. "I took them a pie."

"Of course you did," I say in exasperation. "What's next? You're going to cook them dinner?"

"It's good to be neighborly," she chides. "Do you even know the people that live in your building?"

Not really. "I see a guy with a little poodle on the elevator every morning," I tell her. "The dog's called Rex."

"Well, that's a start. How's Oliver? I haven't seen him for a couple of weeks."

I remember last night's debacle. "Claudia is giving him trouble. She showed up with her new boyfriend to the bar Friday night. Then she proceeded to stick her tongue down his throat."

She heaves a sigh. "I never liked that woman," she says. Her spoon scrapes against the side of her bowl, and I get up and refill it. She smiles at me in thanks and continues her train of thought. "They've been divorced for almost a year. Isn't it time she left him alone?"

"It's Claudia. It's about money. This time, she wants Imperium stock."

Her lip tightens, but she doesn't say anything. She doesn't need to; I know exactly how she feels about Oliver's ex-wife.

Miki:

Neither Finn nor Oliver is around when I get into work Monday morning. "They're going to be off-site all day," Janine tells me. "Finn's in a huddle with the Block team, and Oliver's in back-to-back meetings." She eyes me curiously, and no doubt she wants to ask me about Friday night, but she's far too discreet to gossip about her bosses.

Much better than me, who slept with them.

"Okay." I ignore my stab of disappointment. Finn and Oliver promised me things wouldn't get weird at work, and I hope they're right. Of course, that doesn't matter now. My days at Imperium are numbered anyway.

Neither of them are around, and that gives me a perfect opportunity to see if I can access Ben's information. It's been hard to investigate my brother-in-law's finances with Finn and Oliver working in the same office as me. I'm not going to get a second chance.

After eight hours of non-stop effort, I'm about ready to give up. Finn is the chief architect of Imperium's defenses, and he appears to have thought of everything. I try every trick in the book to get access to Ben's account, and I come up short every single time.

A weird sense of déjà vu grips me. I'm not vain; I'm good at what I do. I've only been stymied this badly once before. Last summer, Wendy was the divorce attorney for a woman whose husband was hiding his money. That system was really tightly secured as well.

There's a knock at the door, and Janine sticks in her head. "Miki," she scolds me, "did you remember to eat lunch?"

Lunch. I knew I was forgetting something.

She shakes her head at me. "You're terrible," she says. "Listen, I need to take off. Are you at a stopping point?"

I still don't have after-hours access to the Imperium offices. I get to my feet, every muscle in my body aching in protest. "Yeah. I'm ready to leave."

"Oh, I forgot to ask this morning. How was the apartment search?"

I didn't look at apartments over the weekend; there didn't seem any point. I'm not going to stay employed at Imperium for long, and I need to save every dollar to pay my divorce lawyer. "Not too great," I mutter, unwilling to get into long explanations.

After all, Janine's loyalties are clear. She's been friendly so far, but if she finds out why I'm really at Imperium, I'm sure her attitude will change dramatically.

THIS MONDAY, my girlfriends are meeting in a bar in Hell's Kitchen. I make my way there after work. Piper, Gabby, and Bailey are already there, half-empty drinks in front of them.

"I'm not late, am I?" I ask, sliding into the booth next to Bailey.

Piper shakes her head. "We're early."

Katie and Wendy show up a couple of minutes after me, and the three of us order drinks. "So, what's going on with everyone?" Wendy asks, looking at her club soda with disgust. "This baby cannot show up soon enough."

"We can stop meeting in bars, if you'd like," Piper offers.

Wendy shakes her head. "Don't mind my grumbling. The pregnancy is making me cranky. I'm a whale, and I need to pee all the time."

I roll my eyes. "You're barely showing."

She laughs. "Yes, Asher used the phrase 'drama queen' yesterday."

Katie's eyes widen. "He did? Asher's a brave man. Or stupid."

"A bit of both," Wendy replies with a grin. "It slipped out by mistake. Don't worry, he groveled." She turns to me. "How's the new job?"

"And the hot bosses?" Bailey interjects slyly. "Still want to sleep with them?"

Last week, I happened to mention that I thought Oliver and Finn were hot. I'm never going to hear the end of it. *And if I tell them about Friday night...*

Gabby's face twists into a frown. "Please tell me you're not going to sleep with your bosses," she says, her voice clipped. "Because that would be really dumb."

Piper raises an eyebrow. "Umm, Gabby? Miki's an adult. Besides," she says, her cheeks going pink, "It's not always a terrible idea. I slept with my bosses, and it worked out okay."

"Technically, they weren't your bosses," Wendy points out. "They were investors in your restaurant. I slept with my partners too, and obviously, it went well." She pats her belly with a grin. "Still, I'm afraid that Gabby's right. The situations aren't the same. If things go wrong, you'll lose your job. It's not worth the risk. Don't dip your pen in the company ink."

"Or whatever the female equivalent of that saying is," Katie adds.

Confession time. "Too late," I mutter, keeping my eyes fixed on my drink. "I slept with them Friday night."

"Both of them?" Piper squeaks. "You're joking, right?"

"Hey," I say indignantly. I point to Bailey, Piper, Gabby,

and Wendy in turn. "Ménage," I say. "Ménage, ménage, and ménage. Are you that shocked that I was curious?"

Katie chuckles. "I've never been interested," she says. "Then again, Adam is the perfect guy."

Gabby looks thunderous. "How did this happen?" she demands. "And where?"

I exchange curious looks with Wendy. Gabby's tone is too heated, too angry. I'm not sure what's going on with her. Her employers are short-staffed, and Gabby's working in Manhattan for the next month. Perhaps she misses Carter and Dominic?

"Don't worry; it was just a one night stand," I reply, my cheeks flushing under their scrutiny. "I don't know why you're so shocked. You ladies threw me an intervention and told me to get a life. So I did."

"No kidding," Bailey laughs. She lifts her glass and clinks it against mine. "Let's toast to Miki and good sex." She takes a sip of her beer. "It was good, right?"

"Pretty spectacular, and that's all I'm going to say about it."

THE GATHERING BREAKS up at nine. Gabby lingers at the table as everyone else gets up to leave. "Miki, will you stick around for a second?"

I heave a sigh. "Listen," I tell her once the others are out of earshot. "I appreciate you watching out for me. But I am an adult. You have to trust that I can make my own decisions."

She looks acutely unhappy. "My company does a lot of crisis management PR," she says. "If a celebrity is caught driving drunk, he calls us. Beating his wife in an elevator? We're on speed dial. I don't see a great slice of humanity."

"Okay." I'm sure there's a point here, but I have no idea what it is.

Gabby takes a deep breath. "I met a new client today. He was into BDSM, and he'd taken photos of his ex-wife without her consent. She's furious and is demanding compensation." She crumples her paper napkin into a ball, then straightens it out and methodically starts shredding it. Her eyes don't meet mine, and a chill travels down my spine.

"And you're telling me this because..."

"Because the guy taking the photos was Oliver Prescott," she says in a rush. "Miki, I don't have anything against BDSM, and I don't care what people do in the privacy of their bedrooms. But this guy took photos of his then-wife without her consent. He violated her trust. Is that the kind of person you want to sleep with?"

I stare at Gabby, my heart hammering with shock. My stomach roils, and I think I'm going to be sick.

She takes in my expression, and her face softens in sympathy. "Oh fuck," she says. "You've fallen in love with them."

"What?" I gape at her, startled beyond belief. "No, of course not. I've only known them for a week, Gabby. You can't fall in love with someone in seven days."

"Can't you?" A small smile creases her lips. "I spent one night with Carter and Dominic, and I couldn't forget them. When I ran into them again in Atlantic City, there was something between us already. A familiarity, a comfort, a deep certainty that I knew who they were. At the risk of sounding like a head-in-the-cloud romantic, my soul knew theirs."

"No." I shake my head violently. "The situations are entirely different. You slept with Carter and Dominic. I flew on a plane with Oliver and Finn."

"What did you talk about?"

"TV shows," I reply. "Doctor Who. The world-building in Dune. Inception's ending."

"Most people," she says, "will have no idea what you're talking about, but Oliver and Finn shared your interests, Miki." She lifts her hand and counts off. "Shared values, shared life experiences, roughly the same age. People tend to fall in love with other people who are like them."

I roll my eyes. "Lancelot and Merlin on the DefCon forums have the same interests as me. Lancelot's even been divorced, for heaven's sake. The stuff you're talking about isn't as rare as you think."

Part of me wonders why I'm trying to prove her wrong, why her assumption that I've fallen in love bothers me as much as it does.

"Okay," she says. "Fine. I'm glad you aren't in love with them. After Aaron, you deserve good people in your life, Miki, and based on what I learned today, Oliver Prescott isn't one of them."

17

Thoughts are the shadows of our feelings - always darker, emptier and simpler.

— F<small>RIEDRICH</small> N<small>IETZSCHE</small>

Oliver:

M y life is like a roller-coaster. I lurch between the highs of the good days and the dismal lows of the bad ones.

I get home a little after five. It's already dark outside, and the only thing in my refrigerator that resembles food is a carton of eggs that's tucked away in the back.

Another day, another pizza delivery.

This morning, I had a contentious meeting with the board. According to the projection Lawrence had drawn up for Ambrose, closing the private security division would cause our revenue to drop by ten percent. "Do you know what'll happen to the stock price if our revenue declines in the first quarter after we go public?" David Blake had demanded.

The first revenue numbers will come out before the board can sell their stock. David's not concerned about Imperium's long-term success, just the value of his holdings.

"Block and Shield will be released before then," I'd argued. "Right now, we're spending a disproportionate amount of time on the private security division. We'll be able to reallocate our efforts to more profitable areas."

Miguel Vazquez, about my only sure ally on the board apart from Finn, had thrown me a bone. "Kent's numbers seem high to me," he'd said. "Oliver, if I were you, I'd double-check them."

Ambrose Sutton's brows had creased in annoyance. "Lawrence Kent is the CFO," he'd snapped. "Are we to trust Oliver's numbers more? It's clear that the two of you," he'd nodded to Finn and me, "want to shutter this division. Let me remind you that the board won't rubber-stamp every decision you make. Our duty is to the shareholders of Imperium."

"Of which there aren't any yet," Finn had replied calmly. "Let me remind you that Oliver and I founded Imperium. Our decisions have got us to this point."

"Finn's right," Barbara Rhodes had interjected. The older woman rarely spoke, but when she did, she was always listened to. Barbara had taken the small grocery chain her father had founded and grown it into the second largest retailer in the country. "So far, your judgment has always been sound."

So far. What happens when Claudia's photos leak? I don't know what faith the board will have in my judgment then.

The meeting had ended inconclusively. My afternoon

meeting, with the PR firm that Susan had recommended, had gone no better. The Aventi employee assigned to my case was a woman called Gabriella Alves, and she'd been hostile and disbelieving of my story. "You're telling me that you run a data security company, but your ex-wife was able to take these pictures without your consent?"

I grab my swim trunks and head to the building's indoor pool. I'm the only one there, which is a relief. I've never been less in the mood for small talk.

I SWIM LAP AFTER LAP, my muscles straining, pushing my body beyond its usual limits in a quest to quiet my mind. As my arms slice through the water, I'm not thinking of Ambrose Sutton and the rest of the board. I'm not thinking of Claudia, Lawrence, or Sebastian Fitzgerald.

There's only one person on my mind. Miki.

After Claudia, I swore I'd never make myself vulnerable again. I never went out with a woman more than once; I wasn't ready to risk my heart.

But Miki slipped in. Our relationship was formed online. I knew things would change if I slept with her, and I did it anyway.

It's ironic. I'm the CEO of a data security company. I know how dangerous the Internet can be. I just didn't think I'd risk losing my heart.

You know what the right thing to do is. Tell her everything.

FINN DROPS by shortly after I get back to my apartment. He's holding a six-pack in his hand. "What a train wreck of a day," he says.

I step aside, and he walks in. "When did our lives get so complicated, Oliver?"

"Money corrodes everything it touches," I reply bitterly. "We wanted to go public, remember?"

"It doesn't seem worth it." He sits down on the couch with a sigh. "I'm beginning to wonder if we wouldn't be better served to call it off."

"Sure, you're saying that today," I reply. "But tomorrow, you'll still be at work at a quarter to seven, and you'll leave at ten at night."

"Maybe not." He opens a bottle of beer and takes a long drink from it.

I pick up my phone. "You want pizza?"

He nods, and I dial the Italian restaurant two blocks down the street and place an order. They know me well. "Your usual order, Mr. Prescott? One extra-large pizza, half Hawaiian, half sausage and mushrooms? It'll be thirty minutes."

"Sounds good."

I grab one of Finn's beers and settle next to him on the couch. "Anything good on TV?"

He's flipping through channels aimlessly. "Not really," he replies. "Nana is right. There should be more to life than work."

He's thinking of Miki too.

Finn and I have shared women in our twenties. We even had a relationship of sorts with one of them, Karina, until she moved back to Brazil. That's not the most important issue confronting us.

There's a knock. "That's fast," Finn comments, as I grab my wallet and head to the front door.

It's not the pizza delivery guy that greets me. It's Miki. "I need to talk to you," she blurts out. "Did you take nude photos of Claudia without her consent? Is it true?"

Fuck.

∾

Miki:

Oliver steps aside, and I enter his living room. Finn's sitting on the couch, his eyes watchful and wary. As usual.

Friday night, we'd sat around on the floor and played a game of strip poker, and the three of us had made love. I thought I knew who they were, but I'm not going to lie. Gabby's revelation has rocked me.

"No," Oliver says calmly. "I didn't."

"Yet you met a crisis management PR firm," I reply.

He holds out his hand for my coat, and I remove it and hand it to him. "We have pizza coming," he says. "Want to stick around? Finn can't find anything good on TV, but there's always Netflix."

I exhale in frustration. "Oliver, don't stonewall me. I slept with the two of you on Friday. Tell me I can trust you."

His expression is stricken. "I didn't take photos of Claudia, Miki," he says. He waves me toward the couch and disappears into his bedroom.

I sit down. Finn looks at me. "Do you really think Oliver would do that?" he asks me.

I'm torn. My heart says *No*. Of course Oliver wouldn't have done it. But I force myself to remain skeptical. I'd trusted Aaron too, and he had made a fool out of me. "I don't know what to believe, Finn."

A pulse ticks in his jaw.

Oliver returns with a large envelope in his hands. He throws it down on the table. "These are the photos," he says.

A sick sense of curiosity compels me to reach for the pictures. I open the envelope. The first photo shows Claudia kneeling on the floor, naked except for a leather collar around her throat. The second photo shows her on all fours, a man in black pants standing behind her.

I swallow hard. Oliver's ex-wife is beautiful and seeing her naked is extremely dispiriting.

"Keep looking," Oliver says.

I pick up the third photo. In this, Oliver's kneeling next to Claudia, a whip in his hands. With a start, I realize what's wrong with the picture I'm looking at. "Your face is exposed."

I've worked with Oliver for a week. He's not as paranoid as Finn, but apart from a habit of leaving his phone lying around in meeting rooms, he's pretty conscious about data security. Like me, he doesn't post on social media, and Janine's mentioned more than once how averse he is to getting his photo taken.

Oliver wouldn't have allowed his face to be visible in this context.

"Exactly," he replies. "No, this is Claudia's doing, not mine. She wants half my share of Imperium."

"What?"

Finn nods soberly. "She's threatening to make these public otherwise," he says. "We think Fitzgerald is behind it. He'd love to get his paws into our company."

"I'm not going to do it," Oliver interjects. "Claudia is demented if she thinks I'm going to bend to her will. No, these photos will go public. I met the PR firm today to see how we could manage the fallout." He crooks an eyebrow. "How did you find out about that?"

"You met my friend, Gabriella," I mutter, my cheeks flaming. I'm feeling really, *really* sheepish. Gabby works with wildly overpaid soccer players, and her job makes her cynical about people's motivations. "She knows about Friday night, and she was being protective."

"That explains the hostility," Oliver says. There's a knock at the door, and he gets up to answer it, returning with a large pizza box in his hands. "Have a slice, Miki?"

"You're not angry with me?"

He smiles warmly in my direction. "Miki, the only person I'm angry with is Claudia. We don't know each other very well. You have every right to want to know the truth."

He's being really nice, and shame trickles through me. Finn gets three plates from the kitchen and hands me one. Flipping the box of pizza open, he grabs a slice and holds it in my direction.

"I should go," I say awkwardly. "I just barged in here."

Finn grins. "Yes," he agrees, "We had quite an epic evening planned. You interrupted us drinking beer and bitching that there's nothing to watch on TV."

I laugh. "When you put it that way." I help myself to a slice of Hawaiian, smiling inwardly when I think of Merlin. Evidently, the ham and pineapple combination is more popular than I realize.

An hour later, I'm curled up between Oliver and Finn, my head resting on Finn's shoulder. We've just finished watching an episode of Sense 8. "Want to watch another?"

When I inhale, I can breathe in Finn's cologne. Oliver's muscles flex when he reaches for a beer. Sitting between them, my desire has been on slow burn all evening long.

Now, I can either do the sensible thing and leave, or, I can succumb to temptation once again.

Oliver's stormy blue eyes rest on me. "Or we could do something more interesting."

He doesn't need to spell it out. I know exactly what he's offering. Finn's fingers are tracing soft circles on my upper arm, and that touch, light and questioning, sets the butterflies fluttering in my stomach.

"My marriage just ended," I whisper. "I don't know what I'm doing."

Oliver's lips twist into a wry smile. "I like you, Miki," he says. "I'm not looking to get involved with anyone either."

"What do you want?" I turn my head from Oliver to Finn.

Finn's response is simple. "You."

My heart beats faster, but after the debacle of my marriage, I'm no longer swayed by charming words and pretty phrases. I want things clearly spelled out. "Are you seeing anyone else?"

Both men shake their heads at once. "I'd like to sleep with you, Miki. I want to keep our relationship monogamous." Oliver cocks his head to one side, his eyes on me. "But I need to be honest. You said you weren't looking for anything serious, and neither am I."

Finn doesn't say anything. I give him a searching look. "Does that apply to you as well?"

"Imperium is going public," he says. "I don't have time for anything else."

Sex with two men, no strings attached. They want the same things I want. *It's a perfect arrangement,* I tell myself. *Say yes.*

I take a deep breath and nod my assent. "Are you into

BDSM? Is there a secret box of sex toys somewhere? Or a dungeon?"

Oliver laughs. "I gave you the tour Saturday morning," he says. "No dungeon, no toys. I threw those out when Claudia and I split up."

"Why do you ask?" Finn says lazily. "Do you secretly want to be tied up and whipped?"

I feel my cheeks heat. "Nothing as intense as whips," I admit in a rush.

Oliver's lips curl into a grin. "Come to my bedroom, Miki. I'm sure Finn and I can improvise something."

Who am I kidding? From the moment I reached for that slice of pizza, I knew I was going to spend the night. And it's not as if I'm risking my career by sleeping with my bosses. My days at Imperium are numbered anyway.

THE THREE OF us make our way to Oliver's bedroom. Once we're there, Finn points to a throw rug at the foot of the bed. "Stand there."

The smoothly dominant tone of his voice startles me. I smile inwardly. *Well, well, well, Mr. Sanders.* It looks like Oliver's not the only one who's done some experimenting.

I obey without speaking. "So you want to get spanked, Miki?" Oliver asks. He moves close to me, his big hands running over the curve of my ass before he gives me a smack.

I jump, more startled than in pain. I'm still fully clothed, and my jeans provide protection. I grin cheekily at Oliver. "Is that the best you can do?"

Oliver's hand grips my shoulder, and he looks into my eyes. "Is taunting me a smart idea, Miki?"

I shake my head silently, my pussy clenching at Oliver's hard, clipped tone.

"Probably not," I admit. "But if I were a sensible person, I wouldn't be in your bedroom."

"Touché."

Finn kicks off his shoes and socks and pulls his belt free from its loops. My eyes widen in alarm, and he chuckles at my reaction. "Don't worry. I'm not going to use it on your ass," he says. "That's too hardcore for me. Take off your clothes."

"Good idea," Oliver agrees. He undresses as well, tossing his clothes casually on a leather armchair in the corner. I lick my lips as he pulls his cock out from his briefs. It's hard. Ready. Delicious.

Finn watches me strip with heated eyes. When I'm done, he beckons me forward with two fingers. "Get on the bed, on your hands and knees."

I get in position, and Oliver adjusts me to his liking, pushing my shoulders so that they touch the mattress. My cheek is pressed against Oliver's Egyptian cotton sheets.

"Are you wet, Miki?" Oliver's fingers graze through my folds, and he spreads some of the wetness from my pussy to my tight rosebud. Instinctively, my muscles clench and Oliver swats me. "Relax," he chides. "I'm not going to do anything you don't want."

I know. If I didn't trust Finn and Oliver, I'd have never hinted that I wanted to be spanked. *My soul knew theirs,* Gabby had said about Carter and Dominic. That sounds a little too Earth-Goddess for me, but there's no denying how comfortable I am around the two men.

Finn takes my wrists in his big hands. He pulls them behind my back, and loops his belt around them, tying them loosely together. "If you're nervous," he says, his palm stroking my shoulder, "you can pull free."

"Okay," I whisper. I'm not nervous. I think I'm going to combust out of sheer lust. My entire body shivers in uncontrolled need.

"What a pretty sight you are, Miki." Oliver's nails graze lightly over my ass, and then he spanks me. At the same time, he pushes two fingers into my dripping wet pussy. I whimper as his thumb rubs my clitoris, a gentle, teasing touch that's too light to get me off. "You like that?"

Oliver replaces his fingers with his tongue, and I sigh in pleasure. While he teases my folds, Finn plays with my breasts, squeezing them in his big palms. He twists my nipples between his fingers, and the action sends a jolt of sharp lust through me.

"I'm going to come," I whimper.

"Not yet." Oliver pulls his mouth off me, and I groan in frustration. "We have all night, Miki. By the time we're done, you're not going to be begging to come. You're going to be begging us to stop."

So. Fucking. Hot.

"She needs a distraction." Finn's voice is amused. I feel the bed shift as he moves, then his hands are on my shoulders, and he's turning me so I'm lying on my side, my hands still awkwardly tied behind my back. "You okay?"

I nod, warmed by the concern. "Good," he says. He removes the remainder of his clothes quickly and efficiently and positions himself so his cock nudges my lips. I part them eagerly, and Finn thrusts into my mouth.

Oliver shifts position as well, moving behind me. "Stroke me," he orders.

I twist my wrists in my binding and take Oliver's cock between my palms. I stroke up and down his length, closing my fingers around his thick girth, pumping his shaft as best as I can.

At the same time, Finn fucks my mouth, his fingers gripping my hair. I lick the underside of his cock and swirl my tongue around his engorged head, squeezing my lips around him.

I'm lost in a haze of pleasure, drugged with lust. Oliver spanks me even as I give him a handjob, and between the swats, he finger-fucks my pussy. Each time he pushes his finger deep into my wet core, I'm rocked forward, and Finn's cock is pushed deeper into my mouth.

Finn grunts. "I'm going to come," he clenches out. I feel his balls draw up and tighten, and then he explodes in my mouth with a muffled moan.

"Some people," Oliver says, his voice dry, "have no stamina."

Finn kisses my lips, flipping Oliver the bird at the same time. "I'd like to see how long you last in her mouth," he says pointedly. He leans against the headboard and pats his lap. "Come here, Miki," he orders.

Oliver chuckles. "Let's put it to the test." He sits on the bed as well, and I position myself across Finn's strong thighs, my head resting in Oliver's lap, in perfect position to suck him off while Finn's spanking me.

Finn pushes my legs apart, spreading them open, and his fingers swoop unerringly between my legs. "Oliver's right," he says. "You *are* soaked. Enjoying yourself, baby?"

Oliver groans as I take him in my mouth. "Okay," he concedes, his voice hoarse with lust, "I might have spoken too soon." He throws his head back and clenches his eyes shut. His fingers stroke my cheek, the touch sweet and soft. "Yes, just like that."

Finn alternates between spanking me and teasing my

pussy. His thumb circles my ass, and pushes at the entrance, and my muscles yield to the firm pressure. "Ooh," I moan into Oliver's cock. Finn's finger in my ass feels naughty and wicked, *and I like it.*

If anal sex feels this good, sign me up.

In my mouth, Oliver pumps faster. From the sounds of his groans, he's not far away from his climax. I suck in my cheeks and lick the underside of his shaft, and his hands grip my hair as he erupts.

At the same time, Finn's fingers speed up over my clitoris. I'm painfully aroused. The men have teased my pussy over and over again, and I'm primed to explode.

Then Finn increases the pace and the pressure ever so slightly, and I can't hold back any longer. My muscles clench and tighten. My entire body seems to hang at the point of release, and then the dam bursts and my climax shudders through me.

One of them frees my wrists and massages my skin. The other pulls me into his lap and puts an arm around me.

It might be casual, and it might not involve commitment, but at this moment, I feel more cared for and cherished than I did during a year of marriage.

I don't let myself dwell on that thought. I think I'm starting to develop feelings for Oliver and Finn, and it terrifies me.

18

Life is really simple, but we insist on making it complicated.

— Confucius

Finn:

This time, she doesn't spend the night. At two in the morning, she gets dressed, ignoring our protests. "My bosses," she quips, "will take an exceedingly dim view if I'm late to work."

"Your bosses are assholes," Oliver says with a grin. He tries to tug Miki back to bed, but she dances out of reach. "Fine," he grumbles. "Give me a second. I'll give you a ride home."

She shakes her head. "Don't be ridiculous," she replies. "It's late. I'll just catch a cab."

"Not alone." I get to my feet and drag my jeans on. "I'll come with you."

"You guys," she says, rolling her eyes. "You don't have to

be all alpha and protective, okay? It's New York. I will be fine by myself."

"Call it what you want," I reply. "If you think I'm letting you catch a cab by yourself at this time of the night, you can think again. If my grandmother found out about it, she'd kick my ass."

Oliver muffles a laugh. "She weighs a hundred pounds soaking wet," he tells Miki. "And Finn's terrified of her. Don't argue, baby. You don't want him to get in trouble, do you?"

Her lips curl into a smile. "I guess not." She gives Oliver a hug and a kiss on the cheek. "See you in the morning, boss."

We hail a cab. Miki gives the driver the address to her apartment, and she leans back against the seat. "I'm probably out of your way," she says. "Where do you live?"

"Around the block. Oliver and I bought our apartments at the same time, right before we founded Imperium."

My grandmother's voice sounds in my ear. *Tell her the truth. She deserves it.*

But I hesitate. This is a really bad time to tell her. It's late, she's exhausted, and we've just had sex. We had good reasons for assuming our online identities, but if I spring the news on her now, she's not going to understand. She's just going to see our betrayal.

Earlier tonight, Oliver had told her that he wasn't looking for anything serious, and Miki had turned to me and asked if the same thing applied to me.

I'd put her off with some kind of vague answer about Imperium going public.

I'd been lying. I don't care about the IPO. The more we get closer to it, the more we clash with the board, the more I realize it's not worth it. I've chased success all my life, but the time I've spent with Miki—both online and in-person—has brought far more happiness.

She's not ready for a real relationship, *but I am*. I want a future with Miki.

But before that, there's something I need to do. Miki's told us—no, she's told Merlin and Lancelot—that she wants to quit her job. I have to stop her from doing that. There's a part of me that hopes that if she spends time with us—the real Oliver and Finn, not just her online buddies—that she'll realize that we didn't mean to break her trust.

Things are spiraling out of control, and I don't know how to fix this mess.

Miki:

Even though it's late, the first thing I do when I get back home is reach for my laptop. Unsurprisingly, Lancelot and Merlin are both online.

Any news on User0989?

I cross my fingers as I wait for their reply. I could ask Mary MacDonald about the circumstances around my hiring, but the more time I've spent thinking about my plan, the less confident I am in it. Mary might tell me something useful, but it's a long shot.

Lancelot types out a reply. *We were able to figure out his identity.*

My heartbeat quickens. *Who is it?*

Imperium's CFO. Lawrence Kent.

No. My first reaction is denial, followed swiftly by shock. *Why would Kent hire me to hack into their systems? He has full access to it already.*

Maybe he's covering his ass?

That seems logical, in a sick and twisted kind of way. For some unknown reason, Kent wants the IPO to fail, but if the client list goes public, he has to make sure that the leak can't be traced back to him.

I'm the scapegoat.

There's a sick feeling in my stomach. I have to go to Oliver and Finn, and I have to tell them what I know.

And then I'll never see them again.

There's more, Merlin types. *User0989 sent Lancelot and me a message earlier today. He offered us a job. Hack into Imperium. We turned him down, but Mouse, if he's getting desperate, he'll up the offer until he finds a taker.*

I was afraid this might happen. *What should I do?*

You can't quit your job just yet, Mouse.

They're right. But the longer I go without telling Oliver and Finn the truth, the more betrayed they're going to feel when they learn everything.

19

The supreme art of war is to subdue the enemy without fighting.

— SUN TZU

Oliver:

The next morning, Gabriella Alves shows up unannounced at Imperium. Janine puts her in a conference room and knocks on my door. "Do you want to see her?"

"Yes." It's a quarter to nine, and Miki's not in yet. My eyes feel like sandpaper, and I've downed my usual three cups of coffee, but the caffeine hasn't yet kicked in. Refilling my mug yet again, I make my way down the corridor.

Gabriella gets to her feet when she sees me. "I wanted to apologize for my attitude yesterday," she says without preamble. "My boss hadn't told me who I was meeting, and when I came in and saw you—" She grimaces wryly. "I jumped to conclusions."

I sit across from her. "You wanted to protect your friend."

She nods. "Miki's marriage just ended. She's in a fragile place."

Last night, Miki had been intrigued by the idea of being tied. She'd wriggled in our laps as we spanked her. Her eyes had turned hazy with lust when we'd fingered her ass. After her ex-husband cheated on her, she's cautious with her heart. But she's certainly not fragile.

"She's stronger than you give her credit for."

Miki matters to me. Last night, Finn and I had told her who User0989 really was, because we realize we need to show her we trust her.

Of course, right after that, we'd lied to her again, and told her User0989 had asked us to hack into Imperium, when he'd done no such thing.

We shouldn't have done that. But like Finn, I'm not ready to lose Miki.

Miki:

I didn't see Leah on Sunday. She'd had a migraine and had canceled at the last minute, leaving my mother and me to eat our traditional Sunday tea in silence. Tuesday morning, before I leave for work, I call her.

She sounds surprised to hear from me. "It's before nine," she teases. "I didn't think you'd be awake."

"I have a job." My cheeks heat. A job for which I'm running horribly late. Hopefully, Finn and Oliver know I'll make up the time because I don't want them to think I'm taking advantage of them. "I'm forced to get up before noon. Listen, I wanted to chat with you about Saturday."

"What about it?"

I take a deep breath. "I watched Ben and you at dinner," I tell her, unsure how my sister's going to react to my interference. "I saw two people that care about each other, but that aren't talking to each other. When was the last time the two of you had fun together, Leah?"

"I can't remember," she says flatly. "I'm doing everything I can to be a good wife, okay? I host dinner parties. I cook beautiful meals. I keep the house decorated. I make sparkling conversation with mind-numbing bores like Jon Sherman."

"Sweetie," I say gently. "You seem trapped. Ben seems trapped. Have you two considered counseling?"

"I can't," she says at once. "Ben works really hard. I don't want him to think I'm unhappy."

"You might not have another choice." I sit on the edge of the bed and stare into Wendy's closet, stuffed to the brim with her clothing from her old job. "I tried to hack into Ben's data, but it's really well-protected. I'm not going to be able to access it." I cross my fingers and hope I'm right about what I'm going to say next. "Ben doesn't look happy, and neither do you, but I don't think he's cheating on you, sweetie. Talk to him."

"I'm terrified," she whispers. "I'm crazy about Ben. I don't think I'm ready to face a world in which he's fallen out of love with me."

I went through a lot of emotions after Aaron cheated. I felt like a fool. I was angry, hurt, and betrayed. But I hadn't shattered. My pride had been damaged, but my heart had survived, intact. I'd never felt the anguish I hear in my sister's voice.

"I'm here for you," I promise her. "You won't be alone.

But Leah, you can't stay in limbo forever. Talk to him. Learn the truth."

I hang up, hoping desperately that Ben isn't sleeping around. I really want Leah to bypass the curse of the Cooper women.

Janine's got a big stack of printouts in her hands as I hurry in. "Killing a forest?" I joke as we cross paths in the hallway.

She rolls her eyes. "Lawrence's computer isn't working again. I don't know why his assistant couldn't have printed this for him. As if I don't have enough to do."

I give her a sympathetic smile and get to Oliver's office. Oliver and Finn are already there, and the clock on the wall tells me it's a quarter to ten. *Ouch.* "I'm sorry I'm late," I say, my cheeks flaming. They're going to think I'm taking advantage of the fact that I'm sleeping with them. "I'll work late tonight to make up."

"I know," Finn replies calmly. "I have no doubts on your work ethic, Miki. I trust you."

A pang goes through me. *You shouldn't,* I want to scream. *I was hired to ruin your business.*

Oliver doesn't seem concerned with my lateness either. "I'm in and out of meetings all day, and I don't think I'm going to get a chance to ask you. Are you doing anything tonight?"

I shake my head. "Not particularly." Trying to sort out why Lawrence Kent wants Imperium to fail. Trying to figure out a way out of this situation along with Lancelot and Merlin. "I was planning to catch up on sleep."

He opens a drawer with an oddly hesitant look on his face. Taking a key out, he holds it toward me. "Want to come over and finish watching the rest of this season of Sense 8?"

he asks. "I think I should be back home at seven, but if I'm not, you can let yourself in."

I stare at the key he's holding. "Is that—?"

"A key to my apartment?" He holds my gaze in his. "Yes."

"You're giving me a key to your place." My voice is thin and high with shock at Oliver's gesture of trust, one I'm profoundly unworthy of. "What if I go through your cupboards?"

His lips curl up in a grin. "I'm not worried, Miki." He deposits the small brass key in my palm, and closes my fingers around it, brushing a kiss on my lips. "I'll see you tonight?"

Oh God. I can't keep up this subterfuge. I have to tell them the truth. I force myself to smile. "Maybe," I reply airily. "Maybe I'll be in your bed when you get back home, naked."

Finn's lips curl into a wicked grin. He pulls his phone out of his pocket and glances at it. "Why wait until tonight?" he asks. "I have twenty minutes to my first meeting. Oliver?"

"Fifteen, but it's with Kent. I can be late." He shuts his office door and locks it. He crooks two fingers at me, patting his desk. "Come on, Miki. We don't have a lot of time."

"Janine could hear us," I start saying, my stomach churning with a mixture of nerves, excitement, and butterflies.

"Janine isn't around," Finn replies at once. "She had to drop off something at Kent's office, and after that, she's heading to the bakery downstairs to pick up bagels and coffee for my huddle with the Block team."

"Miki?" Oliver raises an eyebrow. "If you prefer not to fool around at the office, we'll respect that, of course." He's wearing a navy blue jacket. He removes it and drapes it over the back of a chair, and then unbuttons his cuffs and folds his shirt sleeves. My mouth goes dry at the sight of his strong forearms and his big hands.

"The door's locked?"

"Of course," Finn replies.

Every moment I spend with Finn and Oliver, it feels like there's a giant timer over my head, counting down the minutes. Soon, I'm going to run out of time. I can't keep the truth from them forever, and the knowledge of that fact makes me greedy for everything. "Should I take off my clothes?"

I'm wearing a short, pleated red skirt and a white shirt. I don't normally get this dressed up for work, but I admit it, I wanted to look nice for Oliver and Finn.

"Nope," Oliver replies. "Just take off your panties and hop on the desk." His lips tilt up in a smile. "And spread your legs, baby."

My heartbeat speeds up, and my breathing quickens with anticipation. I slide my panties down my hips and sit on the desk. "Tonight," Finn murmurs, stalking toward me, "we're going to take you at the same time. One cock in your pussy, one cock in your ass. Would you like that?"

His fingers brush at the pulse in my neck. "Yes," I whisper. "I would."

His hands skim over my breasts. He presses them together and squeezes, hard. I gasp and arch my back, thrusting them forward.

Chuckling at my reaction, Finn squeezes again. His thumbs brush over my nipples, and they engorge, pebbling under my shirt. "You like that, don't you, Miki?"

Oliver places his palms on my knees and spreads my legs apart. "You know what I want to do, Miki?" he growls. "I want to bend you over my desk and plunge my dick in your hot little pussy."

A shiver runs through me. "What's stopping you?" I stare into his eyes, emboldened by the raw, naked heat in his expression.

He grimaces. "Unfortunately, the clock is not my friend. Of course," he sits down on his chair, wheeling it close to me, "While we might not have time for sex, I do have time to make you scream with pleasure."

Finn's lips brush over mine, then he trails a path of small kisses to my throat. Oliver runs a finger between my folds, and he thrusts two fingers into my pussy. "Wet already," he says, grinning widely. "You're very good for our ego, Miki."

I groan and part my legs wider, trying to push my hips into Oliver's hand. Finn notices. "No, no," he chides. "Slow down."

"I thought I'd help speed things up," I gasp. "You two have a meeting, after all."

Oliver laughs. He bends his head toward me, breathing on my pussy. Goosebumps rise on my skin. His tongue licks at my slit, and he sucks my clitoris between his lips.

I almost jump off the desk as intense pleasure courses through me.

Finn's arms wrap around my shoulders. "Don't you wriggle away, Miki," he warns. He nibbles at my earlobe, and I whimper again as heat flares through me.

Oliver resumes licking me, his strokes long and steady. I forget everything—User0989, the IPO, Finn and Oliver's meetings, the fact that I'm in their office—in my delirious haze. His fingers piston in and out of my wet pussy; his tongue circles my throbbing clitoris. I tremble uncontrollably as my insides clench.

I'm so close. Every muscle in my body tightens. Then Finn squeezes my nipples between his fingers and Oliver sucks my clit gently between his teeth. The dam bursts and I explode, stifling my moans with difficulty.

Oliver pulls away once my shudders die down, a satisfied look on his face. "That's just an appetizer," he says. "I'm looking forward to the main course tonight."

As am I.

FINN TAKES me out to lunch. "Mary yelled at me because we hadn't properly welcomed you to Imperium," he grins. "Welcome."

I laugh. "Thank you," I say. "I'm surprised that you're stepping away from the office during the day. What about work?"

"It'll keep. I'm enjoying my meal." His smile turns warm. "And the company is excellent."

I stare at the man, a warm tingle coursing through my body. "I don't know what to say to that."

His grin widens. "I believe that 'thank you' is the socially accepted response."

We talk about work briefly, but we soon switch topics and talk about books we like and TV shows we watch. Our conversation feels easy and effortless, and I'm reminded of the many late-night chats that I've had with Lancelot and Merlin.

We get back to the office, and Finn leaves for another meeting. I've just sat at my desk when my phone buzzes. It's User0989. Rather, I should refer to him by his real name. Lawrence Kent.

Well? What progress have you made?

My blood boils. Because of this guy, I'm going to have to quit the best job I've ever had. Because of this guy, I'm going to have to break things off with Finn and Oliver. I'm so furious that my fingers tremble as I type out a reply. *None. I warned you this wasn't going to be easy. Their network is impossible to penetrate.*

Maybe you're not trying hard enough.

He's right. I'm not trying at all. Kent hadn't been at happy hour on Friday night, but I've no doubt that word has gotten around that I barreled out of there, chasing Oliver down. The CFO is probably wondering where my loyalties lie.

According to Lancelot and Merlin, he's already sniffing around on the forums, trying to hire someone else. I can't let him do that.

An evil thought strikes me. *Don't worry; I have an idea. I don't need to crack their network to get what you need. One of the executives keeps his passwords on a post-it note on his monitor. I'll just get the client list that way.*

There's no reply for almost a minute. My grin widens.

If the client list is leaked, Kent knows that Finn will investigate. When he discovers that Lawrence Kent's account was used to download the confidential information, the CFO will automatically come under suspicion.

Kent doesn't want that. Why else would he hire me to hack into a network he already has access to?

Finally, Kent/User0989 answers. *I'll give you two more weeks. Keep me posted.*

I take a deep breath. I'm willing to bet that the next time I visit Kent's office, that post-it note will be gone.

I've bought myself a little more time. *Now, I just need to figure out what to do.*

20

Be happy for this moment. This moment is your life.

— OMAR KHAYYAM

Miki:

I get to Oliver's place at six-thirty. At work earlier, I was only teasing him when I promised to be naked in his bed, but now that I'm here, I'm going to do exactly that.

I definitely need to tell them the truth, and I will. Soon. I have to build up my courage to have that conversation with them. Tonight is just about pleasure. I've been promised a cock in my pussy and a cock in my ass. I'm warring between anticipation and nervousness, but my pussy has no doubt. It throbs with restless need.

I duck into Oliver's bathroom and take a quick shower, resisting the urge to linger. Once I towel myself dry, I make my way to his king size bed and position myself in the middle of it. Totally, utterly naked.

I DON'T WAIT TOO LONG before I hear the front door open. Oliver and Finn must see my coat because they come looking for me. When they enter the bedroom, they both come to a halt.

Oliver grins. "I got to say, Miki. This feels like Christmas."

Finn gives me a half-smile as he takes off his coat and deposits it on the chair in the corner. His gaze is on me, and I can feel the weight of his assessing stare like a touch.

Heat rises in me.

The carpet on the floor muffles the sound of their footsteps as they move toward the bed. Finn reaches me first. His fingers stroke my cheeks, and he tucks a strand of my hair behind my ear. His touch is light, but his quiet scrutiny sends my arousal sky-high.

"This might be better than Christmas."

"No shopping for presents," I agree. My voice is oddly breathless, as if I've run a race. My nipples are just inches from his fingertips now, and my insides tighten with anticipation. Sex with them is better than anything I've ever experienced, and tonight, I get both of them at the same time. I've never thought of myself a greedy person, but my desire for them is insatiable.

Goosebumps rise on my skin as he bends his head toward my chest and captures a nipple between his teeth. I whimper and throw my head back on the bed as his mouth closes over my bud. He licks and nibbles each nipple, and I groan and writhe on the bed.

Oliver joins us. "Are you ready for both our cocks, Miki?" he asks, his breath caressing my ear.

"Yes," I sob out. Finn's mouth on my nipples is making me feverish for more.

"That's the right answer." His lips meet mine, and he sucks my lower lip between his teeth. Sharp lust rises in me; sharp, jagged lust. I moan again, this time into Oliver's mouth.

Finn shifts his position so he's lying on one side of me, propped up on an elbow. His hand slides down my abdomen with excruciating slowness toward the cleft between my legs. His fingers tease me, but he refuses to touch my clitoris, refuses to quench the fire that burns in me. "I want to feel your muscles clench when I thrust inside you, baby," he says. "I want to hear you moan as you come, and I want you to scream our names."

"Yes." The words come out in a rush. "Please don't tease me, please fuck me hard."

"I will," he promises. His voice fills with amusement. "But first..."

"Hang on," Oliver interrupts. He's holding a dark blue scarf in his hand. "Ever thought about being blindfolded?"

Oh. My. God.

Oliver chuckles at my expression. "I'm going to take that as a yes." He ties the scarf over my eyes, and darkness claims me. "Nervous?"

I shake my head, and his lips graze my cheeks. Or is it Finn's? The blindfold adds another layer of excitement.

Hands nudge my legs open and curve under my ass, pulling my pussy close to one of their mouths. Oliver? Finn? A tongue traces a path through my folds. I throw my head back and surrender to the pleasure.

"You like that, Miki?" That's Finn's voice growling the question. Is it Finn licking my pussy? I can't tell. My senses are supposed to be sharper with the blindfold, but lust has overtaken everything.

The tongue circles my clitoris repeatedly, and fingers push into my wet, willing pussy. I bite my lip, trying to stifle my moans. I'm almost ready to burst with the overload of sensation. My hips strain upward, begging for more. "I'm going to come," I gasp out. Lightning bolts of sparkling pleasure travel through my body. "Fuck, fuck, fuck," I chant. The words pour out, an incoherent babble of swearing and begging. "Please don't stop—"

My body dances to their tune. They're taking me higher, higher. My climax hurtles toward me, and I shatter into a million pieces, twisting, flailing, screaming out their names.

I PULL off the blindfold and blink in the sudden light. "Which one of you was it?" I ask, my cheeks flushing as I realize how wickedly wanton it is that I don't know which one of them made me come.

Both men are naked. They grin lazily. "Later," Oliver says. "Right now, I have more important things on my mind." He takes a butt plug and a small bottle of clear liquid from the drawer of his bedside table.

"I see you're prepared for the evening," I quip.

He chuckles. "Of course. Turn around, Miki. I want you on your stomach, ass in the air."

I start to comply, and Finn stops me. "I have a thought," he says. He lies on his back on the bed. Rolling a condom onto his hard cock, he pulls me down onto him.

I gasp as Finn's cock fills me completely. He thrusts a couple of times, but then he stills himself. "I'm going to feel every twitch of your body as Oliver pushes that plug into you," he growls.

"Hold her, Finn," Oliver says. "I don't want her squirming away from me."

The way the two of them are discussing me? *Totally hot.*

Finn pulls me forward and holds me against his chest. Oliver's fingers spread lube into my asshole, and he inserts a finger. I jump, but catch myself and do my best to relax my anal muscles. Finn groans. "God, you're fucking hot," he rasps out.

Oliver trickles more lube over my puckered hole, and then he slowly inserts his finger again. This time, I don't flinch. I lean against Finn's chest, and I focus on the way Oliver's finger feels. It's different.

He adds another finger, stretching me. I whimper, and Oliver caresses the globe of my ass. "You're doing so well, Miki," he says. "Relax for me."

He removes his fingers, and I feel the tip of the butt plug at my forbidden entrance. He pushes it in steadily, and I relax my muscles, as best as I can. There's a brief instant of pain as my asshole stretches against the widest part of the plug, and then it's buried in me.

With Finn's cock in my pussy, I'm almost unbearably filled. "She's so wet." Finn's voice is taut with tension. "Oliver, I'm not going to last here. Hurry the fuck up."

I hear the sound of a condom wrapper tear. Oliver's fingers close over the base of the plug, and he tugs it out. I feel lube drizzle down my crack, and then Oliver's cock slides into me, slow and steady.

His thickness stretches me more than the plug did, but he takes his time and uses plenty of lube. The sensation is slightly uncomfortable but strangely arousing at the same time.

My fingers dig into Finn's biceps as Oliver buries himself to the hilt. He groans, a raw, primal, sound. "You are so tight," he murmurs. He pauses, giving me time to get used to the feeling of both of them.

I'm ready. I want this. I want them. "More," I whisper.

I feel Oliver's chuckle vibrate through his body. "Gladly." He pulls out and slides back in again. Finn rolls his hips, thrusting his cock deeper into my pussy. Then, they start moving in unison, both pulling out at the same time, and thrusting into me with powerful strokes.

I've lost the ability to form words. I whimper in pleasure. An inferno burns inside me, out of control. "Yes," I sob out. I'm so filled by them. The sensations are almost overwhelming. I gasp and pant between them as they pound into me. Their strokes are deep and sure, and I moan with utter abandon. "Fuck," Finn groans. "I can't hold on."

"I'm not going to last either," Oliver grinds out. He snakes a hand to my clitoris. The angle is awkward, but his touch is exactly what I need. I erupt in a burst of pleasure, and they're not far behind. Their bodies stiffen, and their hands tighten around me as they orgasm.

We collapse in a heap of sated bodies. "Spend the night," Oliver says. "Please?"

I can't think about what I'm doing too much. I'm acting on instinct, and my emotions threaten to overwhelm me. "Okay," I reply, forcing myself to sound casual. "But only because I want to watch Sense 8."

21

If you love life, don't waste time, for time is what life is made up of.

— Bruce Lee

Finn:

Nearly two weeks go by. Oliver, Miki, and I spend most of our free time together, watching TV, playing games, and of course, making love.

I'm happier than I've been in a long time.

It can't last. My grandmother gently reminds me that I need to be honest with Miki. I have to tell her that her online friends, Lancelot and Merlin, are really Oliver and me.

My grandmother's right. Both Oliver and I are living on borrowed time.

I've fallen in love with Miki. The more time I spend with her, the more I'm terrified of losing her.

OLIVER and I are at happy hour on Friday when Fitzgerald walks in again. This time, he's alone. Claudia's nowhere to be seen. "I need to talk to you," he says to us, gesturing toward an empty booth.

Oliver raises an eyebrow. "About what?" he asks. "About the fact that you told my ex-wife to blackmail me for Imperium stock? About the suspicious number of similarities between our products and Kliedara's?"

Fitzgerald's lips tighten with annoyance. "I heard you're closing your private security division," he says. "I'm interested in buying it."

I snort. "You've got to be kidding." After all the crap he's pulled, Fitzgerald has to be delusional if he thinks we're going to do business with him. "I wouldn't work with you if we were the last two people on Earth."

Miki isn't here. She was at the bar earlier for a drink, but she left after one pint. "I didn't sleep great yesterday," she'd said, winking at us. "And I haven't spent a single night in my apartment for days. I'm going to go home, change into my pajamas and fall asleep."

I'm glad she's gone; there's a chance that I'm going to punch that smug look off Fitzgerald's face, and I don't need her to witness the bar fight.

Fitzgerald's cheeks redden. "I'm going to get my hands on that division," he snaps. "One way or another. One day soon, Sanders, you're going to look at the wreckage of your life, and you're going to wish you'd cooperated with me when you had a chance." He turns to Oliver. "Well, Prescott?"

"Well, what? Finn's answer seemed perfectly clear to me."

His jaw set tight, he stalks out of the bar. Oliver glances

at me. "What are the odds that Fitzgerald and Kent are working together?"

"My gut says it's pretty high," I reply. "But we don't have any proof."

It's maddening. Without proof, the board won't listen. Unfortunately, to get proof, we need Miki's cooperation.

And for that, we have to tell her the truth.

~

Miki:

"So, Miki." Wendy gives me a searching look. "Tell us what's going on."

It's Monday night. The six of us—Bailey, Gabby, Piper, Wendy, Katie, and I—have gotten together for pizza and beer.

In other words, it's time for the inquisition.

I could pretend that I have no idea what they're talking about, but one way or the other, my girlfriends are going to get at the truth. I might as well just blurt everything out. "Fine. I'm sleeping with my bosses."

I reach for my second slice of pizza. It's got artichoke, spinach, and feta cheese, and is absolutely delicious. Bailey clears her throat. "You don't think we're done with the questions, do you?" Her lips curve into a grin. "We want all the details, Miki."

"What I want to know is," Piper says, leaning forward and surveying me with worried eyes, "are you serious about these two guys? Are they serious about you? Why haven't we met them yet?"

I hold up my hands to ward off the flurry of questions.

"You haven't met them because it's not a real relationship," I reply. "We're just friends with benefits."

"Why?" Katie asks curiously. "Is there no spark between you?"

There are plenty of sparks. The three of us—Finn, Oliver, and I—have spent almost every single night together in the last two weeks. I've barely been on the DefCon forums. The last time I chatted with Lancelot and Merlin was Friday, and that conversation only lasted five minutes. It makes me feel disloyal, but I don't miss my online friends as much as I thought I would.

The truth is, I'm falling in love with Oliver and Finn. Or maybe I've already fallen. Friday night, terrified at the thought, I'd left happy hour early, telling the two men I needed to catch up on my sleep, but I'd ended up tossing and turning all night. I couldn't get comfortable without Oliver and Finn in bed with me.

"Oliver doesn't believe in relationships," I reply. "His ex-wife has made him commitment phobic. And Finn's too busy with the IPO."

"Sure." Bailey's expression tells me she doesn't believe a word of my explanation. "When was the last time you slept at Wendy's place?"

"Friday."

"And before that?" Gabby asks pointedly.

Gabby and I had a long conversation right after she apologized to Oliver. She apologized for interfering, and I forgave her readily. My friends had disliked Aaron, but I'd chosen to bury my head in the sand and pretend that everything was okay. I won't make that mistake again.

She's been working with him closely as they come up with a strategy to blunt the impact of Claudia's photos, whenever she chooses to release them. The two of them get along quite well. "I admit, I was wrong about your two men," she'd told me last week. "They're good guys. Hold on to them."

I flush in response to her question. "I can't remember. Fine, we do spend a lot of time together, but that's because we have a lot in common."

"Hmm," Katie says. "You know, it's okay to fall in love again. If you meet the right guy—or the right pair of guys—don't let Aaron get in the way of happiness."

I eat my slice of pizza in silence. My friends are in happy, stable relationships, and love has made romantics of them all. What they don't know, however, is that my ménage with Oliver and Finn is built on a lie. I was hired to hack into their company. Kent's still out there, the Post-it note on his monitor gone, waiting for me to give him what he needs.

Until I tell Oliver and Finn the truth, there can be no future between us.

Where are you? Finn texts me at nine-thirty, shortly after we settle the tab.

Oliver and Finn had a dinner meeting with some clients. I didn't expect to hear from them tonight, but the moment I see Finn's text, a smile breaks out on my face.

Just leaving, I reply. *You?*

Dinner just wrapped up. Meet us at my place?

"She's sexting her lovers," Bailey sing-songs, her eyes dancing with amusement. "Let me guess; they want you to come over."

My cheeks heat. "Something like that."

Gabby chuckles. "Go get some, Miki. You deserve it."

No, I don't. I've been greedy for the last fourteen days,

but the timer's almost down to zero. Tomorrow morning, the two weeks of grace I won from Kent are going to run out, and he's going to demand answers.

I text Finn back. *Sounds good. I'll be there in thirty minutes.*

It's time for the truth.

22

There is no glory in battle worth the blood it costs.

— Dwight D. Eisenhower

Oliver:

It's been almost a month since Valentine's Day. A month since Miki walked into our party, our lives, and our hearts.

"We have to tell her."

"I know," Finn replies. He's staring out of the window, his hands in his pockets, his shoulders hunched.

"The longer we go without revealing the truth, the more hurt she'll be."

"I know," he says again. "I know what you're saying is right." He takes a deep breath. "I'm afraid we're going to lose her."

Finn doesn't lower his shields very often and admit he needs people. His grandmother, yes. Everyone else, he keeps at a distance.

Not Miki.

"Me too," I admit.

He raises an eyebrow. "I thought you didn't want commitment," he says. "You weren't looking to get involved."

"I wasn't," I reply shortly. "It happened anyway." I take a deep breath. "And I don't regret it."

After the divorce, I let myself get angry. Bitter. I slept with woman after woman, as if sex was the cure to shattered trust. Miki was on the other side of a computer screen, and because she wasn't a part of my real life, I let her in.

I don't know what Kent is doing. I don't know what Claudia might do. Fitzgerald's offer to buy the private security division had surprised me last week, but even though Finn and I have searched hard for any shred of a tie linking our CFO to our biggest competitor, we've come up short.

It stands to reason that Kent's the person leaking our technology to Fitzgerald. But how? Why? These are not questions we have answers to.

At one point, not too long ago, Finn would have gone straight to work after dinner, and he'd have spent the night in front of a computer screen, trying to solve the puzzle.

At one point, beset by forces beyond my control, I'd have gone to a bar and picked up a woman to sleep with, a woman whose name I'd have trouble remembering in the morning.

Things have changed for the better for both of us, but the progress is illusionary. Until we tell Miki the truth, everything we've gained can disappear in the blink of an eye.

SHE WALKS into Finn's apartment, tossing her coat on the couch and pulling her sweater over her head. "Hey, you two," she says, her voice light. "You both look really serious. What's going on?"

I should tell her now, but her cheeks are pink from the cold, and her nipples are hard under her t-shirt. *You're being an asshole, Prescott,* my conscience accuses me. *Tell her everything.*

If this is the last night I have with her, I want to remember everything. The warmth of her smile, the soft flush of her cheeks, the fragrance of her skin.

"Come here," I tell her, a growl in my voice. I push her against Finn's floor-to-ceiling windows. "I want you."

I twine my fingers in her hair and tug her toward me, kissing the delicate skin of her neck, licking the vein that pulses at her nape.

Her breathing catches. "You have me," she replies, a strange expression on her face. She winds her hand around the back of my head, and her lips brush across mine. "I'm right here."

Finn knows exactly why I'm feeling the way I am. There's a serious, intent look on his face as he moves toward Miki. "Take off your t-shirt and bra."

She's in full view of the window. We're on the top floor, and Finn's building is taller than the ones that surround it, but if someone looks up, we could still be seen.

It doesn't matter. Common sense has fled the building. There's a recklessness that rages through me tonight.

A recklessness that's matched by Miki. She whips her top over her head and reaches behind her back to undo her bra clasp, letting the lacy garment fall to the floor. "What now?" she whispers.

I feel my lips lift in an involuntary smile. Taking a step back, I let my gaze run all over her beautiful body. Over the firm, round globes of her breasts, over the rosy pink tips of her nipples. "Take off your jeans," I order.

She obeys wordlessly, a shiver running through her body. I trace the outline of her nipples with my fingertips and pinch the buds.

"Turn and face the window," Finn says. "One of us is going to make you fall apart, Miki. You're going to come, your breasts pressed against the glass, in full view of the city below."

Her expression is hungry, almost raw. "Do it."

Finn's hands caress her back. He cups her ass, and his fingers trail down the back of her thigh. I move to her right, and kiss the back of her neck, moving her hair over her shoulder.

"Do I get to touch you?" There's a smile in her voice as she strokes the outline of our cocks with her hands. "Or is that against the rules?"

"You can do whatever you want as long as you keep your legs parted," Finn replies. He nudges her legs wider apart and slides his hand between her thighs. "So fucking wet," he says harshly.

She whimpers as he strokes her, and she grinds her hips down. "Please," she gasps, her voice almost a sob as he touches her clitoris. "Harder, please—"

She's still rubbing her palm against my shaft. I'm still kissing the back of her neck. She pants and whimpers as Finn pushes his fingers into her pussy, and she whimpers as I bite her shoulder.

Then her fingers grip my bicep, and she shatters with a half-sob. I run my hands over her sweat-dampened skin, and I feel the warmth of her deep in my soul.

"Shall we continue this in bed?"

Miki:

It's dark outside. I'm tangled in Finn's sheets. Finn and Oliver are on either side of me, their bodies touching mine.

"I need to tell you something." My voice comes out high and nervous. I discreetly wipe my palms on the bed.

Both of them freeze.

"I've hidden something from you for almost a month. When I ran into you at the party on Valentine's Day, I wasn't there by chance."

"Miki." Oliver's voice is tight with tension. "Listen, there's something you should hear from us."

I barely pay attention to him. For days, guilt has sloshed through my insides. Both men have given me keys to their apartments. They've cooked for me. They've brought me coffee in the morning and donuts in the afternoon.

I've slept with them. I've given into temptation when I should have resisted, but it's time for the truth, and I won't let Oliver derail me.

"No," I say, cutting him off. "Listen to me. *Please.* Let me say what I need to say."

Finn takes my hand in his. He looks deep into my eyes, "Whatever you think you need to say to us, *you don't need to.*"

Hot shame fills me, and I can't meet his gaze. "I'm a hacker. I hang out on a forum. Last month, someone approached me there." I take a deep breath. "He offered to pay me a hundred thousand dollars to hack into Imperium. He wanted a copy of your client list."

Neither of them says anything, and I'm too afraid to look at them, to see how they've reacted to my betrayal. I swallow hard and force myself to continue.

"A couple of hacker friends did some digging." I cross my fingers as I tell them my bombshell revelation. "They discovered who hired me. The person that offered me a hundred grand to hack into Imperium was Lawrence Kent. Your CFO."

I'm waiting for anger. For bitter reproaches. I'm prepared to hear them defend Lawrence, prepared to hear them tell me that they'll be pressing charges. I'm ready for anything.

Except for their lack of surprise. Finn looks uncharacteristically nervous. His grip on my hand tightens. "Miki, there's something we haven't told you."

The shrill ring of his phone interrupts what he's about to say.

He mutters a curse under his breath and silences the ringtone. He turns back to me, and the look on his face causes my heart to hammer in my chest. What's going on here? Finn and Oliver aren't reacting to my news. *Why?*

Oliver clears his throat. "Before we say anything," he says, "I want you to know that I care about you and I trust you completely."

Finn's phone rings again. "For fuck's sake," he snarls, picking up the instrument. "It's eleven on a Monday night. This better be important." He swipes the screen. "Hello?"

He listens to the person on the other end of the line. His body tenses and his face goes totally white. His fingers grip the phone. "Where is she?"

"What's wrong?" Oliver asks.

Finn turns to him, his eyes bleak. "My grandmother fell in the bathroom," he says. "Her neighbors found her twenty minutes ago. The ambulance took her to Mount Sinai."

Oliver's already getting dressed. "I'll come with you."

"Me too," I reply automatically. I put my arm around Finn's shoulder. "Did they say how she's doing?"

He shakes his head, dazed. "No," he whispers. His fingers tremble as he reaches for his t-shirt. "She's got to be okay."

I've never met Finn's grandmother, but he adores her and talks about her all the time. She brought him up, made him into the man he is today. My heart aches for Finn. "She will be."

Last Christmas, I spent hours at Mount Sinai, as Wendy's mother fought for her life after being in a serious car crash. Her recovery had been something of a miracle.

I cross my fingers and desperately hope for another one.

WE GET to the hospital and try to find someone who can help us, no easy task in the labyrinthine area. Finally, we're directed to surgery, where a helpful nurse tells us that Finn's grandmother is in the operating room.

"I'm Finn Sanders," Finn grinds out. "I'm Joyce Sanders' grandson. I'm her emergency contact."

She gives him a sympathetic look. "Dr. Harris attended to your grandmother," she says gently. "I'll page him. Please sit down."

Dr. Harris, a short man with kind eyes, arrives in five minutes. "Which one of you is Mr. Sanders?" he asks, looking at us.

"That's me," Finn replies. "What's going on with my grandmother?"

"She slipped in the bathroom and broke her hip," he replies somberly. "She's in emergency surgery right now."

Finn goes white. "She was having trouble getting around," he whispers. "She wouldn't listen to me when I suggested she get help. I should have insisted."

"Yes, yes. Mrs. Sanders tried calling for help, but she

couldn't get up. Luckily for her, her neighbors saw that her light was still on past her usual bedtime, and decided to check up on her."

My blood runs cold. It's Monday night. Finn talks to his grandmother twice a week, and he has lunch with her every weekend. Had her neighbors not been paying attention, how long would she have laid there in pain, calling for help?

Finn gulps. "Is she going to be okay?"

The doctor nods. "Hip surgeries are always complicated, but your grandmother is only seventy, and she's in good health. The surgeon's working on her now, and she'll give you an update when she's done, but the prognosis should be excellent."

I squeeze Finn's hand, relief running through me.

Finn still appears shaken. "She has new neighbors," he says. "She took them a pie. I thought she was crazy."

Oliver puts an arm around him. "Nana Sanders is a tough old goat," he says, the affection in his voice obvious to hear. "She's going to be fine."

Finn nods. "I'm going to stay here," he says. "Go home and get some rest."

I shake my head at once. "I'm not going to leave you here alone." A sudden thought occurs to me. "Unless you don't want me here?"

His light blue eyes meet mine. "It would mean a lot if you stayed," he says quietly.

My heart skips a beat at the intense need on his face. "Okay."

In the mad rush of getting to the hospital, I've almost forgotten Oliver and Finn's reaction to my revelation.

They were going to tell me something. *What was it?*

Finn's face is etched with worry. As much as I want to know what's going on, now's not the time to bother him.

Two hours later, a tired-looking surgeon comes to the waiting area where the three of us are huddled, drinking some lukewarm vending-machine coffee. "I'm Dr. Perez," she introduces herself. "One of you is related to Mrs. Sanders?"

Finn rises to his feet eagerly. "I'm her grandson," he says. "Is she okay?"

The doctor nods. "The surgery went well," she says, and Finn exhales, his shoulders slumping in relief. "She's under anesthetic now, but you can see her for a few minutes if you like." She gives Oliver and me a glance. "Only immediate family, please. Mrs. Sanders needs to rest."

"Go ahead," Oliver says, squeezing Finn's shoulder. "We'll be right here."

Finn follows the doctor. Oliver leans on my shoulder. "I'm so glad she's okay," he says softly. "If anything had happened to her, Finn would have been devastated." His lips twist in a grimace. "He wouldn't have been the only one. Nana's fed me more times than I can count. She's always treated me like family."

He pulls his phone out of his pocket and types out a message. "I'm warning Janine," he explains. "I'm fairly sure Finn isn't going to leave Nana's side tomorrow. And I won't be in any shape for my morning meetings."

I don't understand anything. Oliver is acting like I didn't admit to hacking his company. I want to scream at him, demand to know what the hell is going on. Is this some kind of elaborate trap?

He drains his coffee, a disgusted look on his face. "I'm going to go in search of something better," he says, setting his phone on the seat next to him. "You want something?"

I shake my head, not trusting myself to form words. The moment Oliver is out of sight, I pull my own phone out of my purse. Things are not going as I expected. Oliver and Finn were too unfazed by my news. I get the sense that I'm missing something important.

Maybe Lancelot and Merlin will have some insight into their reaction.

Hey, I type. *Are you guys around?*

Oliver's phone buzzes and my lips twitch. He's always leaving it lying around, and Janine's constantly bringing it back to him. I can imagine the way she would roll her eyes at him if she were here.

I wait for either of them to reply, but neither of them does. Maybe they're asleep, I think. After all, it's well past two in the morning.

Still, I keep typing. It feels somewhat cathartic to talk about tonight's weird turn of affairs. *Something's happened. I confessed everything to Oliver and Finn, and they didn't even react.*

Oliver's phone buzzes again. It's probably incoming email, but who could possibly want to talk to him at two in the morning?

They didn't even blink when I told them about Kent. I'm missing something.

His phone buzzes for the third time, and this time, the hair on the back of my neck rises.

I'm missing something.

Finn and Oliver like the same TV shows I do. Gabby had even commented on it one day, and I'd told her that it wasn't that rare, so did Lancelot and Merlin.

Oliver's been divorced. So has Lancelot.

Finn's favorite pizza toppings? Pineapple and ham. Just like Merlin.

They didn't react when I told them I was hired to hack into their company.

They didn't even blink when I told them about Kent.

Because they've always known.

Bile rises in my throat. Disbelief fills my heart, but my brain's finally connecting the dots, and it's painting a damning picture.

Finn and Oliver have been hiding an important piece of information from me, right from the start. Their identities.

They're Merlin and Lancelot.

23

There is no such thing as paranoia. Your worst fears can come true at any moment.

— HUNTER S. THOMPSON

Finn:

I stare down at the frail, wrinkled-lined faced of my grandmother. She's hooked up to an assortment of machines. Her eyes are closed, and her breathing is strained, but she's alive.

For too long, I've lived for work, and I've neglected everything else, but as I stare down at the woman who stepped in and raised me, who gave me a stable and loving home, I know the old Finn is gone.

Spending time with Miki these past two weeks, chatting for hours with her online the three months before that, I've learned for myself what my grandmother's always told me. Work isn't everything. Family, friends, laughter, those are the things that remain when we have nothing else.

Had my grandmother not taken her neighbors a pie in a gesture of welcome, would they have known her well enough to worry when her lights were still on? Would they have checked in on the old lady?

I sit next to her and put my hand on her papery skin. "I started telling Miki everything when your neighbors called, Nana. I know I should have told her before, but I was selfish and greedy, and I couldn't bring myself to give her up."

The beeping of the heart rate monitor is a soothing, steady sound in the brightly-lit room. There's another bed in the space, a curtain dividing us. It's empty at the moment, but I make a mental note to ask for a private room.

"I should have brought her to meet you," I continue. "I was nervous about so many things. I wasn't sure how you would react to the situation, to our ménage, so I hesitated."

A nurse comes in and reads my grandmother's chart. "Dr. Perez is one of our best surgeons," she says encouragingly.

"She's going to need home care, right? Once she's out of here?" My grandmother won't want to leave her home, but her Brooklyn house has stairs that she's going to have difficulty navigating while she recovers. I have so many things to figure out.

She nods. "As well as rehab to get her moving again."

"Don't worry," I say dryly, smiling for the first time since I received that dreadful phone call. "Nana hates being dependent on other people. She'll be up and hobbling around in no time, telling me that she's quite alright and I should stop fussing."

The nurse laughs. "My mother's the same way," she says. "I'll be here for the next ten hours. I'll keep checking on her, but she won't wake for a few hours. Your best bet is to go home and get some sleep."

I'm not leaving, but Oliver and Miki are still in the waiting room outside. I should tell them to go home. I give my grandmother one more look and get to my feet. In the tumult of the last few hours, I've almost forgotten that Miki told us about User0989 hiring her. I saw the surprise on her face when neither Oliver nor I reacted to her revelation.

She's smart and sharp, and she's got to be wondering what's going on, and even though Mount Sinai isn't the best place to have this conversation, I don't think we can put it off any longer.

I EMERGE from my grandmother's room at the same time as Oliver returns from God-knows-where, holding a tray containing three cups of coffee in his hand. "How is she?" he asks me. "I've told Janine to cancel your meetings for tomorrow."

I'm not looking at him. I'm looking at Miki. Her face is white, and her eyes are filled with a terrible hurt when she looks at the two of us.

She's discovered the truth.

Oliver reaches the same conclusion I do. "Miki, we can explain," he starts to say, but she cuts him off with a vehement shake of her head.

"I don't want your pretty speeches," she says, her tone harsh and jagged. "I don't want your fancy explanations. What I want is the truth." She turns from Oliver to me, her face a mask of stone now. "You lied to me."

Wordlessly, I nod. What can I say, really? Every accusation she's going to throw at us is true.

"When you sat next to me on the flight from Houston, was that an accident?"

I take a deep breath. No more lies. Everything comes out

in the open now. She deserves to know. "No. Oliver and I had been searching for you for months. Last summer, you succeeded in hacking into one of our experimental systems. The moment we found out, we started our search for you. The day before Thanksgiving, we finally uncovered your name. We were on that flight to discover what we were up against."

She frowns. "What experimental system? What are you talking about? I've never hacked into an Imperium network."

"It was a prototype, and we kept our involvement a secret. You were searching for Howard Lippman's financial records because your friend Wendy Williams was representing Sandi Lippman in a contentious divorce case."

She draws in a sharp breath, and recognition dawns on her face. "That was Imperium," she says softly. "Of course it was. All month, I've been feeling a sense of déjà vu as I've tried to break into your network. A feeling like I've done this before."

She lifts her chin and gives us a searching look. "Then you befriended me on DefCon. Why?"

"We needed to keep track of who you worked for," Oliver replies. "You were the only person that had ever broken into one of Finn's systems. We needed to make sure that you didn't target us again." He grimaces. "That's how it started."

"It was just supposed to be business," I interject. "It became more. You were my friend, Miki. Our initial motives were suspect, but our friendship was real."

"I'll be the judge of that," she says flatly. "Then I showed up to your Valentine's Day party."

"The IPO was three months away. Claudia had just threatened to make the photos of the two of us public. We were dealing with a difficult board of directors. We believed you'd been hired to hack into our company, and when you didn't tell us anything on the forum, we thought you were a threat."

"So why not confront me right away?" She exhales as she figures it out. "You wanted to see what I was after."

I nod.

"You befriended me for Imperium. Did you also sleep with me for your precious company?"

"No," we both say at once.

"That was unexpected," Oliver says. "That night, when you came after me, I was hurt and upset. We shouldn't have done it, not until we told you the truth."

"But it was real." I stare at Miki, trying to will her into believing us. "We started out under false pretenses, but that doesn't mean we don't care about you." I swallow hard. "Miki, I was afraid to tell you the truth. I didn't want to lose you. I love you."

"No," she says harshly. Her eyes have a sheen of tears now, and she shakes her head again. "No more lies. For a year, my ex-husband lied to me. I thought that maybe I could begin to trust again, but I was wrong."

She pulls her keyring out of her purse and removes our apartment keys from it with shaking fingers. She sets them down on the plastic chair, right next to Oliver's phone. "I think it's safe to say," she says, "that I won't be at work tomorrow. Or any time after that."

"Miki, please." My heart races in my chest. *This can't be the end.* "I screwed up, okay? But I care about you and maybe I'm a crazy fool, but I thought you cared about us too."

She laughs bitterly. "I think it's clear, Finn, that the only thing either Oliver or you care about is Imperium and the billions you stand to make when it goes public." She zips up her coat. "Don't call me."

We watch her walk out of our lives.

24

If your heart is a volcano, how shall you expect flowers to bloom?

— Khalil Gibran

Miki:

I t's almost four in the morning when I get back to Wendy's apartment. I've lived here since November. My clothes hang in Wendy's closet, and those are my shoes scattered all over the bedroom, but the place feels like it belongs to a stranger.

I curl up in the unmade bed. I slept here only four days ago, on Friday night. That day, I'd been alone and restless, but when I couldn't sleep, I'd reached for my phone and chatted with Lancelot and Merlin.

The betrayal cuts bone-deep. I haven't just lost the two men who'd become important to me. I've also lost two of my best friends.

I toss and turn, trying to fall asleep and failing. Finally, I get up and find a bottle of wine in the kitchen. I don't bother with a glass. Taking it back to bed with me, I down its contents over the next hour, feeling tearful, lonely, and sorry for myself.

In the morning, I can give myself a pep talk and try to make a list. In the morning, I can figure out what to do with the wreckage that once again surrounds me.

Tonight, there's just pain.

WHEN I WAKE, the sun's shining through my window, and the radio clock on the bedside table tells me it's noon.

My head throbs and my mouth is dry, and I feel terrible, both physically and mentally. I get up and gulp down a glass of water. There's no aspirin in the apartment, and I blearily contemplate going to the convenience store at the corner of the block to get some.

Last night, I turned off my phone in the cab. I'm not ready to turn it back on, but bracing myself, I do it anyway and navigate to DefCon's forums. I don't want to hear from Lancelot and Merlin—no, from Oliver and Finn—but I'm morbidly curious about whether Kent's reached out again.

He has. There's a message from him, sent at eight in the morning. *Do you have the list?*

Another one, sent at ten. *What the hell is going on?*

By this time, Kent probably found out I wasn't at work. Are Finn and Oliver going to tell him I've quit? Somehow, I doubt that. The two men haven't discovered what the CFO is up to, and until they do, I'm sure they'll play their cards close to their chest.

It's none of my business anyway. I don't work at Imperium. My relationship with Oliver and Finn is over.

There are about a dozen messages from the two men. They've tried repeatedly to reach me.

I don't know why. There's nothing to say.

ONCE I SHOWER, I make my way downstairs and go to the store at the end of the block. It's an independent store in an ocean of chain retailers, but somehow, year after year, it survives. Maybe because the owner, Mr. Greene, is one of the nicest, friendliest people in the city.

He's working the cash register today. "Hello, Mr. Greene," I greet him. "You're not usually at the front."

"Camille quit," he says. "She's moving back to England. I just put up a help-wanted sign. You wouldn't know anyone who's interested, would you, Mackenzie?"

I have no job. No direction. I don't know what I want to do with my life. I should start making a list about what to do next, but I can't think of anything. Part of me wants to flee Manhattan, where everything reminds me of Oliver and Finn. Maybe another city will provide me a fresh start.

"I can't pay much," he says. "Thirteen dollars an hour."

I have a habit of leaping before looking. I jumped into my relationship with Aaron too soon. I took the job at Imperium even though I shouldn't have. I got involved with Oliver and Finn against my better judgment. This time, I'm going to do things differently.

And until I figure out my next steps, thirteen bucks an hour is a start.

"I might be interested," I reply. "Can I fill out a form?"

I'm closing a door. On Imperium. On User0989/Lawrence Kent. On Finn and Oliver.

It's the smart, sensible thing to do.

Yet, I feel as if someone's taken a baseball bat to my heart.

Oliver:

I finally get into the office at two o'clock on Tuesday afternoon. Janine looks up at me. "How's Finn's grandmother?" she asks. "Your message didn't give me any details."

"She fell and broke her hip. She had surgery last night."

She inhales sharply. "That's terrible. Is she going to be okay?"

"I think so. Finn's going to be out the entire week, so cancel what you can, and I'll pinch-hit for him."

"No worries. Miki's going to be out today, I assume? She's got a couple of meetings on her calendar. I can reschedule those for her."

It's no surprise that Janine's deduced that we're seeing Miki. Not much gets by our assistant, but she's both loyal and discreet, and we have nothing to worry about.

When she asks about Miki, a sharp stab of pain pierces through me. I open my mouth to tell her that Miki's never coming back, but I can't yet face the chasm of grief that looms in front of me. "She'll be out for the next week as well," I tell my assistant. "If someone asks, she's out sick."

"Okay." To my relief, Janine moves on to the next item of business. "The only meeting I couldn't reschedule was with Gabriella Alves from Aventi; I couldn't get in touch with her. She's due here in ten minutes. Do you want to see her, or should I apologize on your behalf?"

Gabby is Miki's friend. She has no reason to help me,

but I cling on to that last straw of hope. "No, I'll meet with her."

"OLIVER, YOU LOOK LIKE HELL." Gabby doesn't mince her words. "Did you get any sleep last night?"

She doesn't know. "Finn's grandmother fell and broke her hip," I explain. "We spent most of the night at Mount Sinai." Before she can jump in and ask me questions about whether she's okay, I forestall her. "There's more. Something else happened yesterday."

Her eyes narrow at my expression. "What?"

I tell her everything. Miki's hack of Lippman's information, which led to our plane journey. I confess that our online friendship was initially motivated by our need to keep an eye on her. "But things changed," I end unhappily. "Miki thinks that everything we had together is a lie. It isn't. I'm in love with her."

"Oliver." Gabby shakes her head helplessly. "What a fucking mess. Why are you telling me this?"

"She's not picking up her phone," I reply. "I've tried all morning. She's not answering her texts. I was hoping you'd talk to her."

She gives me a troubled look. "You were one of her online friends, and I know she told you everything, even more than she told us. You know how badly she took Aaron's lies. You know she felt like a fool, like everyone around her was laughing at her and pitying her. And you still didn't tell her the truth."

"I screwed up."

Gabby gets to her feet. "I think you're a good person, Oliver," she says. "I admit I formed a snap judgment about you, and I was wrong. But I'm not going to help you with this. Miki has every reason to feel betrayed, and she needs to work through her feelings on her own. Without pressure from her friends, and definitely without pressure from Finn and you."

She looks at me steadily. "If you care about Miki, then the kindest thing you can do is leave her alone."

25

If you can't fly then run, if you can't run then walk, if you can't walk then crawl, but whatever you do you have to keep moving forward.

— MARTIN LUTHER KING JR.

Miki:

The rest of the week, my only focus is putting one foot in front of another. I wake up at the crack of dawn. I shower and get dressed, and I head to my morning shift at Mr. Greene's convenience store.

My evenings I fill with sappy TV. I avoid my laptop, and I don't log in again to the DefCon forums.

Gabby drops by on Wednesday evening. "I met Oliver yesterday," she says, settling down on the couch and giving me a concerned look. "He told me everything."

"Did he?" I can't seem to summon up the energy to care. "Did he send you here to check up on me?"

"He suggested it. I told him to leave you alone. I just

came by to see if you were okay."

"I'm not," I reply. "But I will be, eventually."

She nods. "Oliver told me once that you were stronger than I gave you credit for. He's right."

A warm rush of pleasure fills me, and I suppress it ruthlessly. Nothing Oliver Prescott or Finn Sanders did was without an agenda. "When?"

"It was when I went to apologize for assuming the worst about him. I told him you were in a fragile place after Aaron. At that time, I remember thinking that he was being presumptuous. After all, he'd only known you for a week or so at that point."

"I think they knew me better than anyone," I reply sadly. I'd poured my heart out to Lancelot and Merlin, night after night. "I'll have to be more careful about who I talk to online."

"So you're not working there anymore?" Gabby probes. "You're done? You don't care what Lawrence Kent is up to?"

"Oliver really did tell you everything, didn't he?" On TV, a kitten jumps on the lap of its owner and falls asleep. I never did get a cat, even though it was on my list. And I went and fell in love, even though I'd sworn to myself that I wasn't going to do that. "That's not my problem anymore, Gabby. I have another job now. I'm working at Mr. Greene's store."

I can tell she wants to comment on my life choices, but she holds her tongue. "Okay," she says agreeably. "Will we see you on Monday for girl's night out?"

"Maybe," I lie. "I get up at five to open the store at six. I don't want to be out too late. Come to think of it, it's almost bedtime."

Gabby gets the hint. She rises to her feet and folds me into a hug. "I know things feel terrible right now," she says gently, "but time really does heal all wounds."

She's almost out of the door when she pauses. "I thought you'd want to know that Finn's grandmother is recovering well," she says. "She's going to be discharged from the hospital the day after tomorrow. Janine told me."

A flood of relief fills me. "Thanks for finding out."

She squeezes my hand. "Whatever decision you make, Miki," she says seriously, "don't make it out of fear. Okay?"

～

Finn:

"Welcome back," Mary greets me with a smile. "How's your grandmother?"

It's Monday morning. I've taken four days off work, probably the longest stretch of my life. On Friday, my grandmother was discharged from the hospital, and I moved her to my apartment. "It's just until you recover, so don't argue with me," I'd told her.

"I wasn't going to," she'd replied, to my surprise. "It'll be nice to stay with you for a week or two until I'm back on my feet."

It'll take more than a week or two, and both my grandmother and I know it. She faces weeks of rehab before she can walk again. Still, things could have been so much worse.

"She's in my apartment," I reply to Mary's question. "I asked her this morning if she was sure she didn't want me around, and she shooed me out. Thank you for finding me a home care worker."

Mary pats my hand. "I was happy to help," she says. "Shayna took care of Bob's mother when she was bedridden. She's wonderful."

"My grandmother really likes her." I transfer my attention to Imperium. I've tried to reach out to Miki a hundred times in the last week, but she won't return my calls, and she won't reply to my texts. I don't blame her for her decision.

My life is in shambles, and there's a gaping empty hole inside me. The only thing I can do is try and fill it with work. "You wanted to see me about Alessandra?"

"I talked to her on Friday," Mary replies. "She's itching to get back to work, but she was hoping to ease back into it by working from home four days a week. I told her I didn't think it would be a problem, but Sachin wanted to check in with you."

"As long as she's ready. I don't want her to feel pressured into coming back. The most important thing is her recovery."

"I checked with her," Mary says. "She assured me that she's ready. I think she's bored. But if you're really concerned, you could visit her and ask her yourself." She gives me a stern look. "It would be a nice thing to do. Sachin visited her in hospital, as did I."

The only thing that's left intact in my life is work. I might as well do it properly. And Mary's right. I should have visited Alessandra after she got back from the hospital. "You sound like my grandmother," I tell our HR Head with a grin. "She tells me off with exactly the same note in her voice. You're right; I should have dropped by to see her. Can you set it up for me? I'll drag Oliver too."

"I already did," she says smugly. "Janine put it on your calendar. Five this evening."

I shake my head at her fondly. "Sounds good. I'll drop by on my way home."

OLIVER and I have seen plenty of each other in the last week.

He's dropped by to check on my grandmother every single day. We've had several conversations about everything under the sun.

But we haven't talked about Miki. That wound is too raw.

He's in our office when I return from my meeting. "Mary's arranged that we visit Alessandra this evening," I tell him.

He winces. "We should have done that earlier."

Miki. Lawrence. Claudia. Fitzgerald. The IPO. There are a thousand reasons why we haven't, but none of that matters.

ALESSANDRA'S HUSBAND Yuri opens the door of their Queens apartment. "Oliver, Finn, it's good to see you."

We've met Yuri several times at happy hour. He's a nice guy, friendly and interesting. "Sorry it's taken us so long to visit."

He waves away my apology. "I'm sure you've been busy," he says. "Come on in. No need to keep your voice down. Alessandra's mom took the baby for a couple of hours."

We remove our coats, and Yuri takes them from us. "You didn't have to send Sofia away on our behalf," Oliver says, walking into the living room. "I'm good with babies. Really."

Alessandra waves from her spot on the couch. "Hey, you guys," she greets us. She's got a plaster cast on her leg but looks otherwise well. "Sorry I can't get up."

"Don't be ridiculous." I sit down on the couch. "How are you, Alessandra? Mary tells me Yuri's driving you crazy and you can't wait to get back to work."

She grimaces. "Something like that." She takes a deep

breath and forces a smile on her face. "It'll be good to think about something else other than the accident."

I exchange a glance with Oliver. Mary had made it sound like Alessandra was in great spirits, but the woman in front of me is distinctly subdued. "Is everything okay? You seem upset. Did we come at a bad time?"

She shakes her head. "No, it's not you." She sighs heavily. "NYPD assigned a detective to investigate my accident. It was a hit-and-run, and they finally made an arrest."

"That's good, isn't it?" I ask her.

"I thought so," she replies. "But Detective Larson said that two days before the guy ran into me, someone wired fifty thousand dollars into his account."

"He thinks someone paid the guy to hurt or kill Alessandra," Yuri says. "Ever since he left, we've been freaking out. I mean, who would want to hurt her? It doesn't make any sense. We're normal people. We're not mixed up in anything."

I stare at the young couple, not knowing what to say. "Anyway," Alessandra says, after a minute or two of uncomfortable silence, "I'm totally looking forward to work. I told Mary that I couldn't deal with the J-train with my cast, but she didn't think there would be a problem with me working from home."

"There isn't," I assure her. "If you're ready to get back to work, we'll make it happen."

Her smile lights up her face. "Thanks, you two," she says. "I really appreciate it."

"I want to see this Detective Larson," I say when we're back in my car.

Oliver's already on his phone. "You want the 105th

Precinct," he says, punching the address into my car's navigation system. "What's bothering you?"

"Alessandra's right. Someone putting a mark on her head doesn't make any sense."

"And?" Oliver prompts.

"And Alessandra got hurt two days before the party at the Waldorf Astoria. I'm going on gut feel here, Oliver. This feels off."

His face wears a thoughtful expression. I drive to the precinct. We find a parking spot, feed the meter, and enter the nondescript two-story brown brick building. Inside, we ask for Detective Larson. "My name is Finn Sanders," I introduce myself. "Detective Larson is investigating a hit-and-run involving one of my employees, Alessandra Mirova? I was hoping I could talk to him."

"Take a seat," the woman behind the counter says, gesturing to the scratched, dented plastic chairs against the wall. "I'll see if the detective is in."

He is. The cop, a burly, balding man, shows up three minutes later. "This is quite the coincidence," he says, leading us to a small conference room at the corner of the building. "I was going to trek into the city sometime this week to talk to the two of you."

"Why?" Oliver sits down, his elbows on the table, and leans forward. "Are we under suspicion?"

He doesn't answer the question directly. "There's no reason for anyone to want Alessandra Mirova dead. I've asked around, the Mirovs are clean. She works with you. Yuri works at the hospital. Everyone in their building likes them."

"Okay." If the detective has a point, he certainly doesn't believe in getting straight to it.

"But then I did some digging around. Your company is

going public. So I was going to ask you. If Alessandra Mirova gets hurt, will that affect you in any way?"

Oliver frowns. "It shouldn't." He glances at me. "Should it? Sachin's project is on track again."

"Because we hired a replacement," I say slowly. I'm on the verge of figuring this out. "Miki worked on Kent's stuff, and she spent a week helping the Shield team. If we hadn't hired her—"

It hits both of us at the same time. "We lifted the hiring freeze because of Alessandra's accident."

Awareness dawns in Oliver's eyes. "Kent told Miki he could get her in. How would he have known? Unless—" His voice trails off.

"Who's Kent?" the detective asks sharply.

"Lawrence Kent," I reply, my voice clipped. "Imperium's CFO. He hired a hacker to access some of our files."

"It might not be Lawrence," Oliver says. "It could be Fitzgerald." He looks at the detective. "Sebastian Fitzgerald. He's the CEO of Kliedara, Imperium's biggest competitor. He'd love for our IPO to fall through."

The detective takes down our information and promises to investigate. I barely listen.

This isn't about hacking and industrial espionage anymore. Fitzgerald or Kent—I don't know which man yet —hired someone to ensure Alessandra was hurt badly enough that she couldn't come back to work.

They're willing to resort to violence.

Oliver told Gabby we'd leave Miki alone. I'd agreed with him, but everything's changed now. Miki knows User0989 is Kent. If Lawrence gets a whiff that she knows his real identity, she could be in danger.

We have to warn her. Before it's too late.

26

No man can reveal to you nothing but that which already lies half-asleep in the dawning of your knowledge.

— Khalil Gibran

Miki:

My phone rings Monday evening. I brace myself to tell my girlfriends that I'm not planning on joining them for drinks, but it's neither Wendy nor Gabby. It's my sister Leah.

"Are you busy?" she asks. "I want to talk to you."

I'm watching the Day of the Doctor for the fifteenth time. "Not really," I reply. "What's up?"

"Not on the phone," she says. "I'm in your neighborhood. I'll be at your place in ten minutes. And Miki, please change out of your Hello Kitty PJs."

"Not going to happen, Leah." I grin despite myself. "Me and my pajamas are a package deal."

Her voice is wry. "I was afraid of that."

"YOU LOOK DREADFUL." Leah surveys me with a frown on her face. "You didn't show up for high tea yesterday either. What's going on?"

"Did you come here to nag, or did you come here to talk to me?"

"The latter," she admits. "You have any wine?"

"There's an open bottle on the counter," I reply. "It's not fancy enough for you though."

"It'll do." She goes into the kitchen and comes back with the bottle and two glasses in her hands. Pouring the wine, she gives it a suspicious sniff before shrugging. "Ah well, what doesn't kill you makes you stronger."

She takes a sip. I wait in silence, wondering what my sister's doing here. "The last time you talked to me, you told me to see a counselor. Remember?"

"Did you?"

She nods. "Ben and I went twice last week."

"And?"

She exhales. "The good news is, he's not cheating on me."

I sip my two-buck-chuck. "You don't look happy, so I'm assuming there's more?"

"He admitted he hid money from me," she says, her voice small. "He said he had to otherwise I'd spend it all." She fills her glass to the brim again and takes a long gulp from it. "He said he's been unhappy with his job for a really long time, and the only reason he's kept working there is that he thinks I care about the Upper East Side apartment, the fancy vacations, all that crap."

"Can you blame him?" I ask her, my voice gentle. "You had orchids flown in from Ecuador for a dinner party."

She frowns. "He hid money from me. You think that's a healthy way to deal with our problems? Marriage is a partnership, Miki. I feel betrayed."

I can't argue with that. "I can understand," I say quietly.

There's a perceptive look on her face. "Because of Aaron, or because of someone else?"

"Someone else." It's been a week exactly since I found out that Oliver and Finn were really Lancelot and Merlin. I think I'm ready to talk about it. "Do you want to hear the story? It might shock you."

"Do it. I have an almost-full glass of wine. I'm prepared for anything."

"Let's get the most shocking thing out of the way. It's not one guy. It's two."

Her eyes go round. "A ménage?" she asks. "Like your friend Wendy?"

"Yeah."

"Wow." She gulps down nearly half her glass. "So, is it a fling?"

"There was a moment when I hoped it would become a real relationship." It's the first time I've said that out loud, admitted that I wanted to be with Finn and Oliver.

"So what happened?"

I tell her the whole, messy story. She listens, forgetting even to drink her wine. When I'm done, I give her a questioning look. "If you were me, what would you do?"

"Do you really want to know?"

"Yes."

"Miki," she says, "you're obviously crazy about these guys. Your eyes shine when you talk about them. I can understand why you feel betrayed, but do you really believe everything they did was a lie?"

In the corner of Wendy's living room are the desk and

the Aeron chair Lancelot and Merlin bought me. All because I'd complained about my neck hurting when I typed.

Was that about Imperium? Not really.

So many nights, Lancelot confided in me about his divorce and how it had wrecked his trust in women. That wasn't a lie.

They didn't have to tell me that Lawrence Kent was User0989, but they had. They didn't have to give me keys to their apartments, but they did.

"It sounds," Leah says, "that they started out doing the wrong thing, regretted it almost immediately, and couldn't figure a way out of the situation. Can you tell me that's never happened to you?"

I look at my sister. "That's exactly what I did at Imperium," I murmur. "I started out doing the wrong thing. I shouldn't have accepted the job offer, but I told myself I had to figure out what Ben was doing. Then I spent weeks trying to extricate myself from the situation."

And they'd forgiven me. On the forum, they'd tried to help me. I remember Lancelot even suggesting I talk to Finn and Oliver. *You're just a tool in this, Mouse,* he'd said. *If they're smart, they'll try and figure out what User0989's end game is.*

"You can hold onto your anger," Leah says gently. "Or you can let it go."

"Are you going to forgive Ben?"

"Yes," she replies at once. "I'm not saying it's going to be easy. It won't be. Our marriage has hit a rocky patch, and it's going to take both of us trying really hard to get us through it." She takes a deep breath. "But I love Ben, and our relationship is worth fighting for."

My baby sister is right. Love is worth fighting for.

I need to talk to Oliver and Finn.

27

There is no love without forgiveness, and there is no forgiveness without love.

— BRYANT H. McGILL

Oliver:

I call Finn's grandmother's caregiver as Finn drives back to the city. Apart from the one woman that Mary recommended, Finn's hired two more people so that his grandmother has someone to keep an eye on her around the clock.

The woman who answers the phone tells me that Nana had been in some pain earlier in the evening, but is sound asleep now. I warn her that Finn's going to be late, and she takes it in stride.

The traffic is crazy, of course. It's rush hour in New York, and it's complete gridlock. The drive from Queens to Manhattan normally takes under an hour. Today, it's half-past eight before we pull up in front of Miki's temporary apartment.

We ring her doorbell, and her buzzer sounds immediately. Finn frowns. "So much for security," he says, entering the elevator and punching in her floor. "Anyone can walk right up to her apartment door."

I can't disagree with him. "Let's try not to open with that, shall we?"

His lips twitch. "Fair enough."

He's nervous, and I am too. Miki was the best thing that happened to us. Everything else pales by comparison. She was furious with us last Monday. What kind of reception will we get now?

I barely knock on the door when it's flung open. "What did you forget this time, Leah?" Miki asks before she realizes it's us. "You're not my sister."

"Can we come in?"

I brace myself for a 'no,' but she nods and steps aside. Encouraged, I step into the room, Finn at my side. On the TV in the living room, Matt Smith and David Tennant are frozen on the screen. "The Day of the Doctor again?" I tease before I can catch myself. "How many times have you seen this episode, mouse?"

She grins, but her smile disappears almost instantly. "Why are you here?" she asks stiffly.

"Two reasons." I explain what Detective Larson had revealed. "Until this is solved, we need to make sure you're okay, Miki. I know you're furious with us, but we have resources, and we can protect you."

"What's the other reason?"

Finn replies. "To tell you again that we're sorry. You told me that Imperium was the only thing that mattered to me."

"Was I wrong?"

"Yes." Finn looks at her, serious and intent. "Do you have a pen and a piece of paper?"

I pull a pen out of my pocket and hand it to him. Miki, with a curious expression on her face, gives him a pink notebook, one I recognize from the plane. This is Miki's book of lists. It's perfect for what Finn and I are about to do. "What are you doing?"

"Showing you that I don't care about Imperium," Finn replies. He writes something on the sheet of paper and hands it to me. "You're my witness, Oliver. I'll get my lawyer to draw up proper documentation tomorrow."

Before I can sign, Miki snatches the notebook from me and reads aloud. "I, Finn Sanders, transfer my ownership stake in Imperium to Mackenzie Cooper." Her head snaps up, and she stares at Finn, shocked. "Are you crazy?"

∽

Miki:

They've lost their minds.

Oliver takes the notebook back from me. "Finn's right," he says. "He's always been the smarter one. You think this is about Imperium, about money. It's not. It hasn't been for a really long time. We fell in love with you, Miki. You are the only person that matters. I will do whatever it takes to try and convince you of that."

My heart stops. They said they loved me at the hospital, but lost in my shock and anger, I hadn't listened. Now, happiness bubbles inside me. *They love me.*

Oliver's writing something in my notebook too. I rip it

away from him again. "Will you stop that? I don't want a grand gesture, okay? Just listen to me."

They look at me intently.

"I did some things I'm not proud of," I say. "You didn't make me accept User0989's offer. That was all me."

"What are you saying, Miki?" Oliver asks, his voice harsh. "Because if this is a really convoluted way to tell us to fuck off—"

Men. Do I have to write this on a billboard outside their office window before they get the message? I roll my eyes at the two of them. "It's not, you idiot. I'm trying to tell you that I fell in love with you. Both of you."

"You did?" Finn stares at me as if he can't quite believe my words.

"I really did. And what you did wasn't great, but neither was what I did." I take a deep breath. "I'd like to get back together."

"No." Oliver shakes his head, and my mouth goes dry. Have I misjudged the situation? "I don't want friends with benefits anymore. It's not casual this time around. It's the real thing."

A smile breaks out over my face, and I hug them, my happiness overflowing in my heart. "I think I'm on board with that."

This time, when we make love, it feels different. There's hot sex, of course, but there's tenderness too. When Oliver pinches my nipples between his thumb and forefinger, he follows it with gentle kisses. When Finn's clever tongue swoops unerringly on my clitoris, his fingers lace in mine. When they shudder out their climaxes, they gasp out my name and cling to me as if they're never going to let me go.

EVENTUALLY, we order pizza. Finn wants his usual ham and pineapple. Oliver gets sausage and mushrooms, and I go gourmet with spinach and sun-dried tomatoes.

"So, what are we going to do about Kent?" I ask after I've wolfed down two slices. "We still don't know what his plot is."

Finn shrugs. "I don't care about Kent."

Oliver and Finn have worked far too hard to give up now. Besides, I don't like the oily CFO, and I really don't want to see him succeed. "I do," I reply sternly.

Oliver gives me a wicked grin. "I forgot, it's your company now. How can we help?"

"Stop calling it my company," I tell him, my eyes narrowed. "I'm going to tear that piece of paper up."

"Back to Kent," Finn interrupts mildly. "The thing is, we can nail him now. He hired Miki to hack into our company."

Oliver shakes his head. "User0989 hired Miki," he says. "All we have linking User0989 to Kent is that an Imperium IP address was used to access User0989's account. There were three people in the conference room at that time. I know it's Kent, but Ambrose is going to want more definitive proof than that."

Finn's lips tighten in annoyance. "Fucking Ambrose," he says under his breath. "Yeah, you're right."

I frown in puzzlement. "What I don't understand is why he wants the list anyway. Lawrence stands to make money from the IPO. He even went to look at a fancy Upper East Side penthouse. So he can't intend for Imperium to fail."

"He did?" Oliver asks, his eyebrows raised.

I tell them what I heard at Leah's party, and Finn nods, unsurprised. "Kent likes that kind of thing," he says, reaching for another slice of pizza. One of mine. Hmm.

Maybe I can cure this pineapple thing after all. "Let's start with what we know," he suggests. "Claudia threatens Oliver with naked photos. Why would she do that?"

"For the money," Oliver replies promptly.

I shake my head. "No, if she wanted money, you'd have paid her off. She asked for Imperium stock. That wasn't Claudia's doing, that was Fitzgerald's. Why does Fitzgerald want Imperium stock? Does he want to force a merger between the two companies?"

"I doubt that," Finn replies. "Sebastian's not that clever. He just wants Oliver to fail."

"Why?"

Oliver rolls his eyes. "Evidently, back in freshman year, we were both at a party, and I left with the girl he wanted. I don't even remember this incident."

Finn leans back in his chair. "Okay. Sebastian wants Oliver to fail, so he gets Claudia to ask for Imperium stock, knowing that Oliver won't pay up. That makes sense. But where does Kent come into this story?"

"Our technology gets leaked to Kliedara," Oliver says. He gets up and fills a glass with water from the tap. "You think Kent's doing it."

I stare at the two men. "You do?"

Finn nods, a surprised expression on his face. "You didn't know? No, of course not, how could you? Someone at Imperium has been leaking our technology to Kliedara for the past year. So far, we've been able to innovate and stay ahead of the game, and it hasn't mattered too much."

"But you think it's Kent?" I probe.

"Just a gut feeling," Finn replies. "I've personally gone over every file Lawrence has downloaded to a thumb drive, and there isn't a connection there. I don't see how he's doing it."

Something nags at the back of my mind and then it strikes me. "Janine," I blurt out. "She was printing something for Kent. I remember her grumbling about being asked to do it." I steal a piece of sausage from Oliver's pizza and think out loud. "I've only been at Imperium for a month. In that time, Kent's computer has been down twice. What if he's faking it and getting people to print out documents for him? Nobody's going to question the CFO."

Finn's eyes brighten. "That's it, Miki," he exclaims. "I bet you're right. That's exactly how he's doing it. I've seen Sachin print out documents for Kent before."

"And I've seen Chris Wilcox take him something," Oliver says. There's a grim expression on his face. "Son of a bitch. Right under our noses."

"Okay, so we know that Kent and Fitzgerald are working together." I chew on my lip, my thoughts all over the place.

"Kent wants to be the CEO," Oliver says.

Finn frowns. "If Oliver's discredited, the board won't pick Kent to be the CEO. They'd pick me."

Oliver lifts his head. "Unless," he says, "you screw up."

That's it. The last piece of the puzzle clicks into place. "If that client list is leaked, Finn will take the blame. Kent hired me to clear his path to the top."

We stare at each other. "What now?" I ask.

Oliver's lips curl into a smile, one that doesn't reach his eyes. The normally good-natured man is furious, and I don't blame him. "Let's call his bluff," he says, his tone clipped.

"What?" I stare at him, wondering if he's lost his mind.

A slow smile curves over Finn's lips. "I agree with Oliver," he says. "Miki, you're going to hack into Imperium, and you're going to give Kent a client list."

A client list.

A strategically modified client list.

Of course.

Let the games begin.

28

Never interrupt your enemy when he is making a mistake.

— NAPOLEON BONAPARTE

Miki:

"Miki!" Janine greets me with a wide smile when I walk into Imperium Tuesday morning. "You're back. How are you feeling? Still flu-ish?"

It turns out Oliver and Finn told everyone I was out sick last week, which is an advantage right now. "It's mostly gone now," I reply, lying through my teeth. A couple of members of the finance team are within earshot, and I want to make sure that Lawrence Kent finds out I'm back. "I spent most of the weekend in bed. I probably would have been fine coming to work yesterday, but I didn't want to give everyone my germs."

She grins. "I appreciate that." She looks at her computer

screen. "Lawrence has been asking for an update on the finance work you're doing. Can you meet with him today?"

That's perfect. At this point, because of my silence on the DefCon forums and my absence from work, Kent's nerves must be on edge. Meeting with him and calming his suspicions is exactly what I need to do.

"Ms. Cooper. Nice of you to show up to work." Kent gives me a supercilious smile, his tone laced with sarcasm. "I sent you a couple of emails last week, but didn't get a reply back."

I refuse to kiss this guy's ass. "I had the flu," I tell him. "I wasn't checking my email."

He gives me a hard look. "With that kind of work ethic, you won't get far at Imperium."

This guy is such a jerk. He'd make a terrible CEO. My determination to foil his plot increases. "Yeah, well, I'm not interested in getting very far at Imperium," I murmur sulkily.

He takes the bait. "You aren't?"

"How would you like sitting in the same office as your bosses?" I ask bitterly. "Two weeks ago, my mother called me for five minutes, and Finn suggested I limit my personal calls at work. Now, Mary MacDonald is hounding me for a doctor's note because I was out sick. I don't want to work in a place that treats me like a child."

Of course, none of this is true, but Kent needs to believe that I'm ready to burn my bridges at Imperium.

He doesn't look entirely convinced. "I thought you were getting along quite well with Prescott and Kent."

"So did I." I manage to make that short sentence sound petulant and whiny. "I guess I was wrong. I asked Oliver about the doctor's note, and he just mumbled something about company policy and ran away to another meeting." I shrug. "Ah well. There are other jobs. You wanted to talk about your project, right?"

For a brief second, there's a triumphant look on his face. *My work here is done.*

I don't log onto the DefCon forums until seven in the evening. Oliver, Finn, and I are at Finn's place. I was a little nervous about meeting his grandmother, but I didn't need to be. Mrs. Sanders is lovely and kind and is honestly the most cheerful sick person I've ever met. She must be in an incredible amount of pain, but there's not a word of complaint from her.

She retires to bed early. Once she's gone, I look at the two men. "Kent totally bought it," I tell them. "He's convinced I hate you." I take a deep breath and click on User0989's icon. "You're sure about this?"

"Absolutely," Oliver replies.

Finn nods as well. "One of these two men," he says, his voice hard, "put Alessandra in hospital. She could have been killed. This isn't about the IPO anymore. These guys are dangerous, and we need to stop them."

He's right.

I start typing a message. *I have good news.*

User0989's reply comes within seconds. *You have the list?*

Yes. Do you have my money?

Of course. You can trust that you'll get paid.

I'm not in the habit of trusting strangers, I reply. I name an escrow service that's popular on the dark web. *I'm going to send the list to them. They'll release a sample to you. If you're satisfied, then the exchange happens.*

Fine, User0989 types. *I'm transferring the money to them now.*

"He's in a hurry," Oliver comments dryly. We wait around Finn's kitchen island, too tense to speak, until I receive a notification from the escrow service that the money is in place.

"This is it." I take a deep breath and send Lawrence Kent the client list Finn created for me. Will Kent spot the changes we made to it? We're about to find out.

He doesn't. I get a reply in less than five minutes. *Perfect,* User0989 types. *Nice doing business with you.*

~~We have Kent exactly where we want him.~~ Time for the final stage of the plan.

Oliver:

The next morning, Ambrose Sutton calls an emergency board meeting. *As I expected.*

This is it.

Five years ago, Finn and I founded Imperium. We worked long hours, we made some smart decisions, and we had more than our fair share of luck as well. We've shepherded our company to the brink of going public.

Kent wants to take that away from me.

Fitzgerald wants to see me fail.

I won't let them succeed.

AT THE DOT OF NINE, Finn, Miki, and I walk into the boardroom. The other five members of the board are already there. Ambrose Sutton is sitting at the head of the table. To his right is Lawrence Kent, and next to him are seated Sebastian Fitzgerald and Claudia, who doesn't meet my eyes.

Yes. The moment I see Fitzgerald there, triumph fills me. We've gambled and we've won.

The moment we stopped asking why Kent would be interested in hurting the IPO, the answer was clear enough. Kent doesn't want to leak the client list to the general public. He just wants Finn and me gone.

As soon as Kent sees Miki, he's on his feet, his face red with rage. "What's she doing here?" he demands. "Ambrose, this is a meeting for the executives. I don't think it's appropriate that Ms. Cooper attend."

"On the contrary," I reply, "Miki's extremely vital to this meeting."

Ambrose Sutton frowns at me. "Lawrence has brought some fairly serious allegations to the board, Prescott," he says.

"I'm aware of the nature of these allegations," I say calmly. "I can assure you that Miki's presence here is related to that."

"Oh, let the young woman attend, for heaven's sake, Sutton," Barbara Rhodes says, rolling her eyes in impatience. She turns toward me. "You're not wasting my time, are you, Prescott? Sanders?"

"No, ma'am."

We take our seats. Kent's expression is nervous as Ambrose Sutton clears his throat. "I want to thank everyone for attending this meeting on such short notice. As I said, Kent called me last night. He told me some things that quite frankly, I found extremely disturbing. Lawrence, why don't you tell the board what you told me?"

"Sure." The man's eyes dart from Finn to Miki to me, then he seems to gather himself. "A month ago, Sebastian Fitzgerald approached me with a serious problem. A hacker had offered to acquire Imperium's client list for him. For a fee." He looks up. "The hacker was Ms. Cooper."

Miki stiffens in outrage at my side, and I place my hand on her lap. There's nothing to worry about. *We've got this.*

David Blake inhales sharply. "Is this true?"

Sebastian Fitzgerald nods solemnly. "Last night, Ms. Cooper sent me Imperium's client list, and I paid her the agreed-upon amount. One hundred thousand dollars." He holds up a thumb drive. "I don't need to tell you what a problem this would create if the breach went public. Of course," he continues sanctimoniously, "I'm not interested in causing harm."

Virginia Mullins looks troubled. "Ask yourself this," Kent says, leaning forward and looking at each of the board members in the eye. "Oliver Prescott and Finn Sanders personally interviewed Ms. Cooper and decided to hire her. Our COO," he says, his gaze swiveling to Finn, "is responsible for our data security. Has either of them done their job to your satisfaction?"

Even Miguel Vazquez, our ally on the board, frowns.

"There's one more thing. Something Oliver Prescott has kept secret from you. This one is a personal matter, but I still think it's relevant because it shows another example of poor judgment. Ms. Weaver, if you don't mind telling the board?"

Claudia looks somber. My ex-wife really missed her calling. She'd do great in Hollywood. "I didn't want to be here," she says, her lips trembling. "But Sebastian convinced me that I need to tell the truth."

Finn coughs into his hand.

Claudia glares at the interruption. "During our marriage, Oliver pressured me to do things that I wasn't comfortable with. He forced me to attend a bondage club with him, and he tied me up several times in our home."

Her voice catches. "He did more than tie me up. He whipped me, and he took naked photos of me."

Barbara Rhodes fixes me with a cool glare. "Prescott? Is this true?"

This is our only wild card. Even if we succeed in discrediting Fitzgerald and Kent, the board members could still end up believing Claudia. Still, I can't cower in fear of the photos, and I'm definitely not giving my gold-digging, cheating ex-wife any portion of my company. "No, it isn't. I didn't force Claudia into bondage, and I definitely didn't take pictures of her against her consent."

"Oh please, Oliver," Claudia says dramatically. "Stop lying. Don't make things harder than they have to be."

Kent jumps in before I can reply. "I called Mr. Sutton last night," he says solemnly. "I'm concerned for our company. Is this the kind of leadership we need ahead of the IPO?"

Sutton turns to Finn and me. "Prescott, I'd like to hear from you."

I smile blandly at Lawrence Kent and Sebastian Fitzgerald. "Let's dissect this fanciful tale, piece by piece. According to Fitzgerald, Miki approached him. Miki?"

She shakes her head. "On February fourteenth," she says clearly, "someone I only knew as User0989 approached me on a hacker forum. He offered me a hundred grand for Imperium's client list."

She looks around the room. "This person also told me that the only way I could get into Imperium's network was from the inside, and he assured me he could get me a job here."

I clear my throat. "Coincidently, at the same time, two things happened. Alessandra Mirova, our security expert on Shield, was in a bad car accident, and Lawrence had *borrowed* another member of the team. Because we were at risk of missing our deadlines, I asked Mary MacDonald to hire two developers."

So far, we've told the truth. Now, we're going to bend it a little. I don't want the board to know that Miki had tried to hack Imperium to find out what her brother-in-law was hiding. That's between the three of us.

Miki picks up the story. "I've known Oliver and Finn for a few months, so naturally, I told them everything. We needed to uncover User0989's identity."

Finn speaks up. "Miki was able to determine that User0989 was someone who worked at Imperium."

Kent's face goes white. "What?" he blusters. "Are you going to take the word of some hacker against Sebastian Fitzgerald's?"

"I want to hear her story," Barbara Rhodes says firmly. "How were you able to reach that conclusion, Ms. Cooper?"

Miki plugs her laptop and casts her screen on her projector. "On the day of my interview, I was supposed to meet Mary MacDonald and Sachin Sharma. It was only after I got into the Imperium offices that Mary told me that I'd be meeting Finn and Oliver." She gestures to the screen. "This was the conversation I had with User0989 that evening, after my interview. Notice anything strange?"

Everyone's head pivots to read the conversation between Miki and User0989.

User0989: *Well? What happened?*
Mouse: *What do you mean?*
User0989: *Don't play games with me, Ms. Cooper. I know you interviewed with Prescott and Sanders at Imperium an hour ago.*

Kent's shoulders slump. He's seen it. "How would someone who wasn't at our offices know about the change of plan?" Finn asks. "So I did a little more digging. That message that Miki put on the screen was, as you can see, sent at five in the evening. We were able to identify the IP address used to access the hacker forum. It came from a conference room that three people were occupying. One of them," he says, "was Lawrence Kent."

Multiple people gasp. "This is preposterous," Kent splutters. "She was paid a hundred grand for the client list that's in Fitzgerald's possession. How do you account for that?"

I grin widely. "Ah, the client list. The smoking gun. Fitzgerald, if you don't mind?" I hold out my hand for the thumb drive. He hands it to me reluctantly, and I plug it in, open up the list and project it on the screen. "Ambrose, you're a client in the private security division. Notice anything about your information?"

Sutton reads the screen with a frown. "If you can't see it," Finn says, "look at the renewal date."

"January first of this year." Sutton's forehead is furrowed. "But we're closing that division. I wanted to renew, but I couldn't."

Finn nods. "Yesterday evening," he says, "I did two things. I gave Miki a copy of a falsified client list to give to User0989. Prior to that, I uploaded the same fake list to our network. Only one person accessed the fake list last night, most likely to verify that Miki gave him the right information." He pauses for a second. "It was Kent."

Multiple conversations erupt around the table. Just then, the doors to the board room fling open, and four cops enter. I recognize Detective Larsen of the NYPD. "Sebastian Fitzgerald," he says, "You're under arrest for conspiracy to commit murder in the hit-and-run accident on Alessandra Mirova. You have the right to remain silent and refuse to answer questions. Anything you say may be used against you in a court of law. You have the right to consult an attorney. If you cannot afford an attorney, one will be appointed for you."

We watch in shock as Fitzgerald is cuffed and led out of the room.

There is a vote, of course, but it's a formality. Kent's out. We've won.

"WHAT NOW?" Miki asks once we're back in our office.

Finn smiles wickedly. "Well," he says, "do you remember the time we fooled around in the office?"

Her eyes fill with desire. "I do."

"Oliver went down on you that day. I've been waiting for my turn."

She laughs breathlessly. "Is this what I have to look forward to? The two of you fighting to pleasure me?" Her smile lights up the room. "In that case, I'm completely on board."

EPILOGUE

True love stories never have endings.

— RICHARD BACH

Miki:

Thanksgiving Day...

Thanksgiving should be a time of gratitude and reflection.

I'm completely on board.

"This is my favorite holiday." I jump out of bed in the morning and open the curtains wide. A weak November sun shines into our bedroom, its rays falling over my two sleeping partners.

Oliver groans and buries his face under a pillow. "Miki, for the love of all that is good, let me sleep."

"I did. It's almost ten." Finn doesn't stir. He's cocooned in a bundle of blankets, with only his right foot sticking out.

With great virtue, I refrain from tickling his toes and make my way into the kitchen. They'll get up once I get the coffee going.

At ten in the morning, exactly one year ago, I'd just arrived at Houston's George Bush Intercontinental Airport, ready to board a flight to JFK. My life had been in shambles. I had no job, no home, and no relationship.

What a difference a year makes.

Imperium's IPO was a huge success. Not Facebook-level successful, of course, but pretty damn good. The stock price has risen almost fifty percent since the IPO. Even Ambrose Sutton, the normally pessimistic Chairman of the Board, concedes that Oliver and Finn have done a good job.

Of course, Ambrose's disapproval had thawed greatly after the Lawrence Kent boardroom meltdown. The older man had been dismayed at his error in judgment. He'd had a long talk with Finn and Oliver later that day, and he offered them his resignation. Oliver had turned him down. "I don't want someone to rubber-stamp my every decision, Mr. Sutton," he'd said. "At the same time, I do know what I'm doing. Keep me honest, of course, but we're both working for the same team."

Oliver and Finn still grumble about the board from time to time, but the relationship has improved by leaps and bounds.

NYPD arrested Sebastian Fitzgerald and charged him with conspiracy to commit murder for his role in Alessandra's accident. Unfortunately, Fitzgerald had access to an army of lawyers, who fought like crazy to get his sentence reduced. Fitzgerald should have been locked up for life, but he only got three years.

Still, Kliedara's board voted to fire Fitzgerald. And of course, Claudia dumped him as soon as the NYPD handcuffed him. Claudia is a gold-digger with very dodgy morals, but even she couldn't turn a blind eye to what he'd done.

Imperium fired Kent, of course. Word got around about why the CFO was let go so close to the IPO. He hasn't been able to get another job, and I doubt that that'll change anytime soon.

As I PREDICT, both Oliver and Finn emerge when the aroma of coffee fills the apartment. They shuffle like zombies toward the caffeine, and I watch them with an indulgent smile.

Finn catches a glimpse of my expression. "Don't look so smug," he says. "I can't remember the last time you woke up before us."

Oliver adds milk and sugar to his coffee and sits down at the table. He doesn't speak until he drains his first cup. "What time are we due at Piper's restaurant?"

"Three. I told her we'd come early to help."

Finn raises his eyebrow. "Piper and Sebastian are Michelin-starred chefs. Won't we just get in their way?"

As if Piper's going to let me cook. My skills in the kitchen are somewhat lacking. And that's putting it kindly. "We're in charge of setting the tables. There's going to be more than twenty people for dinner."

Over the years, our little circle has grown by leaps and bounds. Last Thanksgiving was loud and boisterous. This year promises to be ever more so.

"Hudson's going to be there, right?" Oliver asks, getting up for his second cup of coffee. He refills my mug as well, and I smile my thanks at him. "I want to talk to him about a new office for Imperium." His lips curl into a grin. "Assuming you're okay with it, of course."

I heave a sigh of exasperation. "Stop it," I tell him. "I don't own Imperium. Those stupid pieces of paper weren't legally binding, and in any case, I tore them up."

Finn's eyes dance with amusement. "How do you know we didn't just write another copy?" he inquires silkily.

I glare at him. "Stop joking. It's bad enough that the two of you hired me to be the CFO last month. Everyone thinks the only reason I got the job is because I'm sleeping with both of you."

Oliver shakes his head. "I beg to disagree," he says. "You got the job because you've got the financial background *and* the hacking chops."

Finn clears his throat. "We're talking about work," he points out. "Aren't you always telling me that I'm a workaholic? Pot, meet kettle."

I laugh. "Fair enough. What do you want to talk about?"

He winks at me. "A nice, hot shower," he says. "A beautiful woman washing my back. And maybe some lazing around in bed afterward?"

Hey, it's Thanksgiving. It's a holiday dedicated to food and gratitude, and I'm pretty grateful that Oliver and Finn are a part of my life. "I'm on board with all those things."

FOUR MONTHS AGO, the apartment directly underneath Oliver's penthouse had gone on the market, and Oliver had instantly snapped it up. Technically, I still live in Wendy's old apartment, but the three of us are moving in together in January.

"I don't know why you want to wait," Oliver had grumbled.

"This year, I was miserable in January," I'd replied. "I want a clean slate. New year, new apartment.Besides," I'd added, "If I have to live here during the renovations, I'm going to go crazy."

Which all sounds good in theory. In practice, I haven't been back to Wendy's apartment in over a week, and I have more clothes in the closet here than I do back home.

The renovation was supposed to take two months. Even with all the money Oliver and Finn threw at it, it took three. The new apartment is worth the wait though. An open-concept living space with exposed brick walls, three large bedrooms, and a master bathroom so beautiful that I want to cry in happiness every single time I shower.

It's the shower we make our way to right now. Finn leads the way, and I follow. Oliver doesn't join us right away. I've removed my pajamas and am about to wriggle out of my panties when he shows up, a bottle of champagne in one hand and three flutes in the other. "I don't know if you remember," he says, "but exactly a year ago today, we met for the first time."

"I remember." How could I forget? I thought I'd won the plane lottery when the two tall, good-looking men had sat on either side of me.

He sets the glasses on the counter, pops the cork and fills the flutes. We each take one and lift it in the air. "This has been the best year of my life," Finn says seriously, clinking his glass against mine. "Here's to many more."

I take a sip of the cold liquid. Oliver's eyes gleam with heat. His hand curls around the neck of the bottle, and he rolls the glass over my nipples. "Hey," I say indignantly. "That's cold."

"Want me to stop?" A small smile plays about his lips. Oliver knows me. He knows exactly what I'm going to say.

"No."

"Then drink your champagne, honey." Finn's voice is

smooth and firm. "And let us drink ours." He holds the glass over my chest and drips the ice-cold liquid over my breasts.

My nipples pebble instantly. Goosebumps rise on my skin, and I shiver, my pussy slick with heat. "Are you cold, sweetie?" Oliver asks sympathetically. His thumb smears the champagne into my skin, and his tongue follows, lapping at the liquid. His mouth closes over my nipple, its warm heat a delicious contrast to the sharp cold of the champagne.

My breathing catches. "More," I beg. "Please."

Finn moves me until the back of my knees hit the edge of the large tub. "Sit," he instructs. I perch on the ledge, and fresh goosebumps rise on my skin as my ass meets cold porcelain. "Don't worry, baby," he says, his lips quirking at my expression. "I'll warm you up."

He puts his broad palms on my bare thighs, spreading them apart. Oliver trickles more champagne over me, and the liquid trails down over my breasts, pooling in my belly button, and trickling between the folds of my pussy.

"It seems a pity to waste this," Finn murmurs. He gets on his knees and pushes his head between my legs. He parts me with his thumbs, and his eyes feast on me.

A year later, their open admiration still sends a thrill of shock through me. "Such a pretty pussy," he says. His tongue teases me, toying with the opening of my slit, before sucking my clitoris into my mouth.

I whimper, biting my lower lip as desire shudders through me. I grip Finn's dark hair between my fingers and throw my head back, losing myself in pleasure as he licks, nibbles, and sucks. My breathing comes in short bursts.

Oliver isn't idle. His thumbs smear the champagne all over my nipples, and his mouth follows, heating me up. My body threatens to erupt into flames, and my mind is foggy and clouded with lust.

"Sip." Oliver holds his flute to my lips, and I take a gulp of the cool liquid. "We don't want you to get overheated, do we?"

I close my fingers around his wrist. Pulling his hand near, I suck his fingers, and his eyes fill with dark amusement. "You want a cock in your mouth, baby?"

Absolutely.

Oliver removes his clothes as well. His thick cock springs out, hard and ready, and I lick my lips, holding his gaze in mine. "No hands," he orders. "I want to see your pretty lips wrapped around my dick, honey."

"Bossy," I murmur with a grin. Who am I kidding? I love it. I take his length in my mouth, my tongue swirling around his head.

Oliver throws his head back. "Miki," he groans. "You are killing me here." His hand presses against the back of my neck, not pushing, just touching me, letting me set the pace.

Finn slides two fingers deep into my pussy and twists them to find my g-spot. I whimper into Oliver's cock. "You taste so fucking good, Miki," Finn rasps out. "Champagne has nothing on you."

His tongue circles my clitoris while he pumps his fingers in and out of me. I moan around Oliver's cock.

Blood pounds in my ears as my orgasm nears, and I pick up the pace, bobbing my head faster on Oliver's shaft. It's all too much. Finn's head between my legs, Oliver's length in my mouth—I can't hold on. My climax races toward me like a freight train. My body quivers, my insides tighten, and I can't hold back, not even if I want to. I shatter, feeling Oliver erupt in my mouth at the same time.

"Happy anniversary to us," I breathe when I can think again. I reach for Finn's hard cock. "Can I take care of you?"

He chuckles and lifts me to my feet, helping me into the

shower and turning the steaming jets on. "What makes you think we're only doing one round of this?"

AT THREE ON THE DOT, we show up at Piper's. The kitchen is a scene of frantic activity. To an outsider, it looks chaotic as Piper and Sebastian weave in and out, boiling potatoes, chopping celery and carrots and brining turkey. "Miki," Piper calls out, a relieved expression on her face. "Thank heavens you're here. We're running behind."

"Not to worry, we brought cheese and crackers."

Last year, Piper's tables almost broke under the weight of all the food she made. Judging by the state of the kitchen, it's exactly the same this year. "I talked to Leah twenty minutes ago," I tell my friend. "She's on her way, with pies."

Leah and Ben kept seeing their counselor and it saved their marriage. They both were unhappy with the way things were, but neither of them wanted to admit it. They've made drastic changes to their lives in the last six months. They sold their Upper East Side apartment and bought a bakery in the Hamptons, just as Leah wanted. They've been open since September. Leah's still getting used to her early mornings and is likely to fall asleep at seven in the evening, but she tells me she's happier than she's been in a long time.

As for my parents? Nothing's changed. My dad still cheats on my mom; she still turns a blind eye. They're in Tuscany right now on vacation, probably because my dad feels guilty about his latest bout of adultery. Whatever. I don't approve, but it's not like they're ecstatic about my unconventional relationship either. We've agreed not to discuss it.

"Just as well," Sebastian pipes up. "I'm shit at dessert."

Sebastian and Daniel are Bailey's partners. "Where are the other two?" I ask him.

He grins. "Working, of course. Bailey and Daniel will give you a run for your money, Finn. Crazy workaholics, all of you."

Finn shakes his head. "Not me, buddy. I haven't cracked open my laptop or looked at my phone all day. Piper, how many people are you expecting?"

She stops stirring what appears to be pumpkin soup and starts to count. "Bailey, Sebastian, and Daniel," she says. "Daniel's mom and sister are coming too. Then there's Gabby, Carter, Dominic, and Noah. Katie, Adam, and the twins. Wendy, Hudson, Asher, and Natalie."

"You can't count Natalie," I interject. "She's six months old."

My friend glares at me. "Miki, if you interrupt, I'll lose count."

Oliver grins. "Seventeen so far," he says. "Four kids, thirteen adults. Keep counting."

I squeeze Oliver's arm. "My hero," I say, fluttering my eyelashes in his direction, drawing a chuckle out of him. Piper rolls her eyes at me. "There's the three of you," she says. "Finn's grandmother, Finn's grandmother's neighbors. Wyatt, Owen, and me. Ben and Leah. I think that's everyone."

"Twenty-eight people." Finn whistles through his teeth. "How big is your turkey?"

"Four turkeys," Piper replies. "We can't run out of food on Thanksgiving."

I couldn't agree more with her sentiment.

THE MEAL IS AMAZING. I eat myself into a food coma. I'm idly contemplating yet another slice of pie when Leah slips into the seat next to me. "Great pies," I tell her. "I can't decide which one was my favorite. Probably the apple, but I think I'm going to have another slice to make sure."

She smiles indulgently. "Just as well mom's not here," she replies. "Though once you told her about your three-some, she's at least stopped lecturing you about getting remarried."

I grin. "I told her I'd get graphic about what goes in what slot if she didn't knock off the lectures."

"You didn't?" Leah's eyes go round with shock, then she starts laughing helplessly. "Oh Miki, I wish I'd been there. The look on her face must have been priceless."

"It was." Finn, Oliver, and Hudson are standing near the window, all three men in animated conversation. I'm guessing they're talking about Imperium's new headquarters. "How's the bakery?"

Her smile transforms her face. "It couldn't be better. I sold almost a thousand pies last week. I'm thinking about hiring another assistant."

I'm so happy for my sister. "That's great, Leah."

"Isn't it?" Her eyes are on Ben as he chats with Daniel. "I thought Ben would miss his life in Manhattan, but he loves it in the Hamptons." She sighs. "I can't believe I thought he was cheating."

"Well, there's the Cooper Curse."

"A curse we both broke."

Oliver's laughing at something. Finn's lips are quirked up, his expression one of amusement. I ogle the two men shamelessly. I can't believe we're together. "You're right," I reply, getting up so that I can tell Finn and Oliver how much I love them. "We didn't break the curse. We *shattered* it."

Lovely readers, this is a bittersweet moment; The Hack is the last book of the Menage in Manhattan series. I've very much enjoyed hanging out with Bailey, Piper, Wendy, and Miki, and I hope you have too.

Have you caught up on all the books?

MENAGE IN MANHATTAN

The Bet - Bailey, Daniel, & Sebastian
The Heat - Piper, Owen, & Wyatt
The Wager - Wendy, Asher, & Hudson
The Hack - Miki, Oliver & Finn

If you enjoy my menage romances, may I suggest my Dirty series? Each book features a smart and sassy heroine, and a pair of men who fall in love with her. Like the Menage in Manhattan series, each book in the Dirty Series is a standalone MFM Menage romance.

Flip the page for an extended preview of Dirty Therapy, the first book of the Dirty series.

Dirty Therapy - Mia, Benjamin & Landon
Dirty Talk - Cassie, James & Lucas
Dirty Games - Nina, Scott & Zane
Dirty Words - Maggie, Lars & Ethan

DO YOU ENJOY FUN, light, contemporary romances with lots of heat and humor? Want to read *Boyfriend by the Hour (A Romantic Comedy)* for free? Want to stay up-to-date on new releases, freebies, sales, and more? (There will be an occasional cat picture.) **Sign up to my newsletter!** You'll get the book right away, and unless I have a very important announcement—like a new release—I only email once a week.

A PREVIEW OF DIRTY THERAPY BY TARA CRESCENT

My O is missing. Two therapists are going to help me find it.

Two hours after Dennis proposes, I find my fiancé with his d*ck buried in Tiffany Slater's hoohah, and he has the nerve to suggest it's my fault.

Because I'm frigid.

Sure, I've never had an orgasm with him, or with anyone for that matter, but relationships are about more than good nookie. (Not that it was ever good. Adequate is more like it. Okay, who am I kidding? *Dennis couldn't find his way down there with a flashlight and a map.*)

Now I'm determined to find my missing O with the help of two of the hottest men I've ever set eyes on. Therapists Benjamin Long and Landon West. If these two men can't make me come, then no one can.

I shouldn't sleep with them. I shouldn't **succumb** to their sexy smiles. I shouldn't listen when their firm voices **promise** me all the pleasure I can handle.

I can't get enough. But when a bitter rival finds out about our forbidden relationship, *everything will come crashing down.*

~

CHAPTER 1

Mia:

I'm going to sum up the suckitude of my life with a three-point list.

1. Though I haven't had sex with my boyfriend for over a month, he proposed last night in an extremely crowded restaurant, and I said yes. Because everyone was looking at me and I didn't want to be the girl that broke his heart in a public setting. Even though I wasn't really sure I wanted to marry Dennis.
2. Once I got back home, I started thinking about whether we were doing the right thing. So, I went over to his place to talk to him, and I found him plowing his dick in Tiffany Slater's willing pussy. That wasn't good.
3. I started yelling. Instead of groveling, he yelled back. "You're frigid," he accused me. "I've never been able to make you come." Right. As if it's *my* fault that I have to draw him a map to my clitoris.
4. (Okay, I lied. This is a four-point list.) Worst of

all, when I threw his stupid engagement ring at his pasty-white butt, I missed. Big dramatic moment—ruined.

"So there you have it," I finish reciting last night's humiliating events to my best friend, Cassie, while unpacking a new shipment of cocktail dresses. "Can my life get any worse?"

It's eleven in the morning, or as I like to think of it, 'Treat Time.' Usually, this is my favorite part of the day. The store is quiet, and I can arrange the clothing neatly on hangers, organizing them by color and function. I can fiddle with the display cases of costume jewelry and make sure that everything is perfect.

Cassie, who runs the coffee shop next door, is my supplier of treats. She's watching me now, her eyes wide. "Dennis never made you come?" she asks, honing in unerringly to the most embarrassing part – the lack of orgasms. "Mia, the two of you dated for a year."

"I know."

She takes a bite of her muffin. Chocolate chip, if I know my friend. "Why on Earth did you keep going out with him?" she demands. Crumbs fall on my ornately tufted vintage velvet loveseat. Normally, I'd shoo her out of the way and bust out my hand-vac, but today's not a normal day. "The guy's not a looker, and he has the personality of a wet towel."

I feel strangely compelled to defend my ex-boyfriend, but then I remember Tiffany, and I clamp my mouth shut. "I tried to tell him what turned me on," I mutter, my cheeks flushed with humiliation. "At the start. He called me a pervert."

Cassie's eyebrow rises, and she gives me her 'what-the-

fuck' look. "He called you a pervert?" Her voice is dangerous. "And you still dated him after that?"

Worse, I almost married him.

I avoid Cassie's gaze. This situation would never happen
to my friend. She's bold and uninhibited, and she has every
guy in our small town wrapped around her finger. Me? I'm
the boring one in the corner, grateful for any scrap of attention that comes my way.

"Anyway." Cassie dismisses Dennis with a shrug of her
shoulder. "Forget Dennis. You dodged a bullet there. Let's
get you back on the horse. Friday night happy hour at The
Merry Cockatoo?"

Normally, even the mention of The Merry Cockatoo
would get a giggle out of me. The newly opened bar is on
the same block as my clothing boutique and Cassie's coffee
shop. My landlord, George Bollington, has been waging a
low-grade war with the woman who owns the bar, trying to
get Nina Templeton to change the name.

"We're a family-friendly town," he grouses every time he
sees me. "What kind of woman calls her bar that name?"
Mr. Bollington is so uptight he can't even say Cockatoo out
loud. Because I'm the town's resident good girl, he thinks
he's got a sympathetic audience in me. I get to hear him
grumble about Nina, about the sex therapists who've just
opened a practice in town, about people who chew gum and
listen to loud music, about people who litter... you name it,
and my landlord probably disapproves of it.

I agree with him on the litter, but the rest of it is Mr.
Bollington being a grouchy old man. Except for the sex therapists. That's professional jealousy. Mr. Bollington is a
psychiatrist, and he's grown accustomed to being the only
option in town. He now has competition, and he doesn't
like it.

Speaking of Mr. Bollington, the door bells chime, and my landlord walks in. When he sees Cassie sitting in my store, he frowns. Cassie is another person Mr. Bollington doesn't approve of. "Mia," he says, ignoring my friend, "I just saw your window display." His forehead creases with disapproval. "It's very unsuitable. This is a family-friendly town."

Last week, I'd received some incredible hand-made silk lingerie from a small French manufacturer. Each piece was so gorgeous that it should have been in a museum. I'd spent most of Saturday setting up a window display for the bras, panties, and slips. I should have known Mr. Bollington would get his knickers in a knot about it. (Ha ha. See what I did there?)

"Mr. Bollington, I run a clothing store." I try and keep my voice firm. "Window displays are an important part of my marketing strategy."

He's unmoved. "Need I remind you about the morality clause in your lease, young lady?" he demands. The threat is unmistakable. Take the offending display down, or my landlord will make trouble.

Cassie snorts into her muffin once he leaves. "One day," she gripes, "I wish you'd stand up to him and tell him his stupid morality clause isn't legally enforceable. You're going to take the lingerie down, aren't you?"

"Probably." I'm a people-pleaser. I want everyone to like me. And it seems easier to give in to Mr. Bollington's demands than fight him. It's just a window display, after all.

Cassie lets it go. "Back to more important things," she says. "Friday night. We'll get drinks, get tipsy, and go home with unsuitable men." She winks in my direction. "The kind that will have you screaming with pleasure. The sooner you forget about limp dick, the better."

I feel my cheeks heat. "Yeah, about that," I mumble. "Dennis might be right."

She frowns. "Right about what?"

Oh God. It's mortifying telling Cassie the truth. "I've never had an orgasm with a guy in my life."

Her mouth falls open. Thankfully, she's finished chewing her muffin. "With any guy?" she asks, her voice astonished.

I think back to the three men I've slept with. Brett, my high-school boyfriend, who I went out with for two weeks before he dumped me to date Gayla, a big-breasted blonde cheerleader. Tony, my college crush, who slept with me *once* before confessing that he preferred men. And of course, Dennis, who buried his cock in Tiffany's twat less than two hours after proposing to me. "Nope." I lower my voice. "There's something wrong with me, isn't there?"

"Apart from your horrible tastes in men, no." She gets to her feet and muffin crumbs cascade to the floor. "Friday. Meet me at six. Prepare to party your brains out."

Once she leaves, I stare blankly at the rack of beaded and glittering dresses and think about my ex-fiancé. Even at the beginning of our relationship, I'd never felt the kind of passion for him I read about in books. Maybe he's right. Maybe I am frigid.

Cassie isn't going to tell me the truth. The best-friend rules clearly state that she's supposed to say supportive things.

But there's another way to get the truth. As I vacuum up chocolate chip muffin residue, I make a decision. I'm not the kind of girl who sleeps with a guy she picked up at the bar. Even if I wanted to have sex with a stranger, they never tended to notice me. That kind of attention is reserved for Cass.

No, I'm going to solve my orgasm problem the responsible, adult way. I'm going to see a therapist. Not just any therapist. I'm going to see the sex therapists that Mr. Bollington hates. Benjamin Long and Landon West. Maybe they can figure out what's wrong with me.

∼

CHAPTER 2

Benjamin:

It's been two months since Landon and I opened our practice in this small town, and I can't say that I'm enjoying it so far. While the pace of life is a lot more peaceful than Manhattan, I'm used to the anonymity of the big city. In New Summit, everyone has their noses in our business all the time. Given what we do, that's a problem.

Landon, my partner and best friend, comes into my office at ten in the morning. "I need to talk to you about Amy," he says without preamble, taking a seat opposite me and propping his legs up on my desk.

I give him a pointed look, one that just makes him laugh. Landon knows I like my office tidy and organized, and he takes delight in messing with me. "Make yourself at home," I say dryly. I look him over. His hair is tousled, he hasn't shaved, and his eyes are red. "You look like hell by the way. Late night?"

He grins. "Samantha came over," he says. "She's a tiger, that one. She kept me up all night."

It's far too hard to keep up with Landon's dating habits, but I could have sworn he was seeing someone else. "Weren't you sleeping with Claire?" I ask him.

"Not anymore," he replies with a shake of his head. "She was getting clingy. Talking about clingy, how's Becky?"

I gave him a puzzled look. "We broke up. Didn't I tell you?"

A faintly hurt expression flashes across his face. "No," he says. "You forgot to mention it. When did this happen?"

I do the math in my head. "Three weeks ago."

"Why did you break up with her? The two of you seem to get along well enough."

Landon knows me pretty well, so he's guessed, correctly, that I initiated the break-up. I think about the lawyer I dated for six months. Landon's right—Becky and I got along just fine. We never fought, we never argued, and we never even bickered. It had been an amicable, adult relationship, and it had bored me to tears.

"She wanted to move in," I explain.

Landon raises an eyebrow. "Let me guess," he says, his voice amused. "That suggestion filled you with horror. You thought about Becky's stuff all over your place, her toothbrush next to yours, her pretty lingerie in your closet, and you ran for your life."

"You don't need to psychoanalyze me," I tell him. Landon and I have been friends since college. He knows my flaws, and I know his. After a childhood filled with chaos, I'm almost pathological in my desire for calm. Landon's father cheated on his mother and slept around like a randy tomcat, and as a result, Landon avoids relationships, convinced he wouldn't be able to stay faithful. "I'm quite aware that I'm a little stuck in my ways."

"That's not what I was going to say," he replies, his expression serious. "I was going to tell you that you only pick women that you aren't truly attracted to, so it's easier to walk away from them when you're done."

I glare at my friend. That assessment is a little too close to the truth for comfort. "Didn't you say you wanted to talk about Amy? What has she done this time?"

Amy Cooke is our receptionist. She's new; the receptionist we had in Manhattan hadn't wanted to leave the city. She's still on probation, and at the rate she's going, she's not going to last very long.

"She outed Natalie to her sister-in-law." Landon's voice is angry. "Nat called me in tears this morning. It seems that Amy ran into Doris in church, and proceeded to ask her if Nat's husband knew what she did in our office."

I see red. Our practice specializes in sex therapy, and Natalie is one of our best surrogates. We use her to help clients who are having issues with their sex lives.

Unfortunately, surrogacy is still considered similar to sex work, and while Natalie's husband knows what she does for a living, the couple would prefer that no one else does.

Now Amy has outed Natalie to her family.

"We should fire her," I say flatly. "Amy knows how important confidentiality is. If she can't respect the most basic rules of our profession..."

Landon winces. He's kinder than I am. "Give her a warning," he says. "Tell her that she's out of second chances."

I frown. "You do it then," I tell him. "I'm too angry."

"Not a chance," he says promptly. "She has a crush on me. She'd be more terrified if you yell at her."

"Fine." Amy has to realize how important discretion is in our profession. Otherwise, she is going to get herself fired. Already George Bollington, the psychotherapist in town, is gunning for us. We don't need any more hassle.

My intercom buzzes just then. "Dr. Long? Dr. West?" Amy's voice sounds in my office. "Your ten thirty appointment is here. Mia Gardner."

"Thanks Amy." I put the phone on mute and grin at Landon. "I hope you're ready to put your thinking cap on."

"New patient?" he asks. Landon and I see new patients together, at least until we have a treatment plan in place. "Let's go."

Landon:

There's only one word I can use to describe the woman who waits in my office. *Hot.*

She's in her mid-twenties. Her eyes glitter like green emeralds. Her hair is dark and lustrous, cascading in long, loose waves down her shoulders. Her body is the kind that a man dreams of, curvy and lush.

Except she's a prospective client, for fuck's sake. And though Ben jokes that I'll screw everything in a skirt, I have some boundaries. Clients are always off-limits.

"Ms. Gardner," I greet her with my most professional smile. "I'm Dr. West. This is Dr. Long. Please, sit down."

I wave toward the deep burgundy couch, and she perches on the very edge of it. Her fingers are clenched into fists, and she's yet to say a word.

"What brought you in today, Ms. Gardner?" Ben asks encouragingly.

She bites her lower lip. My cock takes note of the way her teeth indent the flesh, and I stir in my armchair, trying discreetly to adjust myself. God, this is embarrassing. I'm a sex therapist. I've watched people get fucked in this office, and I've never yet had to fight off an erection.

Fuck me. My dick hardens even further at the thought of seeing Mia Gardner naked.

Okay. Focus, Landon. She's here for help.

"Ms. Gardner." I lean forward. "It's okay. You can tell us what the matter is. Everything you say in this office is confidential. We're here to help."

She nods. "I have a problem," she says, her face flushed. Her voice is barely a whisper. "I don't think I enjoy sex."

"Why do you think that?" Ben asks her.

Her eyes drop to her lap. "I never orgasm," she mumbles. "My fiancé thought I was frigid."

She has a fiancé? I don't know why that bothers me as much as it does.

Ben is more helpful than I am. "It's pretty common not to orgasm with a partner."

"It's not just Dennis," she confesses, her hands worrying the fabric of her skirt. "I've never been able to come with any partner."

"Couples sometimes fall into a rut," I suggest. "They find it helpful to tell each other about their fantasies. Role play, kink. Whatever jolts you out of your rhythm."

Her face turns fiery. "Have you tried telling him what turns you on?" I continue.

"What turns you on, Ms. Gardner?" Ben's voice drops an octave, and his eyes glitter with heat. Whoa. Benjamin Long is interested in this girl too. Well, well.

"It's too embarrassing." She can't look at us.

"If you don't tell us, we can't help you."

"I just can't," she wails.

I have a brainwave, which is a miracle, given that most of my blood has pooled in my dick. "Sometimes, when our clients are having trouble relaxing, we use hypnosis."

"Good idea, Dr. West," Ben says, giving me a sidelong look. He turns back to Mia. "Would you like to try that?"

She bites her lower lip again. I can see her debate it in her head.

"We record the session," I assure her. "So you don't have to worry about what you say."

She appears to reach a conclusion. "Yes," she nods. "I really want to solve this problem of mine, and if that's what it takes, let's do it."

Ben's the hypnotist. "Lie back on the couch," he instructs Mia, while I set up the recorder.

She gulps, but obeys. She stretches out on the red burgundy velvet, her skirt riding up to mid-thigh. Her skin looks creamy and soft and very touchable.

"You have nothing to worry about," Ben assures her. "Despite what you hear, we can't make you do anything during hypnosis that you won't do otherwise. It's just to get you to calm down."

He looks deep in her eyes, the lucky dog. "Relax," he says, his voice low and soothing. "Let your muscles sink into the couch." He draws out his sentences, the syllables slow and smooth. "Breathe in. Fill your chest and lungs with air."

She complies, and her breasts strain against her shirt. I want to adjust myself but can't. Until Mia goes under, sudden movements will startle her and pull her out of her trance.

"Good," Ben continues. "Now breathe out slowly. Empty your lungs."

After several steadying breaths, Ben proceeds to the next step. Despite what you see in pop culture, you don't need a swinging watch to hypnotize someone. Just a focal object.

Unfortunately, Ben picks me. "I want you to look at Dr. West's face," he instructs. "Focus on him. Don't move your eyes away from Landon, Mia."

Her pretty green eyes meet mine. There's a hint of

nervousness there, but as Ben goes through each step, it disappears. After five minutes of slow, patient encouragement, her eyes grow heavy, and her breathing evens out.

Ben nods at me. She's good to go.

"We were talking about sex, Mia," I say. "Tell us what you want."

"Dennis was tentative," she murmurs, her voice soft. "Sometimes, I wanted him to take charge."

"Take charge how?"

She hesitates. "I wanted him to push me against a wall," she whispers. "Pull my hands above my head and hold them in place. I wanted him to be forceful. I wanted to be taken."

Stay calm, Landon.

"What else?" My voice is strained. "What do you fantasize about?"

"I want to be spanked," she replies. "I want to be dragged over a man's lap." Her expression turns dreamy. "He'll pull my panties down, and he'll order me to take my punishment like a good girl. And if I don't obey, he'll tie my wrists up so I can't move."

Oh my fucking God.

Even hypnotized, her cheeks go pink. "Then, once the spanking is over, he'll push me down on my knees, and he'll thrust his cock into my mouth."

Ben makes a strangled noise in his throat. Thankfully, it doesn't stop Mia Gardner, because she keeps talking. "Sometimes," she whispers, "I even dream about more than one cock. One in my pussy, one in my ass. Taking me hard."

This girl will be the death of us. Her fantasies are dirty and kinky, and I want to fulfill them.

She's a prospective client, asswipe. Keep your dick in your pants.

Ben's heard enough. He pulls Mia Gardner out of her

hypnotic trance. When she's sitting on the couch again, her back straight, her hands clenched in her lap, he continues gently. "Do you remember what you told us you want?" he asks her.

She shakes her head.

I swallow. Mia is an irresistible combination of good-girl on the outside, and hot kinky vixen when her inhibitions are down. Following procedure, I copy the recording on a flash drive and give it to her. "If you want to listen to it later," I say in explanation.

Ben takes a deep breath to steady himself. "It sounds like you want to spice up your sex life," he says. "Perhaps your orgasm problems are tied to that. Have you tried talking to your fiancé?"

Her fiancé. What a douchebag that guy must be. If I had a woman like Mia in my bed, I'd make damn sure I please her.

Ben says *tied*, and I think of Mia stretched out on the couch, her arms above her head, bound together with a tie. Not mine; I never wear one. Ben's tie would work nicely, though.

"I can't. We broke up."

An unexpected surge of triumph runs through my blood. Yes. She's single. *Tell me more about your fantasies,* I want to urge. Ben and I have shared women in the past. We haven't done something like that in a long time, but for this woman, I'll be happy to make an exception.

"We have some other options," Ben says. "If you'd like, we can explore using sexual surrogates to help you climax during sex."

She sits up. "A surrogate? You mean someone will have sex with me while you watch?"

"We're trained professionals," I reply. "I know it sounds awkward, but it isn't as bad as it sounds."

She jumps to her feet, her palms pressed against her cheeks. "I can't," she says, her eyes wild. "What was I thinking? Oh my God, I need to get out of here."

She rushes out of my office. I stare after her retreating back. "Well, that went well," Ben mutters. "Now I get to go and yell at Amy. What a fucking day."

Start reading Dirty Therapy, book 1 of the Dirty series today! Each book is a standalone MFM menage romance with a guaranteed HEA!

ABOUT TARA CRESCENT

Get a free story from Tara when you sign up to Tara's mailing list.

Tara Crescent writes steamy contemporary romances for readers who like hot, dominant heroes and strong, sassy heroines.

When she's not writing, she can be found curled up on a couch with a good book, often with a cat on her lap.

She lives in Toronto.

Tara also writes sci-fi romance as Lili Zander. Check her books out at http://www.lilizander.com

Find Tara on:
www.taracrescent.com
taracrescent@gmail.com

ALSO BY TARA CRESCENT

MÉNAGE ROMANCE

Club Ménage

Claiming Fifi

Taming Avery

Keeping Kiera - *coming soon*

Ménage in Manhattan

The Bet

The Heat

The Wager

The Hack

The Dirty Series

Dirty Therapy

Dirty Talk

Dirty Games

Dirty Words

The Cocky Series

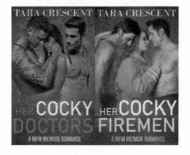

Her Cocky Doctors

Her Cocky Firemen

Standalone Books

Dirty X6